MW01136971

# The Rainwater Family
# from Bergans Ferry

A Novel
Fred Rubio

Copyright © 2016 by Fred Rubio

All rights reserved. No part of this publication may be reproduced, distributed, or transmitted in any form or by any means, including photocopying, recording, or other electronic or mechanical methods, without the prior written permission of the author, except in the case of brief quotations embodied in critical reviews and certain other noncommercial uses permitted by copyright law.

Printed in the United States of America

## To Screenplay Agents

My screenplays, *The Rainwater Family from Bergans Ferry* and *The Elusive Mrs. Hanson,* are available. Please send inquires to

fredrubiowriter@gmail.com

# MY THANKFULNESS

*To God who has blessed me more than I deserve.*

*For my family.*

*To Bill W., who has been my friend since 1979.*

*For everyone that has helped me along the way.*

# TABLE OF CONTENTS

# PRINICIPAL CHARACTERS

*Lottie Rainwater*, a righteous fiery Norwegian mother, helps the less fortunate ones in spite of having very little themselves.

*John Rainwater*, a good man and descendant of a Nez Perce tribal leader, struggles to support his family.

*Mark and Sara*, the Rainwater children, are known as the little avengers. Only Sara and Mark can see angels.

*Sheriff Taylor*, a helpful absent-minded aging lawman, somehow keeps the town free of deviants and looks after the Rainwater and Lindstrom families. One person knows of his past.

*Uncle Will Lindstrom Senior*, an odd loveable patriarch of the two families, walks around in an old suit and top hat with a shovel over his shoulder. He's hell bent to find the Nez Perce treasure.

*Bill*, youngest of the Lindstrom brothers, is a likeable war hero full of fire water and out of control on his 1946 Indian motorcycle.

*Winnie*, an actress and oldest of the Lindstrom daughters, harbors deep secrets involving Lottie and Uncle Bill.

*Lance and Zach Lindstrom*, identical twins, are devious owners of the bank. Which one really died?

# CHAPTER 1

## *LOTTIE'S NIGHT*

Lottie Rainwater walked with her children at a brisk pace down a desolate street in the middle of the night. Her stride was a bit long for the children. The loose gravel bit into the feet of Mark and Sara and their pajamas were soaked by a late spring rain. A persistent wind lashed out at them.

Lottie approached the doorstep of a house nearby, hysterical as she knocked loudly on the door several times.

"Help us, please help us!" shouted Lottie.

No one answered her cries. She took the children down the walkway back to the street, undecided about which way to go.

"Mommy, wait! Where are we going?" asked Sara.

Lottie looked around and then turned to them. "They're taking our house and us away."

Lottie took the children farther down the street and rushed up to an aging two-story house. She banged on the rusty screen door.

"Mom, why are we here? Let's go home," said Mark. "It's cold."

The porch light flickered on. An old woman peeked through the side glass and then slowly opened the inner door partway.

"Please let us in! Everything is gone. Everyone is dead," shouted Lottie. "You must help us."

"Go away! I can't help you," said the frightened woman, quickly closing the door and turning the porch light out. Lottie held on to the screen door handle with both hands as she dropped to her knees.

"We need your help," pleaded Lottie. "Don't leave us." Her arms dropped to her side. She seemed to be in a daze as she trembled from the cold rain. Sara and Mark turned to each other. Sara had tears in her eyes as they helped their mother back up onto her feet.

"Mom, let's go home," said Mark.

"Home?" said Lottie.

The children guided their mother down the steps and onto the dark street. Lottie looked at Sara from time to time as they walked back home.

"Mommy, I'm going to take care of you, I promise." Lottie gave Sara a faint smile.

From the distance a man hurried toward them. As he came closer, Sara shouted.

"Daddy!" Sara embraced her dad as he ran up to her.

"We ran from one house to another house, Daddy, said Sara. "Is Mommy sick again?"

"You're all okay now. I'll take you home." John stepped forward and embraced Lottie and Mark.

"Lottie, are you all right?" John asked.

Lottie, speechless, kissed Sara on her forehead and then gave Mark a hug. Lottie then turned to John.

"Help me, John. Please help me." He embraced her, holding her tightly.

"Everything will be okay. You're safe, Lottie." He draped his raincoat over the children and Lottie.

\* \* \* \*

Lottie was in her early thirties. Her mother was said to be of Norwegian Dutch heritage. She was adopted by the Lindstrom family as an infant. Lottie had long flowing auburn hair, hazel eyes, and a dimple on her right cheek.

Her height gave her an assertive look. Lottie's good looks were the envy of some women in the Northwest town of Bergan's Ferry on the Copper River in Idaho. The year was 1953.

Lottie was a God-fearing woman dedicated to her family, and she was driven to help the down-and-outers in spite of not having much herself. Under that exterior lived a fragile woman. She had her faults. She's wasn't good at taking advice and was too proud to accept much help. She also had a sharp tongue at times.

Some people said that Lottie strutted around town as if she knew exactly what she was doing. Sheriff Taylor, a comical aging lawman, knew different. He did his best to keep her on an even keel.

Lottie blamed herself for not being able to carry little Mark to full term. She also wanted to know why her mother gave her away at birth and to find out who her mother really was.

That night, financial burdens, deaths in the family, and the secret about her birth got the best of her. A few of the townsfolk said she was just nuts all the time. Some said she had a nervous breakdown because of the hardships. Many people felt that Lottie always gave her best to her husband and her children.

John Rainwater came from the Nez Perce Indian tribe. He was tall like his forefathers and ten years older than Lottie. He left the reservation when he was a boy and secured a modest education. John was a good man and had been married to Lottie for twelve years. He worked part time at the sawmill across the railroad tracks and raised rabbits behind their house.

There was some animosity toward the family because of John's Indian heritage. Back in the 1950s, it wasn't popular in some circles for an Indian to marry a white woman.

Sara, eight years old, was tall for her age. She had dark brown hair and somewhat light skin. She always stood up for her brother and didn't take any guff from the other kids.

Mark, eleven years old, was no taller than his younger sister. His skin was darker like his father's, and he had some of his dad's facial features. He had difficulty in school and got picked on by some of the kids. Mark didn't listen well to others. His dad thought he took after his mother.

\*\*\*\*

Several days passed since that night on the outer streets of Bergan's Ferry. Lottie sat in her rocking chair much of the time just staring out the window. There was little conversation or emotion, which was unlike her. She was afraid to go outside after dark and didn't want any visitors. The children tried their best to cheer her up. Lottie wasn't an outgoing assertive person anymore.

John remained lost on how to handle Lottie's unruly behavior. He wasn't sure what might happen next. After talking with the hospital staff and the Lindstrom family, Lottie was gently taken away.

# CHAPTER 2

## *UNCLE BILL'S VISIT*

The Rainwaters' old house stood near the edge of town next to the railroad tracks. Five sets of tracks separated the house from the sawmill. The house shook when the trains passed their house. The Midnight Freight Express was the longest and loudest train.

The house had seen better days. Paint was peeling off the coarse siding from the harsh winters, and the wood rain gutters were rotted in spots. The living room ceiling drooped as if it was beckoning for help. The Frigidaire was on its last legs, and the only heat source was a cast iron wood stove in the living room. The toilet was in the woodshed that was attached to the back of the house. It was the coldest seat in town in the winter time. It was an old house, but they kept it squeaky clean.

Behind the house were several rabbit pens. White Angora rabbits were kept in their cages, and the spotted rabbits were in separate ones. John sacked up the rabbit manure and made a little money at the farmers market. The pelts were once popular for sweaters and purses, but it didn't work out too well for the rabbits. But rabbit stew was still popular with some folks.

Mark would go out and try to catch small spotted bunnies in the wild. Sara would let the rabbits that Mark caught back out of their cages. She felt that those rabbits should have their freedom back. One couldn't blame her for that.

Near the Rainwaters' house was a road that was rarely traveled. It ran south alongside the railroad tracks. It then veered west up a gradual grade into the hills and then ended. No one knew why the road was built, and no one cared.

\* \* \* \*

In the early morning sunlight, a dust cloud could be seen in the distance on the gravel road that came down from the hills. Just in front of it appeared to be a motorcycle that swerved from side to side as though it was screaming down the road by itself. It was a loud machine.

The red motorcycle slowed down and stopped abruptly in front of the Rainwaters' house.

The rider looked around as if he was hesitant to dismount his motorcycle. The engine's healthy idle shook the bike. He turned the key to the off position, and the engine became breathless.

He grabbed a pack of Lucky Strikes out from the side pocket of his leather jacket. The left jacket pocket and sleeve were torn and the collar was discolored. His left hand shook as he lit his cigarette. As he slowly exhaled, a puff of smoke rose from the burnt oil on the exhaust manifold. They were both in tune. After a few puffs, he pinched the burning end of the cigarette off and wedged the cigarette behind his ear.

He was a man in his thirties. His name was Bill Lindstrom. Bill was a veteran from World War II and was called back into service at the start of the Korean War. He was wounded in action and received the Purple Heart. Bill had been back from the war for five months. His injury still plagued him.

Bill was the sharpest-looking first lieutenant in his brigade. Now he was unshaven and had long sandy brown hair. A scar was etched across the bridge of his nose from when he was in a bar fight the first week he returned home. He defended the Rainwaters' reputation that night and then some. Bill still had a chip on his shoulder against the government as they overlooked the seriousness of his back injury.

He was unlike his two older brothers. He was very likable and generous. He loved his family and the Rainwaters as well, but he always felt that he didn't quite fit in at times.

Today Bill had a hard time dismounting his motorcycle. The heels on his old railroad boots were worn. One heel came loose as he stepped away from his motorcycle. He stumbled a bit as he stood there.

\* \* \* \*

As a kid, he was given a pair of new railroad boots. They were too large for his feet, but he wore them only when he rode his 1936 Hiawatha motor scooter. The steel nails holding the heels on caused a lot of friction on the pavement when he would dig the heels into the pavement to slow down the scooter, as it had no brakes. One could see the sparks flying from his heels at night.

\* \* \* \*

Bill pulled out a small flask from the inside pocket of his leather jacket. He took one healthy swig. He started to take another one but quickly placed the flask back in his jacket pocket when he saw John.

John walked up and shook Bill's hand. A few moments of silence passed.

"Good to see you, John. How are you?"

"I'm okay. Out for a morning ride, Bill?"

"I guess I am," replied Bill.

"Anything up there on top of the hill?" asked John with a grin.

"Not a thing, just more trees. And how's the kids doing?" asked Bill.

"They're okay, considering," replied John.

Bill removed his goggles and squinted a bit from the morning sun in his eyes.

"Your bike is still like new, Bill."

"It sure is. I had it stored at my old man's place while I was overseas. This bike still has a lot of fire in it."

"And the driver has a lot of fire water in him." Bill gave John a funny look.

"Well, maybe so, John."

"Bill, you're the only war hero this town has. We would hate one day to have to scrape you and that bike off the cement. There's been enough deaths in the family. People say that you've been pushing life too hard. That booze is going to kill you, Bill."

"John, Lottie buzzed me one time about this before, and I told her it was none of her business. I didn't get a chance to tell her that I was sorry for snapping back at her. I know that Lottie means well. I care about her as if she was my blood-related kinfolk."

"That means a lot to me," said John.

"I came here to let you know that I'm sorry to hear about Lottie. Gloria said she's at a hospital."

"Lottie is at the sanatorium at River Falls," said John.

"The same nut house my dad was in after the accident? Oops. I'm sorry, John, I shouldn't have used those words." Bill became uneasy.

John smiled. "That's okay, Bill. We all slip once in a while."

"So what happened?" asked Bill.

"Well, Lottie suffers from depression, as you know. Two weeks ago, she ran out of the house one night with the kids. She woke up half the neighborhood. She was screaming about everything."

"Then a week ago, she did the same thing. She's been really out of control. I didn't know what Lottie might do next."

"My dad didn't tell me much. He hasn't been himself lately, you know," said Bill.

"I just saw your dad at the bank," said John. "It seems he always likes to talk to me."

"Yeah, he always liked you, John. As you noticed, he still walks around town in that worn-out suit with that shovel over his shoulder. The top hat is real cool. The top hat is older than we are." They laughed.

"I see that," John said. "He's still digging here and there for the Nez Perce treasure."

"Anyway, how long will Lottie be at the sanatorium, John?"

"Don't know. She was so upset when Gilbert died in Korea. And your brother and mother went so quick after that. And then our mortgage problems. A lot of people consider you a war hero, Bill."

"Gloria's husband was the real hero, John. He got shot and died. I got shot and lived. Why was I spared? I was the single one."

"Lottie feels there's a reason why you made it back alive."

Well, in lieu of what has happened over the years, I guess God has been good to me. I sometimes forget that."

Mark ran up to Bill and John.

"Hi, Uncle Bill!" said Mark. Bill let out a big smile and gave Mark a hug.

"How's my little man doing? And are you helping your dad around the place?"

"I'm okay. I help dad feed the rabbits every day. Wow, that's a real big motorcycle, Uncle Bill. Is it yours?"

"Yes sir, and it's paid for," replied Bill.

"Is it fast? Real fast?" asked Mark.

"This Indian Chief motorcycle can go over eighty miles an hour. See the Indian name plate on the gas tank here." said Bill.

"Did the Indians make this motorcycle," asked Mark.

"No, Mark. The factory people were looking for a good name for a motorcycle, so they came up with this name. It was built in 1945."

"Dad's people were great Indian chiefs a long time ago. Right, Dad?" John looked at Bill and smiled.

"Dad says you're a great warrior, Uncle Bill."

9

Bill got back on his motorcycle. He put his goggles back on and adjusted the strap. With one crank, the engine started, and then he shifted into gear. He stopped the bike after a few feet and looked back at John and Mark.

"So you think I'm a great warrior, John?"

"I sure do."

"Well, if you say so," replied Bill.

Bill gunned the engine, and the rear wheel threw gravel as he took off down the road.

"Dad, Uncle Bill smells funny at times. Mom says it's the whiskey. Did Jack Daniels make Uncle Bill's whiskey?" John laughed and then hugged Mark.

"Could be, Mark."

As they walked back to the house, Mark turned to his dad.

"When can we see Mom?"

"As soon as we get the car fixed, Mark."

# CHAPTER 3

## *SANATORIUM*

Lottie was sitting in front of Dr. Rose's desk. The old wooden chair creaked when she moved. Lottie had been in the state sanatorium for two days. She wore a drab khaki gown, and her hair was tied up in a ponytail. Makeup was absent from her face. Her birthmark was visible.

The plastered walls of the office were painted an off white, and water stains adorned the ceiling. In the middle of the ceiling hung a fan entangled with cobwebs. Two florescent lamps were suspended from the ceiling. The dimly lit office, like the rest of the building, had a musty smell. The doctor's rustic vintage desk matched the rest of the building. The only thing on the walls of the office was a picture of President Theodore Roosevelt on a horse. A patient's scream echoed down the long dark hallways.

A robust, odd-looking female nurse with big feet was standing by the office doorway. Lottie attempted to speak but was told by the nurse to be silent. Lottie wasn't used to being so quiet, and she didn't like dealing with the controlled environment.

Dr. Rose entered the office and sat behind his desk. He was a man in his forties and had that refined look, but the bright plaid shirt with the spotted bow tie took away any beauty he was born with. He opened Lottie's file, glanced through it, and then placed it to the side of his desk.

He looked up at Lottie from time to time. He took a pen out of his ink-stained shirt pocket and placed it on the desk.

Lottie looked upward for several moments as if she was

counting the nails in the ceiling. The doctor looked up at the ceiling and then at her.

He cleared this throat. "Mrs. Rainwater... Hello." Lottie looked back down and then gave him a look. There was complete silence for several moments. Dr. Rose started to become a little impatient. He took a notepad and placed it next to his pen.

"Mrs. Rainwater, how are you doing this morning?" He moved his notepad to the other side of the desk. "Hello, Mrs. Rainwater, I'm not saying anything more until you say something, okay? I know you can hear me."

Lottie leaned forward in her chair. She gave him an intense stare and then blurted out, "Didn't they teach you anything in medical school? You should ask me if a cat has my tongue."

"That's a new one on me. It sure is," he replied. Lottie settled back in her chair.

"Will they cut my hair off and place that electrical thing on my head, like in the movies, Doctor? You know, shock treatments and all that?"

"We don't do that sort of thing here, Mrs. Rainwater."

Lottie tried to compose herself. "This is just too much. I want to go home. There's nothing wrong with me. Nothing. I can have someone pick me up right now. I don't need this place. My kids need me at home."

"Mrs. Rainwater, we're here to help you. We have some issues to work out. I hope your stay here will be as brief as possible."

Lottie's eyes appeared to be sunken as Dr. Rose continued.

"In the middle of the night, you took your children and ran out of the house. You ran from house to house banging on doors and screaming for help. You did the same thing two or three more times. Your husband said that prior to these events you'd been extremely depressed and argumentative. John wasn't sure what you might do next. Do you remember doing any of this?"

She shook her head. "I don't remember any of that. Sure, I have a few problems, Doctor. Who doesn't? Things are real tough for us."

"May I call you by your first name?"

Lottie nodded.

"Please tell me about the deaths of your love ones, Lottie." She looked away and started to ring her hands.

"Is there something else that is a burden to you right now? I'm very willing to listen."

Lottie suddenly stood up. The nurse by the door stepped closer to her.

"I just found out that the lady who adopted me thirty some years ago was actually my grandmother! How do you like that, Doctor?"

Lottie kicked the rickety wooden chair and stormed out of the office. The robust nurse quickly followed her.

The next day, Dr. Rose and Lottie sat on a bench on the sanatorium grounds.

"It's nice here," said Dr. Rose. "It's a nice park setting. The blue jays always fly in at this time of the year. And they make that screechy sound at times. I sit here often before leaving the office and just try to forget everything for a while. Life tends to get too complicated at times."

"You need to do that too, Dr. Rose?"

"Yes I do. I guess I'm just trying to keep some of my sanity."

"The pansies look like little people with smiling faces," said Lottie. "They seem to cheer me up. I'm sorry I flipped out last Friday."

"I understand, not a problem. That was nothing. A few weeks ago, a man tipped my desk over during a session. Then he tried to shove my chair through the office window."

"Did the big ugly female nurse grab him, Dr. Rose?"

"No. One of the big ugly male attendants grabbed him," he

laughed.

"Is that patient still here?"

"Oh yeah," replied the doctor.

"Lottie, let's talk about your loved ones who passed away in such a short time. Please, take your time."

"Well, my grandmother who adopted me had three daughters, and Winnie Lindstrom is oldest of the three. Winnie is my real mother."

"And your grandmother just died," said the doctor.

"She went to the grave with this long-kept secret three months ago. I was always told that a stranger gave me up for adoption. My mother must have sworn my grandmother to secrecy all this time. I guess my mother didn't want to be bogged down with a baby. She should've told me at some point. I didn't deserve that."

"This would have been a shock to anyone. Where was Winnie all this time?" asked Dr. Rose.

"My mom is an actress. In the early days of her career, she traveled a lot. Sometimes she went overseas, so I didn't see her for months at a time. When she did make it home, she would show me a good time. She acted like a sister to me. I sometimes wondered why she spent more time with me than her flesh-and-blood sisters, Gloria and Rosa. After I got married, she seemed to slowly drift away from the family. She lived in Europe for a time. But she did write."

"How did you find out that Winnie was your mother?"

"My children accidentally discovered all this when they were up in our attic. They're great snoopers." Lottie looked down for a few moments.

"Are you okay?"

She nodded. "Anyway, my children were in the attic going through some things in a box that belonged to my grandmother. I guess they set aside some envelopes from the box to get at some old miniature toys on the bottom. I just happened to go upstairs to look for something, and I came across the kids as they were going through everything. I opened one of the envelopes and found my birth certificate. It also contained some photos of my dad. He was a handsome man. I didn't even know that the box was up there."

"Why was that box in your attic?" asked Dr. Rose.

"I don't know. Someone must have put the box there."

"Have you told anyone of your findings?"

"Not yet. I just don't how to approach my mother. I hope to put all this all together very soon."

"I understand. If my notes are correct from speaking with your husband, your brother-in-law died in Korea just about the time your grandmother passed away. Is that correct, Lottie?"

"Yes. Gilbert was killed two weeks before he was to be shipped home and retire from the Army. He was such a great guy. Then my Uncle Lance died a few months ago. Doctor, they died all around me. So fast. They're gone. Why?"

"I don't know. Life just isn't fair at times," said Dr. Rose. "Wish I had a better answer. Your husband said that you're very close to the Lindstrom family."

"Yes I am. Zach and Lance were identical twin brothers. You seldom could tell them apart. They both commandeered the bank away from their father when he was in the sanitarium years back. So I wasn't close to them like I am to Bill, the younger brother."

"How did Will Lindstrom treat you?"

"He treated me as if I was actually his daughter," replied Lottie. "I guess now I'm actually his flesh-and-blood niece.

Many of us refer to him as Great Uncle Will," said Lottie. "In fact, many of the people in town do too."

"And what about the other two daughters?" asked the doctor.

"Gloria and Rosa are wonderful," replied Lottie. "I always called them my sisters. Now I guess they're my aunts. What a change."

"The reason we went into great detail about your family is

that it makes it easier to sort things out, Lottie. Let us call it a day. Tomorrow we'll talk about how all this has affected you."

"Dr. Rose, what's going to happen to me? Am I Looney Tunes?"

"What do you mean?" replied the doctor.

"Some of these people have been here so long. Others look so normal. Which am I, Doctor?"

"Lottie, we will take it a day at a time, okay? Oh, someone delivered flowers to the office. They're for you. I believe it was Sheriff Taylor."

Lottie's eyes lit up.

"His name sounds familiar," said the doctor. "Real familiar."

"Doctor, he's a friend of my family and of the Lindstrom family. He's very much like my Great Uncle Will. A little awkward at times but a very nice man, and he's funny. We're not sure how he keeps law and order around town, but somehow he does. The sheriff seems to oversee our two families. Can I get the flowers now?"

"Of course," replied the doctor.

Lottie got up and quickly walked down the walkway to the main building. The doctor took his bow tie off and looked at it. "Good God, this is an ugly gift from my niece," he thought. The doctor looked around for a moment.

"The heck with the smoking rules." He reached into his jacket and pulled out a cigarette. "Who says I can't talk to myself and have a smoke?" He leaned back and lit up.

Lottie returned to her dorm room with her flowers and placed them on her dresser. A young woman sat on a cot next to the wall.

"Are you the new girl?" asked Lottie.

The girl looked up at Lottie and then looked back down. Lottie sat next to her.

"My name is Lottie. And your name is?"

"This is my first day. Why am I here?" asked the woman.

"I don't know," replied Lottie.

"My name doesn't matter anymore. They say I'm messed up."

"Your name matters to me," said Lottie.

"It's Kathy Larson. This is my first day. I'm really scared. I don't know what to do."

"I was too when I first came here to this place," said Lottie.

"Are you crazy?" asked Kathy. "You must be if you're in this forsaken place," said Kathy. "This is a real nut house."

Lottie laughed. "I guess it kinda is."

"I don't know if anyone cares anymore about me," said Kathy.

"Someone cares, Kathy. And God cares about you too. See those flowers on the dresser that I brought in? Those pansies have pretty little faces just like yours."

Kathy smiled.

"The office had me bring those flowers up here for you, Kathy."

"For me? Who sent them?"

"No one knows, but someone out there must care about you."

Lottie got up and stepped over to the dresser. Kathy followed her. She took the flowers and gave them to Kathy.

"Thanks, Lottie." Kathy's hands trembled as she held on to the flowers. Her eyes sparkled with joy. "I don't think anyone has ever given me flowers."

"Well someone has now," said Lottie.

"Are you worried about things?" asked Kathy. "Like what's going to happen next."

"I am. I guess I have problems too. Stick with me. We'll work things out together." Lottie gave Kathy a hug.

# CHAPTER 4

## *A GATHERING*

Sara and Mark were in the woodshed stacking kindling in the wood bin. John was outside splitting wood. Sara stepped out of the shed and walked over to her dad. Mark followed her.

"Daddy, when can we see Mommy?" asked Sara.

John placed the ax down. He walked over to the bench next to the woodshed and sat down. The children joined him.

"Kids, we can visit her next week. Uncle Bill will take us in his car."

"But why is Mommy in the hospital?" asked Sara.

"Your mom is in the hospital to get some rest and sleep," said John.

"But Mommy can sleep here," said Sara. John is lost for words. "Great Uncle Will is here!" said Mark.

Uncle Will Lindstrom walked in from the road toward the back of the Rainwaters' house. He was a tall, good-looking man in his early seventies. He was rather stout and of Scandinavian descent. He had thinning gray hair, blue eyes, and always had a warm smile.

Most of the time, Uncle Will wore a tired dark blue suit complemented with a top hat when he came to town. He was considered the patriarch of the two families, and other people who knew him well felt that he was like an uncle to them. Years ago, Uncle Will fell off the back end of his truck and hit his head on a tree stump. He was never quite right since.

After passing the bank on to Zach and Lance, Uncle Will assumed his carefree sons would protect his personal investments for his retirement. They didn't. Now that his son Lance had passed away, Zach, his other son, ran the bank. Some say right into the ground. As Uncle Will walked along the side of the house, he spotted John and the children. He walked over to them.

"Hi, Great Uncle Will," said John.

"How are my wonderful little people doing?" asked Uncle Will.

He gave Sara and Mark a hug. John stood up and gave Uncle Will a hearty handshake.

"Still driving that big red Mack Truck?" asked John.

"I sure am."

Mark carried a chair over to Uncle Will. As he sat down, Sara pulled on his coat sleeve.

"Mommy can't come home yet," said Sara. "She's tired and has to sleep in the hospital, Great Uncle Will. How come?"

Uncle Will became a little uneasy. He looked at John as if he was looking for answers.

"Well, us grown-ups need a quiet place to sleep at times," said Uncle Will. "The trains make a lot of noise around here when they steam by this house at night. The hospital is a quiet place for your mom to rest so she can become strong again. She will be home very soon. Everything will be okay."

"The kids at school say Mom is crazy. I get mad when they say that," said Mark.

"Don't believe them, Mark. I was in the same hospital years ago. Did you kids ever see me crazy?" asked Uncle Will. Mark shook his head. John gave Uncle Will a grin.

"We don't think you're crazy. You always tell us funny jokes all the time," replied Sara.

A white patrol car pulled up in front of the Rainwaters' house and parked behind Uncle Will's truck. Sheriff Taylor got out and looked at the truck and then quickly walked around the house to the woodshed in back.

"Sheriff, what brings you here?" asked John.

"Just making my rounds to ensure there's peace and order. That's what a lawman does," replied the sheriff.

"Sheriff, did you put any bad guys in jail today?" asked Mark.

"Not today, little Mark. But I'm ready. Would you kids like to go down to the candy store? Here's fifty cents."

"Yeah! Could we, Dad?" asked Mark. John nodded.

The children gave Sheriff Taylor a hug. He held them for a few moments as if they were his own. Then the children ran out of the yard and down the road.

Sheriff Taylor was a man in his late fifties with long silver hair and was considered handsome by some women. His facial features presented an authoritarian look. He wasn't a very tall man and wore square-toed cowboy boots with two-inch heels. Most of the time, he wore a buckskin leather jacket. He always was openhearted.

The sheriff carried a long-barrel 38 revolver and kept four rounds in his coat pocket and a couple in the glove box of his patrol car. He always had a nightstick on the front seat. He liked being known as a hard-core lawman. He seemed to be a little awkward at times, but he did keep the town safe from the undesirables. His two deputies rarely needed to assist him. He'd been friends with the Rainwater and Lindstrom families for over twenty years.

Sheriff Taylor and Uncle Will were always at odds with each other, but it was all in fun. Now Sheriff Taylor made his case to Uncle Will.

"There's an old truck up front. It's big and odd looking, like the owner. Nothing personal, Great Uncle Will. And there isn't a license plate on the back of that truck."

"The plate is gone?" asked Uncle Will. "It must have fallen off on the way over here, Sheriff. You know the roads are rough."

"Registration and driver's license, please," said the sheriff.

Uncle Will reached into his coat pocket and then into his pants pockets. "It's gone! Someone stole my wallet! Or it's in my other pants? Sheriff, it's not a crime to forget, is it? I'm just an old forgetful man." John tried to keep from laughing. The sheriff shook his head.

"Great Uncle Will, I'm giving you the benefit of the doubt. You see, I can do that because I'm the law in this town and county."

"I'm beholden to you," replied Uncle Will. "Thank you." The sheriff sat down with John.

"John, I was out that way on a call, so I brought some of Lottie's favorite flowers to the sanatorium for her," said the sheriff. "I said it was from all of us."

"Thanks. You're like family to us," said John.

Uncle Will chimed in. "That being said, Lottie is family to me, so you and I are kinda related, so to speak. Right, Sheriff?"

"I'll never be related to you in any way, shape, or form."

"We will see," said Uncle Will. "Plus you owe me a root beer from three weeks ago. You lost that checkers game."

"All of a sudden, this old man's memory comes back," said the sheriff. "The only way he wins at checkers and poker is when he cheats. And I bet his license is expired. Do you have any coffee brewing in the kitchen, John?"

"I do have some hot coffee brewing. Come inside."

"We'll be in there in a minute," replied the sheriff.

"Sheriff, how is Lottie doing?" asked Uncle Will.

"I'm not sure. I'm kinda worried," said the sheriff.

"Prayers will help her through all this," replied Uncle Will.

\* \* \* \*

Lottie sat on her bed in one of the sanatorium dorm rooms. "This is a far cry from home," she thought. Her bed was a military- type cot with a scrawny mattress stretched over one thin layer of springs. There were six cots in the room and a small dresser behind each one. A coat rack stood in the corner of the room. A small brass framed picture of Lottie's family was on her dresser, along with a hair brush and a comb.

She took the picture, looked at it for a moment, and then held it near to her heart. Lottie seemed a little jittery, as if she was waiting for something to happen.

The robust nurse could be heard coming down the hallway toward her dorm room. The wood flooring groaned under the weight of her big feet as she walked. The nurse stopped at the doorway of Lottie's dorm room. A tall, frail, older-looking male assistant accompanied the nurse. The nurse gave Lottie a long cold stare. Lottie slowly stood up.

"Are you ready?" asked the nurse.

"You mean it takes both of you to walk me downstairs to meet with the doctors?" remarked Lottie. "One might think you're escorting me to a firing squad out back in the courtyard."

Lottie held on to the picture of her family with both hands as she left the room. The thin man led the way. The robust nurse walked just behind Lottie.

Dr. Rose, Dr. Gore, and a beautiful secretary were sitting at a long table in the board room. Dr. Gore was an elderly man. He had a grayish white complexion, and the eyebrow above his left eye was missing. The young secretary was sitting very close to Dr. Gore and had a bad case of acne. She seemed out of place in that sanatorium.

The board room had a large bookcase against the wall with a broken bookcase ladder. Four high, narrow windows were on the opposite side of the room looking out toward the sanatorium grounds. The board room door was partway open. Lottie entered the room.

"Lottie, please have a seat," said Dr. Rose.

Lottie walked up to the large oak table. She gave Dr. Gore and the beautiful secretary a funny look.

"Which chair creaks? I don't like creaky chairs."

Dr. Gore looked at Dr. Rose. The nurse at the door blurted out. "Just pick one chair out and sit down, lady."

"Please, Dr. Rose, could you have that excuse for a woman leave this room?" asked Lottie.

Dr. Rose shook his head and tried not to laugh. Dr. Gore looked over at the nurse and nodded. The nurse left and slammed the door behind her. Lottie sat down with an assured look on her face. Dr. Gore glanced at Lottie's folder for several moments and then looked up.

"Mrs. Rainwater, you've been here for a few weeks. How are you doing, considering everything?" asked Dr. Gore.

"Well, I'm learning how to work out my problems, and I'm not so depressed. Dr. Rose helped me sort out a lot of things. He said that I'm making great progress, Doctor."

Dr. Gore slid the folder over to the secretary. She glanced through the folder for a few moments and then started to pick her face. Lottie became distracted as she watched the secretary.

"Mrs. Rainwater, do you have any questions? Mrs. Rainwater, any questions?" Lottie looked back at the doctors.

"Oh, I'm sorry. Yes I do. Why do you people put starch in the sheets? That makes the linen so hard. One would have to be crazy to do that. It's like I was sleeping under a sheet of canvas." The doctor turned to Dr. Rose.

"Starched sheets?" said Dr. Gore. Lottie wished she could take back her words.

"She's a special lady," remarked Dr. Gore.

"Yes she is," replied Dr. Rose. "She has done quite well. I recommend that she be released. Hopefully tomorrow morning."

"Everything looks in order, Doctor," said Dr. Gore.

"Can I go home?" asked Lottie. "I know I'm much better."

"Mrs. Rainwater, since you don't like our starched sheets, you can go home."

"Thank you so much, Doctors." Dr. Rose escorted Lottie out of the board room. As they passed the nurse near the door, Lottie stuck her tongue out at her. The nurse's face became more distorted.

# CHAPTER 5

## *THE GARAGE*

Jerry's garage was a family-owned business that had been around since 1910 and was located on the edge of town next to the old bridge. It looked like most auto repair shops. It had one shop door that slid on rollers and had a few cracked window panes. The main door was on the far right.

The rusted rooster weather vane on top of the metal roof still turned with the direction of the wind, and the Richfield gas pump next to the shop still worked. Twenty cents per gallon for supreme was the going price for gas in Bergan's Ferry.

Off to the side was a 1939 dark blue Hudson parked next to a huge old red Mack Truck. The metal pole with the business sign leaned to one side. It had its share of scrapes from cars that came too close when they were backing out.

Jerry Ward was always accommodating to the Lindstrom family, as they helped him years ago in starting his business. Uncle Will drove up and parked his 1942 Packard sedan in front of the garage. He leaned back in the plush Packard seats and closed his eyes.

Uncle Will was a truck driver in his early years and then inherited enough money and clout to open the bank in Bergan's Ferry. He did well in the banking business. Everyone liked and trusted him. In 1928, he purchased a new chain-driven Mack Truck. It had a two-tone paint job, red and black. It was one of the most heavy-duty trucks one could buy at the time. He occasionally rented it out and then retired the truck near the end of the depression. Uncle Will couldn't let go of the old truck, so he had it refurbished and repainted in 1949.

He drove the Packard around most of the time and took the truck out mostly on special occasions. Little did Uncle Will know that in the near future, his truck would be involved in a jailbreak.

After a quick catnap, Uncle Will got out of his car as Jerry came out of the shop. Jerry seemed quite eager to talk to Uncle Will.

"Great Uncle Will, how are you this morning?"

"I'm good. The sun is up, and we're both still above ground by the grace of God."

"That we are," replied Jerry. "I fixed the starting problem on Big Red. It had a bad starter and two bad cable ends from the batteries. So it looks like you can still keep the old truck around."

"I guess I'm still attached to it," replied Uncle Will. "After Ingrid died, I figured it would be good to hang on to the truck. Just something to tinker with. She liked riding in the old truck the last couple of years in the town parades. It brought back a lot of memories from the old days for the both of us. I heard that John's car was towed in."

"Yes it was. It's inside. Bill towed it in yesterday. That old Ford needed a lot of work. But something really strange happened."

"Oh, what was that?" asked Uncle Will.

"The engine had a blown head gasket on the left bank of cylinders. I ordered the parts, and they were at my shop this morning. Don't know how they came so fast."

"I'll be glad to pay for the repairs, Jerry."

"Thank you, but the parts were already paid for."

"Who paid for the parts?" asked Uncle Will.

"Don't know," replied Jerry. "That's not all. I decided to get some coffee and hash at the diner this morning before tackling the job on the Ford. When I came back from the diner, the hood was closed. The old gasket was on the work bench.

I raised the hood and got the surprise of my life. The head gasket was installed, and the radiator was topped off with fresh water."

"That's amazing, Jerry."

"And there were also brand-new water hoses installed. They sure ain't cheap. I didn't order the hoses, as I wanted to keep the repair bill to a very minimum."

"Who did the work?" asked Uncle Will.

"Sure wasn't me. How could someone change that head gasket in the time I was at the diner? It's at least a four-hour job. And I could tell that our tools were never touched. My son is still out of town, so it wasn't him."

Uncle Will walked outside and sat down on the bench next to the shop. Jerry sat with him.

"Any ideas?"

"Not a one," said Jerry. "And this isn't the end of this story."

"You're really getting in a lot of storytelling this morning."

"I guess I am," replied Jerry.

"Okay, I'm all ears," said Uncle Will.

"When I was walking back from the diner, I saw Sheriff Taylor in his patrol car parked in front. I didn't get a chance to talk to him, as I was several feet away. The sheriff saw me walking down the sidewalk, but he left anyway. He didn't even wave. Sheriff Taylor is a good man, but he's a little odd at times. People say he loses his keys to the patrol car and jail at times. I think he's sharper than that. Or is he?"

"Well, he is," replied Uncle Will.

"I'm going to deliver the car to the Rainwaters right now."

"I'll follow you out there to their place and bring you back," said Uncle Will.

"That would be great," replied Jerry. "You don't seem to be all that surprised about the miracle car repair and the sheriff just taking off after he saw me. You know the sheriff pretty well."

"Well, I believe so, Jerry. You know, his eyesight isn't that great, and he refuses to wear glasses."

They laughed. Uncle Will got up and walked into the shop. Jerry followed him. Uncle Will looked at the engine for a few moments and then picked up the old head gasket from the work bench.

"Looks like the old gasket. That is something, Jerry."

"Let me know if you ever find out who did this good deed for the Rainwaters," said Jerry.

"I sure will, Jerry. The Rainwaters will be quite pleased about all of this."

# CHAPTER 6

## *MARK'S ORDEAL*

Mark and his sister Sara walked down the church steps just behind their mother.

"There's the stupid kid," said the boy walking behind Mark. He stopped and looked at the boy, and then Mark turned away.

"Leave him alone," said Sara. "My brother isn't stupid!"

\* \* \* \*

Lottie was bedridden for five weeks before she gave birth to Mark. He weighed almost two pounds at birth. Gloria said that you could have held him in your hand. Mark was in an incubator for two months. It was a crude one compared with today's standards. Lottie was informed that little Mark wasn't going to make it. The doctor said that they should take Mark home to let him die there in peace. The family was devastated. Lottie became partially bedridden again.

Gloria and Rosa took turns caring for Mark. The sisters would cradle him in their arms for long periods of time. The family believed that prayer and the close physical connection would help Mark survive.

Mark stayed a small kid for some time. One time, the sisters dressed him up as a little girl for Halloween. They put him in a dress and put lipstick and rouge on him. They paraded him around that night through the neighborhood. He stopped complaining about his image as soon as his bag of candy got fuller and fuller.

At the age of seven, Mark entered the first grade at Holy Disciples Parochial School. After a few weeks, the nuns realized that Mark was really struggling with the basic classes. It was hard for him to form his thoughts, and his memory wasn't the best. The doctor stated that Mark's ability to learn was probably hindered by his premature birth.

Toward the end of the year, he wasn't required to participate in many of the classes at times. He sat in the back row and drew on the blackboard with the colored chalk. Mark showed a lot of promise when it came to art. But the other subjects were a failure for him. He didn't want to accept the fact that he would have to do the first grade over again.

\* \* \* \*

As Sara and Mark walked farther down the church steps, they noticed Sister Mary behind them and stopped.

"Hi, Sister Mary," said Sara.

"Sister Mary, my mom said that I failed the first grade," said Mark. "And I have to go back again. The kids will call me stupid and everything."

"I'm sorry, Mark. Your mother is right. You will have to go back through the first grade again." Sister Mary hugged him for a few moments.

"But I say my prayers every night," said Mark. "I carry wood in every day for the stove. And I feed some of our rabbits too."

"I know you do," said Sister Mary. "Just try to remember that God loves you just the way you are no matter what."

"Really?" said Mark.

"That's right, so we will help you get through all this, Mark. Okay?" Mark nodded.

"We should join your mother," said Sister Mary.

* * * *

Sister Mary came from a well-to-do family and joined the Dominican order when she was eighteen. She wore a white tunic with a black apron covering the front and back of it. Her headdress was a black and white veil.

The only skin you could see was her face and hands. Some people said that the nuns looked like big penguins.

Sister Mary had been friends with the Rainwaters since they were married. Lottie and John hardly had two nickels to rub together when they were married. Sister Mary arranged a nice reception after their wedding. She also helped get John a job at the hospital back then.

Even though John was not a believer at first, he always volunteered to drive the nuns around wherever they needed to go. He was their favorite chauffeur and was good at changing flat tires. It was a common occurrence on those old cars back then.

* * * *

Mark, Sara, and Sister Mary joined Lottie at the bottom of the church steps. "Did that Wagner kid bother you again?" asked Lottie.

"That boy is a bully, Mommy," said Sara. "He pulled on Mark's shirt in class last week. That's how it got ripped."

"And then he tried to kick me," said Mark.

"I'll talk to the principal next week about him," said Lottie. "Okay, how about I make you kids your favorite pancakes when we get home?"

"Okay, Mom," said Mark.

"Sister Mary, you're also invited," said Lottie.

"Thank you, Lottie."

Lottie was sitting on the swing under the tree in the backyard. She looked up at the clouds. Mark came out of the house and walked over to her.

"Honey, did you get enough pancakes this morning? You only had one small one."

"I didn't feel like eating much," answered Mark.

"You didn't give your share to Blackie, did you?" asked Lottie.

"No, Mom. What are you looking at?"

"I'm just seeing if those clouds look like little puppies or bunnies. You ever do that?" asked Lottie.

"I see one cloud. It looks like a little angel," said Mark.

"Where?" asked Lottie.

"Over there, Mom. Next to the real big cloud."

"I don't see that one, but you and Sara always seem to see angels down here."

"Blackie can see angels, Mom. If he sees an angel, he barks two times only. Sometimes he's the only one that can see them."

"Really, now," replied Lottie.

Mark sat down by the swing with his head down for several moments. "What's wrong, Mark? Is there something bothering you? You can tell me."

"The kids at school say you're the crazy lady and that I'm a stupid Indian. Some of their moms don't want them to come to our house to play with me."

"You have our dog Blackie to play with, and you like to play with some of the little spotted rabbits."

"I guess so," said Mark. "Mom, one boy said we were trash people by the railroad tracks." He got up and held on to her.

"Mark, you're part Nez Perce Indian. You got that from your dad. One of your dad's ancestors was an Indian chief, and the Norwegian Dutch part is from me. And you're not stupid. You will do better very soon. When I drove Sister Mary back to the convent this morning, she said that she will help you in school. Did you hear me, Mark?"

"Yeah, but Sara is real smart and she can read real good. I can't read much. School is so hard. I just want to stay home with you, Mom."

Lottie placed Mark on her lap. He wrapped his arms around her neck. Lottie kicked her feet off the ground and started to gently swing back and forth.

Mark was half asleep as they swung. Lottie looked up at the clouds with tears in her eyes.

# CHAPTER 7

## *LOTTIE'S DRESS*

Lottie has been out of the sanatorium for a week. She felt free as she walked down the streets of Bergan's Ferry. She received an odd look from one lady as she walked by. Gossip got around quickly in the small close-knit town.

Her shopping bag was in hand, and she had a few dollars in her handbag from John. He insisted that she shop for a new dress even though they really couldn't afford it. John stated that it would be her homecoming present. She didn't miss the sanatorium gowns that were a drab green khaki-like material.

There was only one store in town that sold women's clothing and accessories. Sisters Sue and Erma Wart were the owners. The store was located on Main Street. Some people preferred to shop as Sears and Roebuck in River Falls.

The sisters never married. Sue was a few years younger than Erma. She was a little taller and much leaner. But her hair was a mess at times. The beauty train didn't stop very long at Erma's door when she was born. She also was a customer of the local town bakery. But to be fair, she did have a great smile when she wasn't devious.

Some people remarked that the sisters at times could really be insulting and snide. They also had another thing in common. They both had warts on their faces. Sue had two warts on her left cheek, and Erma was just covered all over. It was a coincidence that their last name was Wart. That's what most people said.

Lottie stopped in front of the Warts' clothing shop. She looked

34

at the window display. Mannequins were clad in brilliant-colored dresses. One mannequin was clad in a swing dance outfit from the thirties. Hats of all kinds were suspended from the ceiling, with scarfs streaming from many of them.

There were two long tables in the middle of the shop as you walked in. Sweaters and blouses were displayed on one table, and slacks and pantsuits on the other table. Farther back was a glass table with accessories, such as purses, gloves, and the like. Coats were displayed on the north wall, and two cherry wood-framed mirrors decorated the east wall of the shop.

Most of the dresses were on display racks. The shoes were displayed in back on fancy step-type shelving. Hosiery and under garments were on round tables in the corner. Two wedding gowns were on display, but the Wart sisters may never have any need of them. The floors were stained oak planking with earth-tone-colored broadloom throw rugs.

As Lottie looked at the window display, the sisters within the shop gave her the eye. Erma wasn't fond of someone being married to an Indian, and I'm sure they were jealous of Lottie's good looks.

As Lottie entered the shop, she greeted them.

"Good morning," said Lottie. The one sister looked at the other sister. Erma cleared her throat.

"I'm sorry, did you say something, Mrs. Rainwater?" asked Erma.

"Yes I did, ladies. I would like to look at some of your dresses."

Lottie took a dress off the rack. The Wart sisters stepped back behind the counter. They turned to each other and laughed.

"That Rainwater woman should be looking at a couple of heavy-duty straitjacket," said Erma. Lottie turned her head slightly as if she heard what they said. Sue approached Lottie.

"Did you finally see something you liked?"

"No. Not yet."

Lottie took another dress off the rack and held it up.

"That dress is for a younger woman," said Sue. "You do understand, Mrs. Rainwater."

"I understand. This dress wouldn't be for you," replied Lottie to Sue. The sister became upset and quickly stepped back behind the counter.

"Well, that woman is a mean one," said Sue to her sister.

Erma approached Lottie. Lottie placed the dress back on the rack and took another one down. Lottie smiled, as this one seemed to be her color.

"Did you finally see something you like?" asked Erma. "Are you sure it's not too tight for a woman like you?"

"It's the right size for me," replied Lottie. "A slim size, if you know what I mean." Erma struggled to keep her composure. "It's priced a little higher than I can spend. Could I make payments on this dress? It is so nice. It would make me feel like a million dollars."

"Of course, this wonderful dress would make you feel worth something," said Erma. "We only allow credit for our good customers. You do understand?"

"You say 'good' customers," remarked Lottie. Erma nodded with a faint smile.

Uncle Will looked through the dress shop window. "Oh, not him," said Erma, standing behind the counter. He entered the dress shop and took his top hat off.

"Lottie, I've been looking for you." Lottie, surprised, turned to Uncle Will.

"Hi, I didn't know you would be in town today." Lottie embraced him. "It's always good to see you."

"How are you doing?" asked Uncle Will.

"Much better. It's good to be back home."

"I saw you through the window looking at the dress. It would look good on you," declared Uncle Will.

Lottie looked at the price tag again and then laid the dress down.

"This dress is way beyond my means. But it's so nice."

"We'll take this dress, Miss Wart," said Uncle Will. "Please put this in a real nice box and put a big green ribbon on it. Put it on my tab."

"Sir, you don't have a tab here anymore," said Erma. "Besides, you could use a new suit yourself."

"You sisters are very rude. My son is part owner of this building, so you might have to find a new place to rent in order to sell your high-priced clothes. My suit is fine. Do you understand, ladies?"

Uncle Will gave them a crazy look and laughed. Erma stepped back. "I understand, Mr. Lindstrom."

Erma took the dress and gently folded it and placed it in a white box. She attached a large green ribbon on the box.

Lottie had the dress box in her arms, and Uncle Will was quite the sight with a shovel slung over his shoulder as they walked down the city sidewalk.

"Let's step in the diner here and have some coffee, Lottie. We can talk for a bit."

They entered the diner and sat in the corner booth. Lottie placed her dress box at the end of the table, and Uncle Will stood his shovel up against the wall. The waitress brought coffee.

"Hello, Great Uncle Will, and a hello to you, Mrs. Rainwater. Any luck with the digging today? Are you rich?" asked the waitress.

"No, not yet nice lady. Thank you for asking." The waitress smiled and left.

"It's good to have you back home, Lottie."

"Thanks again for the dress. You didn't have to do that."

"I know. Consider it an early Christmas present."

"So, how have you been?" asked Lottie.

"Oh, okay."

"I worry about you at times," remarked Lottie.

"How's that?"

"Well, you know, driving that big truck around and moving things. You're not a young man anymore. You're seventy now, and you should really take it easy."

"Are you counting my years?"

"Well, kinda," replied Lottie.

"Really now. Maybe I have an angel looking out for me," he replied.

"That angel didn't do a good job looking out for you back when you fell off the truck," said Lottie.

"Evidently the angel was off that day," replied Uncle Will with a grin. Lottie shook her head.

"Please be careful, Great Uncle Will."

"I will, Lottie."

"People see you walking around town with that shovel on your shoulder. Some people still think you're crazy. And your suit gets so dusty digging all around."

Uncle Will looked at his suit and then smiled. "It's a little worn, Lottie. I thought for sure there was something in that vacant lot the other day. I'm going to find that Nez Perce treasure mighty soon. If it's around here, I'll find it. I guess I'm known as the crazy treasure hunter. Right?"

"Well, that's what some people say," answered Lottie.

"You know what? I latched on to a real old treasure map," said Uncle Will. "All I have to do is decipher it. Then the big dig will start."

"A treasure map? I hope the map is authentic. Can I ask you a personal question?"

"Well, why not, Lottie?"

"How are you really doing since Lance's death? Zach doesn't say much to us or anyone else."

Uncle Will looked down at the table for several moments. He had a sober look on his face. "Well it's not easy. Too many deaths in this family. Too many."

"You really miss Ingrid, don't you?" asked Lottie.

"She had her faults, he replied. "But she was a great mother. Yeah, I miss her."

"I still have Bill, Gloria, Rosa, and Winnie. And let's not forget about you, Lottie. You make five, plus the rest of the families. Not sure of a lot of things concerning Zach."

"How about Sheriff Taylor?"

"He might make one more," said Uncle Will with a grin. "I guess he's my best friend even though he accuses me of cheating when we play checkers and poker. I'm really a blessed man."

"Can I ask you one more question?" asked Lottie.

"Now you're going to have to invite me to dinner, Lottie."

"Why did you give up the bank after your accident? I've heard two different versions over the years from other people but not from you. I was shocked that they would do something like that."

"While I was in the sanatorium, Lance, Zach, and that lawyer took over the bank. They said that I was incompetent, losing my mind, and that stepping down from the bank was for my own good."

"I know they did," replied Lottie.

"They pressed hard to have me committed. Then I thought it might be good for me to get straighten out. The doctors thought there might have been some brain damage from my accident. There were a lot of old people in the sanatorium who had been there for a long time. I felt so sorry for them. That wasn't exactly a vacation for me. Is that giant nurse woman still there? You know, the one with the big feet?"

"She's still there," replied Lottie.

"Sure wasn't my kind of gal," said Uncle Will.

"It was quite a while after you left the sanatorium that we learned how they mismanaged your investments."

"Those two were real slick, Lottie. They knew what they were doing, Lottie. Most of it is all gone. Not much left."

"Why were you so quiet about this over the years?" asked Lottie.

"I just didn't want to talk about it. It's was embarrassing to be taken advantage of by your own flesh and blood. There's still some things that I need answers to. Don't worry. My place is paid off, and I own my truck and the Packard. And I make a few dollars here and there. Besides, who needs riches when I have people like you around me?"

"You're the best," said Lottie.

"Maybe I'm still a little goofy, but I know who loves me, and that's what is important to me."

"Come home with me. We have rabbit stew and some rhubarb pie," said Lottie.

"Sounds good, Lottie. What's so funny?"

"I guess we both have a certificate from the sanatorium saying we're sane," remarked Lottie.

"I guess we do," said Uncle Will. "We have graduated."

# CHAPTER 8

## *THE RIVER*

There were five sets of railroad tracks between the Rainwaters' house and the Bergan's Ferry lumber mill. The railroad switch yard was always busy. Twenty-some men worked there, and about 150 people were employed in the sawmill. The mill was on the river's edge of the Copper River. It was built in 1903.

The four long, large bays were kept open depending on the weather. The exterior of the mill was painted white with brown trim. With all the ceiling lights illuminated, the working bays at night looked like a massive lighted ship docked at the river's edge.

The machinery seemed loud at night while everything else around the mill was silent. Every few seconds, the logs were ripped apart by the giant turning saw blades, and sawdust flew everywhere. The smell of fresh-cut wood filled the air as it fell to the side.

The steam whistles sounded off, signaling the shift change, and the workers made a mad dash to their cars parked nearby. Many workers who lived across town walked to work.

Logging trucks lined up during the day on the road in front of the Rainwaters' house to wait for clearance to cross the busy railroad tracks. Many of the trucks were beat up from the rough logging roads. At times, the logging trucks could carry only two pieces of a tree. The base of a cut tree often reached seven feet across. Minutes later came the rest of the tree in the second truck.

When the railroad tracks were clear, the trucks crossed over the tracks and dumped their logs into the river alongside the sawmill.

Mark and Sara would sit on the porch steps of their house and watch the parade of log trucks go by. Sometimes Mark would ask the truck driver where the trees came from. Sara thought it was sad in a way to see them in pieces. The once-majestic trees that towered into the sky were now limbless and bruised.

The copper mines were coming to a close, but shipping started to grow on the river. Mark was not allowed to cross the tracks by himself, as there was a lot of traffic in the rail yard. And for sure he wasn't allowed to be on the river's edge by himself. But one day, Mark couldn't resist the urge to go fishing.

There wasn't a lot of train or logging traffic on the weekends. John was at the mill, and Lottie was busy in the kitchen. Mark felt that he wouldn't be missed.

He ran across the railroad tracks with fishing pole in hand and then he tripped and fell. He and the pole, along with the cans of worms, went flying. He picked himself up and gathered the worms up. He walked the rest of the way.

Mark finally got to the river's edge. He set the can of worms down and baited the hook. As he cast his line out, he wasn't able to get enough distance with his short pole. Mark walked toward the log booms that jetted out from the river's edge into deeper water.

He stepped on to the log boom and cautiously walked out to the edge of the logs. As he cast his line out, it backlashed. While Mark tried to untangle the line in his reel, a large wake from a passing tugboat hit the log boom. As the logs pitched up and down violently, he lost his balance and fell in. Mark tried to cling to the side of the logs as he cried out for help. A hobo quickly stepped across the log boom toward him.

\* \* \* \*

A hobo back then would hitch a ride on the trains. They would find a boxcar with an opened door. For many of them, it was their mode of travel.

These people for the most part were homeless and had very little family. Many worked their way across the country working part-time jobs here and there. Much of the travel and work was seasonal. Not many of them caused trouble, but the railroads did their best to discourage illegal travel on their trains. Sometimes the railroads were ruthless against them. Some hobos lived and traveled in small groups.

\*\*\*\*

The hobo, wearing a worn-out jacket and hat, kneeled alongside Mark at the river's edge. They both were soaking wet. Mark was on his side. He coughed up some water and had a hard time making out the hobo, as the sun was in his eyes. Mark tried to talk.

"You're okay. Just rest," said the hobo.

After a bit, Mark tried to get up.

"No, not yet," said the hobo.

"How did I get here, mister?"

"I heard your screams. I was nearby, so I got across the log boom as fast as I could. I jumped in just as you went under. I got you out of the water and carried you here."

"I can't swim."

"I noticed that," replied the hobo.

"Are you going to tell my mom?"

"Perhaps not," said the hobo. "You can sit up now. Feeling better?" asked the hobo.

"I'm okay. Thanks mister. You're a hobo."

"I guess I am. Is it Mark?"

"How did you know my name, mister?"

"I just do. Many people in town here know your family," replied the hobo.

"Where's my pole?" asked Mark.

"It's at the bottom of the river where you almost went. I'll take you home."

"We live just across the tracks in the old house," said Mark.

The hobo helped Mark up. They slowly walked back toward the mill, across the tracks, and stopped just short of Mark's house.

"Can you come home with me? Mom can make you a sandwich. She likes to help people like you."

"Thank you. Maybe next time," replied the hobo. "Sam is my name. Now don't go across the tracks or go near the river by yourself. Understand, Mark?"

Mark nodded. The hobo shook Mark's hand. As he walked back to the river, the hobo turned around and waived.

"Thanks, Sam," said Mark.

Mark stood in the woodshed and looked through the kitchen door window. His shirt and black corduroy pants were dripping wet. His wet black hair drooped over his face. He was about to turn around, but Lottie noticed him. She opened the door and pulled him inside the kitchen.

"You're soaking wet. What happened?"

"Nothing, I was walking through a mud puddle, Mom."

"Tell me the truth," said Lottie.

"I... I was fishing. I was on the log boom by the mill. I fell in. I won't do that again, Mom. I won't."

"How many times have I told you not to go across those tracks and not to go to the river by yourself?"

"I lost my pole, Mom."

"Honey, we could have lost you." Lottie knelt down and wrapped her arms around him. "Mark, you could have drowned. You know you can't swim. How did you get out of the water?"

"The hobo saved me, Mom."

"Was it Larry or Harold," asked Lottie.

"He said his name was Sam," replied Mark.

"God bless that man's soul," said Lottie. "I would give anything to thank him in person. Go to the washroom and take those wet clothes off."

Sara entered the kitchen and dropped her library books on the kitchen table and sat down.

"Easy there. What's wrong Sara?" asked Lottie.

"The Brewer sisters were at the library. The one sister made fun of me again. They said that I'll grow up and be a retard like Mark. So I kicked her. Is that true, Mommy? And they're always calling us bad names."

"You will be just fine, and Mark is not a retard. Pick up your books and do your homework. Wait... What is that slip of paper?"

"A note," answered Sara.

Sara handed Lottie the note. She quickly read it and then folded it.

"So I have to see the head librarian next Monday about your fighting. Well that's all I need. One wet kid and one kicker."

Sara took her books and left the kitchen. John came through the kitchen door from the woodshed as Lottie sat at the kitchen table.

"What's with the long face, Lottie?"

"Sara got into a fight again. She was at the library. The Brewer sisters were there. She's okay. But that's not all. Mark was at the river trying to fish and he fell in. He's okay, John. Just wet," said Lottie.

"Where's Mark?" asked John.

"Mark is in the washroom, John, changing his clothes." Mark opened the washroom door a crack and peeked out.

"Mom, I'm done changing my clothes."

"Come out here, Mark," said John. "Right now." Mark hesitated and then slowly walked over to his dad.

"Son, are you okay?"

"Yes, Dad, I'm okay." John hugged him.

45

"Go upstairs," said John.

Mark left the kitchen and ran up the staircase. John turned to Lottie.

"I'm thankful that he's alive, but I owe Mark a lickin'. He never listens, and then there's still the problem at school," said John.

"John, he's just a little kid."

"Well, I'm not going to give him a lickin', but I'll give him a good talking to, Lottie."

"If I could have carried him for a full nine months...maybe he would have been a normal kid," said Lottie. "We owe so much money to the hospital, the sanatorium, and then there's the house. What are we going to do? We're broke!"

Lottie started to cry. She stood up and walked into the living room and sat down on the davenport. John joined her. He held her as the evening sun started to fade away.

"Lottie, don't blame yourself. It's not your fault. You're the best mother the kids could ever have. The doctor said that he should improve as he grows older. Maybe I can get our rabbit business going a little better."

"John?"

"What is it, Lottie?"

"I don't ever want to go back there. Don't let me slip away again."

"I won't," said John.

As John held her, Lottie thought about the time when she held him as they sat in their '33 Ford pickup truck years ago. That winter day, they were going up the road that led to nowhere looking for a Christmas tree. A large elk darted across the road and hit the truck. The elk flew up against the windshield of the truck, crushing it. John went forward and hit his head against the steering wheel. The truck came to a standstill.

Lottie sat there for several moments. She had broken glass all over her and was bruised up as well. She pulled John off the steering wheel. He was bleeding and unable to move. Lottie held him as she kept a handkerchief against his head. She turned the headlights on, hoping that someone would see them. Out of nowhere came Sheriff Taylor in his police cruiser.

# CHAPTER 9

## *THE DOUGHBOY DINER*

The Doughboy Diner building in Bergan's Ferry was built in 1910. It originally was an IRS office. A high-ranking IRS director wanted the building to be one story with ten windows and a high, arched ceiling with chandeliers. The inside walls would be trimmed with wallpaper borders that had little duck images. A small basement, with a stout iron door and lock, was built to store classified paperwork and the director's expensive haunting rifles. He liked the hunting in the area until he caught his foot in a bear trap in the hills.

In 1917, the Army took over the lavish IRS office. It was now the Northwest Army Outpost Recruitment Center. After World War I it was closed, as only three men ever enlisted in the area. Years later, the building was purchased from the government and made into a diner. The new owner named it The Doughboy Diner.

Before and during the First World War, the Marine and Army soldiers were nicknamed "Doughboys."

The chandeliers were still intact. The new owner decorated the walls with World War I and early Northwest pictures. The wallpaper-border duck theme was restored, and there were also shelves everywhere with little duck figurines.

The diner served the best hash in the region, and the buckwheat pancakes were the best. Thick potato soup and chili dogs were one of the lunch specials. Bottled beer was available but not on Sundays.

On your left was a soda fountain with four stools. The soda fountain was always crowded on the weekends. A large milk shake was twenty-five cents, a banana split was thirty-five cents, and a Nehi soda pop was ten cents. It was a favorite place among many.

Next to the soda fountain was a coffee bar with cake and donuts on display. The small brown donuts were four cents each. They were the ones that you broke in half and dunked in your coffee. The coffee was ten cents a cup, to include three refills.

The kitchen was located in back just above the old basement. No one believed Uncle Will that the explosives and ammunition, stored there by the Army in 1917, still remained there. The key was lost and no one could break down the iron door. Directly above the old basement was the kitchen grill.

Uncle Will said he hopes he's out of town if the grill catches on fire and spreads. The owner said there's nothing down there and that the US government wouldn't overlook something like that. The sheriff thought different. The bakery, next to the kitchen, baked fresh bread every day, and there was always carrot cake for the weekends.

Just about everyone showed up at the diner. On Friday nights, people were allowed to dance in front of the Wurlitzer jukebox until eleven o'clock. The jukebox could hold over seventy records.

Uncle Bill rode in one morning on his Indian motorcycle after a Wednesday night drunk. He drank two cups of coffee and wolfed down a large plate of hash. Then he fell asleep in the booth with his face resting on the empty plate.

The Wart sisters would run in and run out with a white paper sack full of boysenberry-filled rolls during lunchtime. That's the only time they ever exercised.

The diner was Sheriff Taylor's second office. At times he would have a checker game with Uncle Will, and Lottie would often meet her sisters there. A so-called writer, who arrived every morning for his coffee, found out that his favorite little table next to the window was gone. A waitress said it went to table heaven. He was quite distraught.

Zach Lindstrom was at the Doughboy Diner with his cronies at a long table in back of the diner. Zach, the oldest son of Uncle Will, was in his late forties. He wasn't quite as carefree with the bank business as his deceased brother Lance. It was said that Zach had some of his own personal wealth buried somewhere.

When Uncle Lance was alive, he was a chronic gambler. When his dad was in the sanatorium, he attempted to sell the Mack Truck to pay off a gambling debt, but Sheriff Taylor got wind of it. Another time, Uncle Lance forged a customer's signature for a safe deposit box full of gold coins. The elderly customer became aware but died that day when he stepped in front of a truck. The only thing the two banking brothers had in common was that they both liked White Owl cigars and money.

The cronies sitting with Zach were some of the old businessmen of the town. One young businessman was new at the table. The Rainwater children, with their buckets in hand, walked through the diner to the bakery in back. They waived at Uncle Zach as they walked by. Uncle Zach gave them an odd look.

"Isn't that the Rainwater children?" asked an old businessman.

"Sure is," replied Uncle Zach. "Their father makes them pick those berries to sell to the bakery in back. They get next to nothing for their effort. What a waste. The girl is the bright one of the bunch, but the boy isn't real quick," remarked Uncle Zach.

"The father is an Indian. Right?" said the old businessman.

"That's correct my man," replied Zach. "Their mother ended up being married to a so-called descendant of a great Indian chief. I'm sure everyone in this town is mighty impressed."

"I heard that you're foreclosing on their house," said the young man at the table. "Didn't their mother take care of you when you were sick a while back?"

"No one asked her to do that," answered Uncle Zach. "They're way behind on their mortgage payments. Business is business, and I'm getting that house back that my deceased brother once owned. I can guarantee you that."

"I thought you were close to the family," said the other businessman across the table.

"My parents adopted her when she was a baby," said Uncle Zach. "She's just another upset woman running around in this town."

The Rainwater children, on their way out, stopped at Zach's table. Zach at first pretended that he didn't notice the children.

"Hi, Uncle Zach," said Mark.

"How come you don't talk to us anymore when we see you?" asked Sara. Zach looked away for a few moments.

"Go home and play Indians and cowboys or something," said Uncle Zach. "You and your dad should be good at that!"

They all laughed except the young man at the table. Mark and Sara left with saddened faces. The young businessman spoke out.

"I didn't find that so funny, gentlemen."

The young men got up and left. The rest of them looked at each other and laughed.

"He's too soft," said Uncle Zach.

"That he is," said one of the cronies.

Sara and Mark were sitting on the bench outside the Doughboy Diner. The young businessman on his way out joined them.

"You kids are doing a good job selling berries. Don't pay any attention to what those old guys said in there."

"You're the coffee man," said Sara.

"I guess I am. My name is Mr. Morrison."

"Our mom says you're a good man and you bring coffee for the people on Saturdays," said Sara.

"Well, thank you," said Mr. Morrison.

"Are you our Uncle Zach's friend?" asked Mark.

"After today, no I'm not. I must get back to work. Have a good day, kids."

"Okay," said Mark.

# CHAPTER 10

## *THE TOWN AND THE LESS FORTUNATE*

There was only one stoplight in the Northwest town of Bergan's Ferry. The stoplight was by city hall and the Red Scarf Lounge. There was one lighted crosswalk in front of the hospital.

The bank on Main Street was in a good location. A cement wall separated the bank from the police station. The bank was never robbed. The two buildings were the oldest in the state.

The police and fire department barely met their expenses, and the sheriff paid for the upkeep on his police cruiser. People couldn't figure out how he did it. Sheriff Taylor said that it was his way to help out, as the town was strapped for cash. The other cruiser was maintained by the county. The small hospital was subsidized by taxes but ran in the red at times. The repairs on the streets were always a drain on the city budget.

Last year, a sinkhole formed in a parking lot and took out half the liquor store and city hall with it. A street-corner minister said it was a warning from God.

Taxes paid for the two schools in town. The Catholic school was subsidized by the larger parish in River Falls. The sisters during July held free classes for anyone. Some of the townsfolk donated their time to do repairs on the three schools. It seemed that many people in Bergan's Ferry tried to take care of each other regardless of faith or social standing.

The mayor wanted to replace Sheriff Taylor one time because he never wrote enough traffic tickets to raise money for a new jail. He wasn't worried, as no one wanted his job.

Two-hour parking was allowed on Main Street, but it seemed no one ever checked their watch. The city couldn't find the white chalk sticks to mark the car tires.

The Doughboy Diner was a popular place in spite of the rude man who ran the diner when the other manager was gone. Haunting season was good for the town. They sold a lot of bullets and beer, but they hadn't sold bear traps for a long time.

There was only one gas station right in town. Just about every young boy in town wanted to wear the cool-looking Texaco gas station uniforms with the star on the cap.

One could get their windows washed, tires aired, under the hood checked, and road maps all for free. The station had recapped tires for ten dollars each, and new Dayton tires were twenty dollars each.

The town seemed to attract the less fortunate people in the surrounding area. There were few benefits available for the poor as compared with today. Churches and other kind-hearted people provided many of the services.

The Rainwaters and most of the Lindstrom family were very active in the giving. Gloria and Rosa didn't have much, but they devoted a lot of their time to the cause. Winnie was gone most of the time working small acting roles and trying to rejuvenate her Hollywood career.

Bill wasn't able to work full time at the gun store because of his war injuries but was getting a small compensation from the Veterans Administration. He always came up with the bacon for the Saturday-morning breakfast for the needy.

Uncle Will didn't have a lot to live on after his sons mismanaged his investments, but he helped when he could. One small-store owner always let the Rainwaters run a tab on their groceries.

On the edge of town was the Rainwater house. That part of town showed little material beauty, but in the eyes of the downtrodden, the Rainwaters' house was their hope and nourishment.

It was Saturday morning and time for the not so rich to be served. The Rainwaters' front yard was full of activity.

John and the young businessman, who once sat with Zach and his cronies in the diner, brought out the folding tables and chairs to the front yard.

Sara came out of the house with cups and glasses and placed them on a round table by the benches. Linda, Gloria's daughter, brought out the plates and utensils.

The smell of crisp fried bacon, flapjacks, and eggs could be smelled a mile away. Blackie, their dog, sniffed around for food. He was a German Shepherd that could swim much better than Mark and could outeat him. Blackie had a keen sense when it came to recognizing special people around him. Sara and Mark still believed that Blackie could tell if one was an angel.

Many people already knew that every other Saturday morning was a fine meal, weather permitting. In the winter months, the breakfast was held in a vacant building on the edge of town near the Rainwaters' house. It was owned by the young businessman who helped out at the breakfast.

The wind died down and the clouds started to move to the west, letting the morning sun surround the Rainwater family and their incoming guests.

Lottie was in the kitchen with Rosa and Gloria. They had pancakes cooking in two of the three frying pans. On the table was a large pan of scrambled eggs.

"Wish we knew who drops off the two buckets of eggs on the doorstep every other week. What a generous person," said Rosa.

"Will we have as many people as before?" asked Gloria.

"Could be", said Lottie. "Last time, we had about thirty people, and they all had two or three pancakes apiece. And that was a lot of pancakes to cook."

Lottie took the pancakes out of the two pans and placed them on a large hot plate. Rosa prepared more batter.

"It's hot in here," said Lottie. Rosa walked over and opened the window.

"I can smell the bacon," said Rosa.

"What did you say?" asked Lottie.

"Bill must have gotten the outside grill going for the bacon, and he's also frying the potatoes," answered Rosa.

"That will get the people in," said Gloria. Gloria opened a can of coffee and shook her head.

"This coffee isn't getting any cheaper. How are we going to afford all this coffee again?" asked Gloria.

"I know," replied Lottie. "It's about sixty cents a pound now."

"The young businessman was so helpful with his coffee donation last month," said Gloria. "What's his name, Lottie? Morrison, perhaps?"

"Gloria, it's your turn to act stupid," said Rosa. "You ask him his name."

"Nope, not me. Brother Bill will know," replied Gloria.

"I knew his name at one time," said Lottie. "Ah, I just don't know. Since I got out of the hospital, my memory isn't the same."

"Lottie, it's a nut house," said Rosa.

"It's not a nut house," replied Lottie.

"Then what is it?" asked Rosa.

"Easy ladies," said Gloria.

"Okay, you win. Let's cook these pancakes," said Rosa with a stern look.

"You're not the boss. You're not the oldest," said Gloria.

"Well, I'm the second oldest," replied Rosa. "Anyway, our oldest sister sure isn't here helping us out. She's too busy trying to be a movie star again. She could really be more helpful to this family."

"We've talked about this before," said Lottie. "Winnie is not much help, but she loves us and we love her. I don't want to hear any of this about her."

"Okay, we get it," said Rosa.

Rosa sat down at the kitchen table. Lottie stepped away from the stove and sat with her.

"You're a little cranky today, Rosa," said Lottie. "I can hear it in your voice. We all miss Mom and everyone else. I can't pretend that I know exactly how everyone is feeling. Gloria is hurting too. We all are."

"I'm sorry. I'm just not doing so well at all. Just so many deaths in such a short time." Gloria stepped over and gave Rosa a hug.

"We're all going to stick together and get through all this," said Gloria.

"What are we going to about our brother?" asked Lottie. They all looked at each other.

"I don't know," said Gloria. "Bill is drinking himself into the grave and then some."

"Bill seems to always talk to you, Lottie. You're the outgoing one," said Rosa.

"Maybe I can get him aside next time I see him. Let's get back to work. These pancakes won't cook themselves. It's my turn to be the boss now."

"You wish," said Gloria. They laughed.

Uncle Will once remarked that he was a very blessed father. He never had to be concerned about his daughters not getting along with each other. The girls always ended up sticking together after a disagreement. He also said he didn't have to cook very often with all the girls around. And at times, Greta from the diner would drop by his place with a cake or a pie.

Everything was set up in the yard. Cup, glasses, and the large coffee pot were on the small table. Benches and tables were dress right dress. John checked out the table and chairs again. He wanted to make sure everything was perfectly straight. The plates, utensils, and the napkins were on the large round table.

Blackie went out to the edge of the road and barked a few times and then returned. People started to gather in the front yard. One young lady had a small boy with her. An old couple walked in ever so slowly. He was blind. There were several people from out of town.

Larry and Harold, the hobos, were there. They'd been staying in the halfway house behind the Baptist church. They'd been coming by the Rainwaters' house for three years now. At times, they would stay for the summer if they could find odd jobs. The churches would help them out with clothing. In the fall, they planned to hop a freight train to Seattle.

Now all the people were seated at the tables. Lottie rang a bell two times. They all became attentive.

"Good morning everyone. I'm Mrs. Rainwater. This is my husband, John. And my two children, Mark and Sara. I think you know the rest of our family. It's our pleasure to share with you what we have." Lottie said a short prayer of thanksgiving.

"Thank you for being here with us," said Lottie. "The food is on its way. Please enjoy."

Many of these people being fed were there before and were glad to help. One of the men stood up and got the plates from the table and placed them before each person. A woman placed the cups and glasses. The little boy got the utensils and placed them on the right side of each plate. Sara and Mark got the salt and pepper shakers and placed them on the tables.

Rosa brought out the pancakes. Many people called them flapjacks. Gloria brought out the eggs, and one of the guests helped with the fried potatoes.

Linda was the waitress of the five tables. She refilled the water and coffee cups and brought anything else the people needed. The ketchup, butter, and syrup were used up mighty fast. Linda also mixed some cocoa powder in the milk for the kids. Blackie walked around looking for handouts.

The breakfast wasn't complete unless you had two pieces of crisp bacon on your plate prepared by Bill. He seemed under the weather that morning, as he was very quiet and his cheeks were quite red. He never combed his hair when he had a hangover. This morning, his hair was a mess.

A neighbor from down the road came to the breakfast and walked up to Lottie and Rosa. He stood there with his arms crossed. Rosa gave him a faint smile.

"Hello, Mr. Stanford. What brings you this way?" asked Lottie.

"I just wanted to know a few things."

"Know what, Mr. Stanford?"

"You know, Mrs. Rainwater," said Mr. Stanford.

"Spit it out, Mr. Stanford," said Rosa. "We don't have all day." Rosa turned around and walked off. Lottie could hardly keep from laughing.

"It may not be my business, but I heard that things are tough for you," said Mr. Stanford. "You seem to feed these people all the time. This must cost you a bit of money."

"Well, Bill always comes up with the bacon," replied Lottie. "The farmer across town always has a good potato crop every year. So he's willing to bring potatoes. Great Uncle Will brings milk for the kids when he can.

Someone always drops two buckets of eggs off every other week on our porch. We don't know who that person is. Rosa only works part time at the dealership but always has the money to buy the bread and butter. The other stuff just seems to show up at our doorstep. It just happens. It's a miracle. It really is."

The neighbor just stood with his mouth open.

"Is that enough information, Mr. Stanford?" asked Lottie.

"Well... Ah, perhaps things like that may happen," replied the neighbor. "But it's not like these people contribute to society."

The neighbor looked around and shook his head.

"These people are children of God," said Lottie. "They don't need to explain their circumstances to me. Look around. These people are talking to each other, smiling, and are thankful. Look at you!"

"Well, I'm very glad that I don't have your problem with all these people," said the neighbor.

"You just might be part of the problem, Mr. Stanford. What have you given to the world?" He gave Lottie a funny look and then walked off.

Mr. Jack, a hobo, walked in with help from a young man. The man helped Mr. Jack to a table. Blackie rushed up to the man and barked twice. The young man smiled at Blackie and then walked away. Gloria walked over to greet Mr. Jack.

"Mr. Jack, it's great to see you," said Gloria.

"Thank you, Miss Gloria. My pleasure," replied Mr. Jack.

Mr. Jack was a hobo for a great part of his life. When he was a young boy, his mother left him and his dad. His dad started to drink and then lost his job a year later. Jack came home from school one day and found his dad sitting in an armchair. He was dead. At the age of fifteen, he was on his own.

He quit school and started to do odd jobs here and there. He lived with his aunt for a while, and then she passed away. He had nowhere to go, so he enlisted in the Army in 1918 and went to France. This was supposed to be the war to end all wars. So they thought.

Mr. Jack witnessed the endless slaughter in and out of the trenches on both sides. Hundreds of large artillery pieces leveled towns and everything around, to include the soldiers. This was the everyday norm in Europe.

He received a Purple Heart for his injury and then came back from the war. He still was shell-shocked from all the death he had seen. He worked in a factory that made parts for a car company. The Great Depression hit in 1930, and then he lost his job. Mr. Jack, like many people, spent time in the soup lines and lived off of charity. There were no jobs to be had, so he gathered a few things and hitched a ride on the Great Northern train heading west.

From there on, his lifestyle was that of a hobo. As he got older, he could no longer jump up on the door sill of a moving boxcar. In fact it was very hard for him to get up onto a boxcar when it was parked. He needed help most of the time. But today he managed to sit at the table and enjoy a great breakfast. Minutes later, John joined him and Gloria.

"Mr. Jack, you didn't finish your breakfast. Was everything okay?" asked John.

"Oh, I didn't have much appetite. Not feeling so hot, but it's always great to see you and all the family. And, of course, to have a fine meal here at the house."

"We always like seeing you, Mr. Jack," said Gloria. "Any good stories today?"

"I don't know," replied Mr. Jack. "My memory seems to come and go these days."

Mr. Jack's breathing was heavy. He took his old hat off, and sweat was running down his forehead. He grabbed his left arm as if he was in pain.

"Are you okay?" asked John. "We're going to help you up and walk you over to the porch. There's a real comfortable rocking chair you can sit in."

"Okay," said Mr. Jack.

John and Lottie helped him onto the porch and then into the rocking chair. Gloria felt his forehead.

"Rosa, please get a towel with a little ice in it."

Mr. Jack's face was pale white. John had a worried look on his face. Rosa came back with the towel with ice and tried to cool him down a bit.

"Mr. Jack, I hope this is better," said Rosa.

As Sara and Mark gathered around Mr. Jack, he looked up at them and smiled.

"I don't have any family anymore," said Mr. Jack. "You're like family to me. Perhaps I do have a real old story for everyone. I enlisted in the Army in 1918 and then was sent to France. It seemed like all hell broke out over there. When we left the trenches to try to advance, our captain was hit. I carried him back to the trenches but got hit myself by machine gun fire. That's why I limp so badly today."

"You're a war hero," said Sera. He smiled.

"The depression hit, and there were few jobs. I started to drift here and there. My Purple Heart is in my side coat pocket. It's in a small case. Please take it out."

John gently reached into Mr. Jack's pocket and pulled out a small worn case.

John handed the case to Lottie. She opened it. "Oh my. It's beautiful, Mr. Jack."

"You deserve a medal for taking care of people like me," said Mr. Jack. "Please take the medal."

"The medal?" asked Rosa.

"We can't do this," said Lottie.

"Please take it, Lottie. It would make me happy if you did."

"Well, it would be an honor for us to hold on to this medal for you," replied Lottie.

Mr. Jack's breathing became more difficult. John stepped back with Gloria. Her eyes teared.

"Call the hospital, Gloria," said John.

"You never told us your last name, Mr. Jack, after all these years you've visited us, remarked Lottie."

"No one knows who I am anymore," said Mr. Jack. "I spoke to

Winnie one time when she was here. She can tell you more about me.

I'm Private Jack Warner, Company A, 2nd Infantry Division, US Army, France, 1918."

"I'm writing all this down on paper," said Rosa. "Sister Winnie knows some of the big newspapers. She will have your story printed."

"People will know who you are," said Gloria.

"They will?" asked Mr. Jack.

Mr. Jack turned his head to the front yard. The young man who helped him to the breakfast was standing there. He stepped a little closer to the porch as Gloria held Mr. Jack's hand.

"Maybe I could've done a better job of my life. I hope to be forgiven," said Mr. Jack.

"God will be kind to you," said Lottie.

"Will you remember me?" asked Mr. Jack.

"We will," replied Lottie. Mr. Jack looked over at the young man standing near them.

"He's going to take me home," said Mr. Jack.

"Who, Mr. Jack?" asked Lottie.

Mr. Jack's head dropped to one side. His eyes closed. Lottie noticed that the young man standing there was gone. He was nowhere to be seen.

"Mr. Jack has left us," said Lottie. "He's in heaven now."

# CHAPTER 11

## *A NIGHTMARE*

In the middle of the night, Lottie heard a vehicle leave the sawmill at a high rate of speed with its siren blaring. Minutes later, the phone rang. Lottie walked into the kitchen.

"Who could this be so late in the night?" thought Lottie.

She hesitated for a moment and then picked up the phone.

"Yes, I'm Mrs. Rainwater. What? Hospital? Beaten up?"

Lottie dropped the phone. She stood there motionless.

\* \* \* \*

Lottie stood at the front desk of the hospital emergency ward desk. A nurse approached her.

"I'm Mrs. Rainwater. I'm here to see my husband!"

"This way, please," said the nurse.

The emergency ward nurse led Lottie through the emergency door, down the hallway, and into John's room. A nurse was adjusting an IV drip line that was inserted into his arm. She took John's blood pressure, made a notation on his chart, and then left. A doctor was at John's bedside.

Lottie rushed up to John's bedside. "What happened to him, Doctor?"

"It appears that he was beaten at the sawmill," said the doctor. "Sheriff Taylor has the details on the men who did this to him. He should be here very soon. John has bruises on his head and some cuts on his cheek, as you can see. He also has bruised ribs."

"Will he be okay? He's going to wake up, right, Doctor?"

"The large bruise on the left side of his forehead is the problem," replied the doctor. "We hope to know more very soon."

"You don't know?" said Lottie.

"I'm sorry, Mrs. Rainwater. At this point, I wish we could tell you more. You can stay here for a while. I'll be in again to check on him. Let us know if you need anything."

Lottie placed a chair next to the bed. She sat there and held John's hand. Minutes later, Sheriff Taylor walked into the room. Lottie stood up and hugged him for a few moments. The sheriff walked over to John's bedside.

"John is hurt real bad," said Lottie.

"I'm so sorry. How's he doing?" asked the sheriff.

"The doctor hopes to know more very soon. How did this happen to John?" asked Lottie.

"A witness said that John was jumped by three men at the sawmill," said Sheriff Taylor. "I have all three of them in jail. I accidentally broke my nightstick over the head of the one who resisted arrest. He also was the one who hit John several times as he was being held by the other two thugs. I'm going to press the prosecutor to go hard on these guys."

"Why did they do such a thing?" asked Lottie.

"I don't know, Lottie."

Sheriff Taylor pulled up a chair and sat down. After a time, the doctor returned. He examined John again and made further notations.

"Feel free to stay in the waiting room," said the doctor. "The chairs are more comfortable."

"Let's go in the waiting room, Lottie," said the sheriff.

The sheriff took Lottie into the waiting room. She stood there for a few moments and then paced the floor.

"Lottie, let's sit down."

"Sheriff, what are we going to do? I feel so helpless."

"All we can do is wait and pray right now, Lottie."

After two hours, the doctor entered the waiting room and sat next to Lottie.

"Mrs. Rainwater, your husband is still unconscious. The good news is that his condition is stable. It would be best if you went home and got some rest. It's been a long night for you."

"No, I'm not going anywhere."

"Lottie, it would be best for you to be home with the kids," said the sheriff. "That's what John would want."

"Will he make it through this, Doctor?" asked Lottie.

"Lottie, we will do all we can for John. I'll call you if there's a change in his condition. Please, get some rest."

\* \* \* \*

Lottie walked into the living room. Linda was sitting on the davenport. Lottie took her coat off and sat down with her.

"Thanks for staying with the kids, Linda."

"How's John, Lottie?"

"He's in a coma. The doctor said he wasn't sure how long that would be. He has bruises all over his face. The large bruise on the side of his forehead is the big problem."

"How did this happen to him?" asked Linda.

"He was beaten up at the mill. Sheriff Taylor arrested the three men who did this to John."

Mark came down the bedroom stairs and hugged Lottie. Sara followed him.

"Why did Linda come here tonight?" asked Mark.

"Mommy, where's Daddy?" asked Sara. Tears welled in Lottie's eyes. She was lost for words.

"Sara, your mom had to see your dad in the hospital tonight, replied Linda. "He had a little accident at the sawmill. It's nothing real bad. Your dad is going to be fine."

"Your dad just needs some rest," said Lottie. Sara started to cry. Lottie took her into her arms. "Everything will be okay, Sara."

"Is Dad coming home soon?" asked Mark. Lottie looked over to Linda and then at Mark.

"Don't worry, honey," replied Lottie. "He will be home soon. Maybe in a day or two," replied Lottie.

"I can take them back up to bed," said Linda.

"Okay," replied Lottie.

"Come on, let's go, kids."

\* \* \* \*

Lottie and Bill are at John's bedside. "It's been almost two weeks now since John has been here in a coma. I try to visit him every day and talk to him all the time. Do you think that helps, Bill?"

"I don't know, Lottie. It surely won't hurt to talk to him. Perhaps John can hear us at times."

"I tell John that you and the kids are taking care of the rabbits, Bill. I just talk about how my day was. Sometimes I talk about things we've done together over the years. I just hope he can hear me. I tell him not to worry and that we are all okay. I don't know what to say to the kids, Bill. They want to know when their dad is coming home. I tell them again that I don't know. It's hard on them. Sara cries sometimes when we leave his room to go home. Dr. Rose had a talk with our doctor. He assured me that they are doing all they can to bring John out of the coma."

"John was always such a strong man," said Bill. "John said one time that his grandfather called him Strong Hawk."

Lottie leaned over and kissed John and gently squeezed his hand. "John, please come back to us."

Lottie and Bill left the hospital and walked across the parking lot and got into his car.

"I don't know if I can handle all this, Bill. The house mortgage, the kids, and all that. I'm going to have to find a job or something. We can't go on like this."

"Lottie, some of us together can scrape up a few bucks every week for you. Of course, we can't count on Zach."

"Bill, we are so behind on the mortgage."

"Well, that's a big one there, Lottie. But you need to be more willing to receive some help at times."

"Have you received any help, Bill?"

"I know where you're going with this, Lottie. I just found an AA meeting in River Falls. I've been sober for two weeks. I really don't have a problem, but Dad said I best go. I can quit drinking any time I want, Lottie."

"Then why didn't you quit sooner, Bill? You know the booze is killing you." Bill looked away for a few moments. "Hey, I know it isn't that easy. I guess that's why they call it an addiction. I have a hard enough time just keeping my mouth shut at times." Bill laughed.

"Now the truth comes out, Lottie. Now I'm going to tell everyone what you just admitted to."

"Well, I'm not an angel, you know. Bill, you can do it. All of us will keep you in our prayers. You know that. Right?" He nodded and then poked Lottie in the shoulder.

"Lottie, your turn. Give me a smile."

"Okay." Bill, you look a little too thin. I'll fix you something to eat after you take me home."

"That will work for me, Lottie."

Lottie and Bill got up from the kitchen table.

"Thanks Lottie, you can really whip up a meal in a hurry. It was great. Those beans and fried potatoes are my favorite. Sure beats my cooking."

"You're welcome, Bill. Mom taught me well when it came to cooking. I'm going to check on the kids to see if they're doing their homework."

"And I'm going outside for a quick smoke."

"Okay," said Lottie.

Bill left the kitchen and went out on the porch. He had one cigarette left in his pack. He shook his head. He lit up. After a minute or two, he pinched the end of the cigarette off and wedged it behind his ear. Bill then sat down in the rocking chair and looked up at the stars.

Blackie came up to Bill, wagged his tail, and then licked Bill's hand. Lottie joined Bill as Blackie left.

"Blackie is quite the comforter," said Bill.

"Bill, you're also a great comfort to our family, you know. And to everyone else."

"Really, Lottie," replied Bill.

"You're always there for us," said Lottie.

"Well, I guess I'm good for something," said Bill.

"That time in the tavern when you first came back from the war, you defended our name," said Lottie. "You know the man who called our family all those terrible things. It was a noble thing to do, but it was a little risky on your part."

"I sure won't forget that," replied Bill. "He left town after that. I'm glad he did. He was a big one. Yeah, he hit me once in the nose, and then I got him with a roundhouse to his head. He hit the floor pretty quick."

"Sheriff Taylor saw all that blood on you and thought for sure you were shot or stabbed," said Lottie.

"It was just a broken nose with a lot of blood, Lottie."

"It seems like things just don't always work out the way we think they should," said Lottie. "I never thought the mill would have a slowdown or we would get behind on the mortgage. And then I never thought I would end up in the sanatorium. You know what Rosa called the sanatorium, Bill? She called it a nut house. That didn't set well with me at first."

"Yeah, I know," replied Bill. "I'm guilty of saying that too in front of John. And who knew that I would be dragged back a few years later into another war and then get shot. Now I can hardly get on or off that motorcycle of mine. People say I shouldn't give up and demand further help from the VA hospital."

"I hope you don't give up," said Lottie.

"Gilbert was gone, just like that," said Bill. "Brother Lance and Mom went so soon thereafter. And I would never have thought I would be in an AA meeting with a bunch of ex-drunks."

"When is your next meeting, Bill?"

"Next Friday, I believe." It's in River Falls.

"What kind of people are in the meetings, Bill?"

"Many of them just seem to be regular people from all walks of life," replied Bill. "It kinda surprised me that most of them had jobs."

"Do you think we will make it through all this?"

Bill shook his head. "I don't know. Hope so. Lottie, it seems like something has been bothering you for some time. I mean something other than John being in the hospital, the bills, and all that. Is there anything you would like to say or something I can do?"

Lottie looked at Bill for a few moments. She got up and walked to the edge of the porch. She took a deep breath and then turned around.

"There's nothing. Nothing at all," said Lottie.

# CHAPTER 12

## *LOTTIE'S INTERVIEW*

There were no resources that Lottie could draw from in order to halt the foreclosure on their house. Lottie never worked full time at any job. She was a homemaker at an early age. Back then, it was common for the husband to be the only breadwinner. The most important job of all was for the wife to be home with the children and also run the household.

Lottie was hesitant to seek employment. Underneath that assertive way of hers was a woman afraid of rejection and unsure of herself. Also, her appearance seldom showed the fragility of her health that often fueled her depression.

Lottie stood in front of the mirror in her bedroom. The new dress that Uncle Will bought her was so pretty, but she wondered if she would be overdressed for the interview.

The only interview she ever had was for a part-time job behind the soda fountain at the diner. She was fifteen then and didn't have a care in the world at the time.

Lottie parked her car on a side street. She made a point to be early, as she didn't want to be late. She got out of the old Ford and walked half a block to Main Street. She just missed the early-morning downpour that hit the town an hour earlier. There was a fresh breeze with a lavender scent as Lottie walked by the town's flower shop. She was determined that morning to have the best day possible.

She stood next to the curb wondering how to get across the standing water created by the downpour. Just as she started to walk up the sidewalk a bit farther, a Plymouth sedan veered toward the curb and sprayed water all over her. Erma Wart, the driver of the sedan, had a smile on her face from ear to ear as she quickly drove by.

Lottie, drenched with water from head to toe, stepped back, took a handkerchief out of her handbag, and tried to wipe the water off her face. Out from the Chinese laundry came the owner. He was a small Chinese man in his early fifties and worked hard to make a go of it.

"You not hurt?" asked the man.

Lottie shook her head. "I'm okay. Just dirty and wet."

"My name is Chu. I see whole thing. That Wart lady from clothes store...a bad lady. Come inside and sit down."

"Thank you so much," said Lottie. She sat on a chair near the counter.

"Bring towel for her," said Chu to his wife.

Moments later, Chu's wife gave Lottie a towel. Lottie tried to wipe the muddy water off her dress but just made it worse.

"Her dress doesn't look so good," said Chu to his wife.

"What happened?" asked Chu's wife.

"That Wart lady splashed water all over me with her car when I was standing next to the curb," said Lottie. "What am I going to do? I have a job interview in a few minutes. My dress and my hair are a mess."

"I help you. My name is Lin," said Chu's wife.

"I'm Lottie, Lottie Rainwater."

"Come with me," said Lin. "I fix everything for you."

Lottie followed Lin to the back of the cleaners. She sat Lottie down in front of a small table.

"Wait here, Mrs. Rainwater," said Lin. "I try to find you a nice dress that doesn't belong to customer." Moments later, Lin came back with a wild-looking dress.

The dress was bright green with a large yellow and orange

butterfly design.

"Put this on," said Lin. "I take your dress for cleaning."

Lottie held the dress up. She was hesitant to put the dress on. She sat back down with the dress over her lap.

"You don't like the dress?" asked Lin.

"Well, okay. It's fine. Thank you," said Lottie.

After Lottie put the dress on, she sat down and Lin combed her hair.

"I go up front," said Lin. "My daughter will do the rest."

A young girl, with silver and blue hair, approached Lottie.

"You look nervous," said Lin's daughter. "I relax you."

As she messaged Lottie's lower neck and shoulders, Lottie dozed off. The daughter then combed Lottie's hair.

"You like colored hair?" asked the young girl.

Lottie, half asleep, nodded. She was unaware what the girl exactly said. The girl sprayed Lottie's hair in spots with one bottle and then with another spray bottle. After finishing the rest of her hair, she applied a healthy amount of bright rouge and lipstick to Lottie's face.

"We're done. Now you have the modern look," said the daughter.

Silver and blue streaks adorned Lottie's auburn-colored hair.

"Do you have a mirror somewhere?" asked Lottie.

"No. No mirror."

"Well, thank you."

Lottie stood up and grabbed her handbag and walked up to the front of the shop. Mr. Chu looked at his wife and then at Lottie.

"Our daughter did her hair?" asked Mr. Chu to his wife.

"Yes she did. That's the modern look, husband," replied his wife. Lottie was puzzled by their response.

"Looks like I'll make my interview just in time," said Lottie.

"Thank you so much for fixing me all up. I'll return the dress as soon as I can."

Lottie walked quickly down the sidewalk and stopped at the business front of 405 North State Street. She pulled out the job ad from her handbag and looked at it for a few moments. She then walked into the office and stopped at the receptionist desk.

"I'm Mrs. Rainwater. I have an eight o'clock appointment for a job interview with Mr. Green." The receptionist checked her calendar.

"Yes, here you are, Mrs. Rainwater. Please have a seat next to the bookcase and someone will be with you very soon."

Lottie sat down and went through her handbag looking for her mirror.

A snobbish-looking woman walked by Lottie, took a double take, and then turned around. "And you're here for?"

"I'm waiting for a job interview," replied Lottie.

"Sure you are," said the office lady.

"Do you have a mirror of some kind that I could use for a moment?" asked Lottie.

"I suppose so," answered the lady. She returned with a mirror with a crack in it.

"Thank you," said Lottie. She looked into the mirror. "Oh my God." Lottie dropped the mirror. It shattered into several pieces.

"Oh great," said the office lady.

The receptionist approached Lottie before she had a chance to pick up the pieces of the mirror. "Mrs. Rainwater, Mr. Green is ready to see you."

"This way," said the receptionist. Lottie followed her down the hallway and into an office. "Please have a seat."

Lottie leaned back in the worn-out wicker chair. She looked around the office. Stacks of old newspapers were in one corner of the office, and two old filing cabinets in the other corner. The carpet had seen two or three wars. There were pictures of ducks on the wall with two shotguns mounted next to them. Lottie looked down at her dress.

"He can't see me this way," Lottie thought.

"Oh, what the heck. Some people think I'm crazy anyway."

"What was that?" said Mr. Green, who came through the door just behind her. She turned around.

"I'm sorry. Nothing... I didn't hear you come in, sir."

He sat behind the desk and picked up her folder. He was a decent-looking man in his fifties. He combed one side of his hair across the top of his bald head. On his desk was a thick-framed pair of glasses like the ones you would get free in the Army. He had a lisp from time to time when he spoke. He was known to have more than forty duck pictures in his home.

"Hello, I'm Mr. Green. On this job, your duties will be filing, bookkeeping, and receptionist. Okay. Let's see here... Married, high school, math one. You took bookkeeping?"

"Yes I did," replied Lottie.

Lottie became a little irritated, as Mr. Green didn't look up at all as he went through her application.

"I suppose I should put my glasses on. I'm nearsighted. I don't even know how you look." He placed his glasses on and looked up at Lottie.

"Holy smokes," said Mr. Green. He stared at Lottie for several moments.

Lottie thought she would break the ice a bit by complementing Mr. Green's duck pictures on the wall.

"Well, you have nice pictures of ducks and...some really nice giant shotguns hanging on the wall," said Lottie.

Mr. Green turned his swivel chair to one side and looked at the pictures.

"My uncle directed the IRS office in town here decades ago," said Mr. Green. "Of course, now it's a diner. He liked ducks and guns. So do I. He's eighty-five now and limps around the best he can, as his ankle was crushed from a bear trap on one of his hunting outings back then. I only got two of his shotguns." He continued talking while he looked up at the duck pictures.

Lottie felt she didn't have a chance to get this job. After all, she sure didn't look the part today, and Mr. Green seemed a bit engrossed in his duck pictures.

"Mr. Green, I'm over here."

"Oh yes," said Mr. Green. "Sorry."

"Mr. Green turned around and faced Lottie. He was still distracted from Lottie's outlandish look. Mr. Green looked at her application again.

"Your name does sound familiar. You have no work references."

"I'm sorry. No I don't, Mr. Green."

"Oh, you're that woman," remarked Mr. Green. "My secretary must have jumped the gun on this application. You know what I mean?"

"Yes I do know what you mean," answered Lottie. "That's too bad. I wore my favorite dress today just for you, sir. It's so pretty as you can see. Do you like it?"

"It's a special one, right? It's quite different," replied Mr. Green.

"How do you like my hair? It's the new modern look." said Lottie. "My appearance is quite breathtaking for you, I'm sure, Mr. Green."

"I'm lost for words here, Mrs. Rainwater."

Mr. Green loosened his tie. Sweat rolled from his forehead. He moved her application forward on his desk.

"I think the receptionist part of the job is out," remarked Mr. Green. "Thanks for coming in. Ah, I'll call you..."

"Of course, you will," replied Lottie.

As Lottie reached over and grabbed her application, she accidentally bumped his ink bottle, spilling ink all over his desk pad.

"Oops. Did I do that? I'm so sorry. Thank you very much for your time," said Lottie.

Lottie left the firm and walked across the street and sat down at a bench next to the post office. Rosa noticed her and walked up to her. "Lottie, is that you?"

"Unfortunately it's me," answered Lottie. Rosa laughed and then sat down with her.

"I was just coming out of the post office, and I wasn't sure if that was you or not. It's not Halloween yet, or is it?"

"Really funny," answered Lottie. "And you're quite right. It's not Halloween today. I guess you can be funny at times."

"I guess," replied Rosa. "What are you doing here so early in the morning?"

"I just had to rest a bit before I drove home," replied Lottie. "It's been a tough morning for me. A terrible thing happened to me before my job interview. That Wart sister purposely drove through some standing water next to the sidewalk as I was on my way to the interview. The man in the Chinese laundry helped me get cleaned up. His wife gave me a dress for the interview, and her daughter did my hair and makeup. I was half asleep when they did this. I'm thankful that they helped me."

"Chu's wife is half blind and can hardly see a thing," replied Rosa. "I'm sure she meant well. Her daughter is a little different. How did the interview go?"

"What do you think?" replied Lottie. "Not well."

"I'm sorry," said Rosa.

"I waited in his office for twenty minutes, and then I dozed off," said Lottie.

"He didn't catch you talking out loud to yourself?" asked Rosa.

"Perhaps," replied Lottie. "It wasn't a big deal. You know how I think out loud at times, especially if I'm half asleep."

"Brother Bill is even worse than you when it comes to that," remarked Rosa. "You both are so much alike."

"I knew I didn't have a chance in that interview, so I toyed with him a bit, Rosa. He really got shook up. I'm sure I made a lasting impression on Mr. Green."

"Well, I guess this whole family isn't quite right," said Rosa.

Lottie smiled. "I think you're right. I should get home and clean up before Linda brings the kids home. I don't want to scare them to death."

"Oh, I almost forgot. Winnie called and said that she will be home to visit us in two weeks," said Rosa.

"This will be a very special gathering for all of us," said Lottie.

# CHAPTER 13

## *WINNIE'S CONFESSION*

Lottie invited the Lindstrom family over to her house for the family meeting. She hoped that everyone would come. She wanted to share her revelation with them. Also, she didn't want to confront Winnie by herself. Lottie wasn't sure if she was up to it.

Rosa, Gloria, Winnie, and Linda sat around the coffee table in the living room. Looking at the Lindstrom girls, one could tell that their good looks also came from their mother.

Gloria, the youngest daughter in the Lindstrom family, had a great smile and was as pretty as her sisters. She was always at Lottie's side. Linda, Gloria's daughter, like many teenagers, knew everything, but she never got in trouble and always helped Lottie with the kids. Linda also was a great help to the unfortunate people who showed up on Saturdays for the morning breakfast.

Rosa was in her mid-forties. She had blue eyes and her share of gray hair. She could be somewhat cranky at times, but she did have a dry sense of humor. Rosa always helped when asked and also had a very special laugh.

Winnie was in her fifties and never married as far as anyone knew. At the age of eighteen, she was quite the looker. She won Miss Idaho and was spotted by a talent agent out of Hollywood. They sent her to drama school in Los Angeles, and then after a few years her career took off.

She had one problem. She depended on her beauty to carry her through her career. She never really refined her acting ability as well as she should have. After several years as an actress, she realized that she had to address some issues concerning her career. By that time, she had only supporting roles here and there, but it was a living. She took what she could get.

Winnie wasn't much help to the family after their dad lost the bank to her two older brothers. She was never close to those two, but she did like Bill very much, as well as her sisters. Now her big car was getting old, and she had to watch her money. One day, Winnie said that she might have to work at the diner slinging hash to the customers. Rosa thought different, as Sheriff Taylor would never let that happen.

Winnie still looked like a million bucks and always contacted Sheriff Taylor when she was in town. Some of the men in town were quite jealous of the sheriff for having Winnie as a close friend. The sheriff always said that Winnie picked him and that it was his civic duty to please her when he could. What else could he do?

No one expected Uncle Zach to show up. He said he just had too much work at the bank and didn't want to be concerned with unimportant family matters. They knew that Bill might not show, as he was probably at the Friday-night AA meeting in River Falls.

Of course, everyone wished that their mother was still alive and sitting there with them. Ingrid was a great mother but seemed to like other men a little too much in her early life. Uncle Will never liked being with Ingrid when she was heavy on the sauce. At times, he stayed overnight at the bank. He remarked one time that perhaps he should have chosen a girl with the prettiest insides, not the prettiest outsides. It is said that Ingrid didn't cook supper for him for two weeks after that.

Meeting time at the Rainwaters' house was at seven in the evening. Lottie brought the coffee and some cookies to the coffee table. She served the coffee and then sat down next to Gloria and Linda. Winnie and Rosa sat across from them. Winnie didn't seem as relaxed as she usually was.

"Looks like we are it," said Rosa. "I heard that our dad is not feeling well, so I guess he won't be here tonight."

"Again, it's nice to see you, Winnie," remarked Gloria. "Any big movie contracts coming your way?"

"Well, not yet. I haven't had a movie role for about ten months. My agent insulted me the other day and said I was getting long in years. Can you imagine that?" As Linda giggled, Gloria elbowed her.

"That's okay, Linda," said Winnie. "My agent is probably right. I'm not the skinny glamorous young one anymore."

Lottie, who was usually the outgoing talkative one, remained silent. As the girls talked back and forth, Lottie thought about how and when she was going to present all this to them. How would she approach Winnie about the thirty-some-year lie? Would Winnie, the actress, deny everything after all these years?

"Lottie, what did you want to see us about?" asked Rosa. "It must be important. You wanted all of us to be together here tonight."

Lottie looked around the table and then closed her eyes for a few moments. She was uneasy as she spoke.

"I don't know how to say this," said Lottie. "I wish our dad was here tonight and, of course, our mother.

When I was adopted by the family, all of you took me in as if I was always one of you. I could not have asked for more. But someone has kept a secret for many years. That one is sitting right here among us. Yes, right here."

Winnie looked at Lottie and then looked away.

"That's what I want to talk to you girls tonight about," said Lottie. "Just before I entered the sanatorium, I found out my true identity."

"Identity... What do you mean?" asked Gloria.

"Winnie has been silent for over thirty years, and so was our mother," said Lottie. "Winnie knows what I'm talking about."

"I don't know what our little sister is saying," replied Winnie. "You know how she is."

As Lottie stood up, she threw her coffee cup against the wall, shattering it. She glared at Winnie as she spoke.

"Winnie, you do know!" screamed Lottie. "You kept the truth from us all these years!"

"Oh gee. Lottie's going off again," said Linda in a low voice.

Rosa pinched Linda's arm. "That wasn't nice," said Rosa.

"I'm sorry," said Linda.

Winnie became rattled.

Lottie rushed into the kitchen. Gloria followed her. As Winnie started to leave, Rosa stood up and took her arm.

"Sit down, Winnie. We need some answers."

"Are they talking about me in there?" asked Winnie.

"Probably are," answered Rosa. "And all of us will be talking about this for a long time. Right?"

Winnie sat back down. Nervously, she opened her purse and took a cigarette out of her stainless cigarette case.

"I have to go outside for a quick smoke."

"Don't forget to come back," said Rosa.

Lottie and Gloria were still in the kitchen.

"Lottie, what's going on?" asked Gloria. "I hate to see you this way." She held Lottie for a few moments.

"I just wish John was here," said Lottie. This is so hard for me to do alone."

"You're not alone, Lottie. Is there anything I can say or do for you?"

"Nothing you can do, Gloria, I'm the one who has to get Winnie to tell us what is really going on."

"Let's get back in there," said Gloria, "I'll be right next to you. Everything will work out. Okay?"

Lottie nodded.

Gloria, with her arm around Lottie, brought her back into the living room. Gloria sat down and turned to Lottie.

"Come on," said Gloria. "Please sit."

Lottie sat down as Winnie came back in from the porch. Winnie stood there for a few moments.

"Please sit with us," said Gloria. "She has something to say to us." Winnie reluctantly sat down.

"I do have something to say," said Winnie. "Lottie is more than just an adopted family member. Lottie is...my daughter. Yes...my daughter." Rosa, Gloria, and Linda were stunned.

"Your daughter! How did this happen?" asked Gloria.

"Our mom adopted Lottie when she was born. She agreed not to disclose that it was my baby," said Winnie. I was young and really into myself. I was worried about my image. In Hollywood, image is everything."

"What did dad know about this?" asked Rosa.

"Our dad was told it was some woman who didn't want her child," answered Winnie. "I'm not sure if he ever caught on that Lottie was my daughter. Back then, things were quite simple and no one asked questions."

"So that's why you spent more time with her instead with us," said Gloria.

"I should have said something later on," said Winnie. "We had such a great relationship as sisters. I just kept putting it off."

"Lottie, we just never knew," said Rosa. "Looks like Mom is still full of surprises."

"I thought Lottie would have a chance to live a normal life with our mom instead of being dragged all over the country," said Winnie. I was afraid of what people might say. Now you know. "I really messed up."

"That wasn't right. You just didn't want Lottie at all," said Rosa. "How could you do that to her? You're terrible! I won't accept your excuses."

"Rosa, calm down," said Gloria. "Give Winnie a chance." Rosa turned to Lottie and then to Winnie.

"Okay, okay," said Rosa.

"Well, who's Lottie's father?"

"Not now, Linda," said Gloria.

"It's okay, Gloria," said Winnie. "I'm going to get to that very soon. I went to London in 1921 with a theater group from the states. The war was officially over, and everyone in Europe seemed to be hungry for entertainment and good times again. I did well in the theater. As a result, my name really got into the spotlight. I was really accepted by my fellow actors.

I met Lottie's dad at a party. He was working at the embassy in London. His name was Joe, Captain Joe Wagner. He was from Ashford, California. After a couple of dates, I just knew that he was the one for me. We saw each other quite often. I had to leave for the states sooner than I thought. We agreed that we would get married soon as Joe came back to the states in a few months."

Winnie's voice became shaken as she spoke.

"I arrived in LA, and then a month later I received word from Joe's mother that he was killed in an auto accident. I also found out that I was pregnant. I never met his mother. She passed away a few months after that. I can still see Joe's face. He had hazel eyes, just like Lottie. I still think of him after all these years."

Tears formed in Winnie's eyes.

"I still don't get how you got Mom to adopt Lottie and keep this secret for such a long time," said Gloria.

"There's something else I haven't told all of you that has been bothering me for many years," remarked Winnie. "Bill already knows what our mom did back then. Bill didn't really know when or how to explain all this. Perhaps he was waiting for me to say something."

"There's more?" said Rosa

"Yes there is," replied Winnie.

So our mother wouldn't say a thing about Lottie being my daughter, I blackmailed her. In turn, I wouldn't say anything about

Bill's birth to anyone. Bill is not our dad's son. I found out by accident that Mom had an affair prior to Lottie being adopted. So that's how I blackmailed her. I'm not real proud about that."

"This is really getting too crazy," said Rosa. "No wonder Lottie is having a hard time dealing with things. You are one terrible lady." Winnie struggled to continue on.

"Mom told Bill when she was on her death bed about her affair," said Winnie. "He was shattered. Bill finally told our dad last night. I think in the back of his mind, Dad always knew about the affair. You know he doesn't like to start trouble."

"So Bill is really our half brother," remarked Gloria. "So now Bill has another thing to deal with besides the booze."

"Lottie, looks like you have blood-related aunts and uncles now instead of brothers and sisters by adoption," said Winnie.

Gloria gave Lottie a hug. "You can still call me Sis if you want," said Gloria.

"Lottie, I feel the same way," remarked Rosa.

Lottie smiled.

"And I guess Linda is actually Lottie's cousin. How am I going to keep all this straight?" said Rosa.

"I haven't been much help to the family," remarked Winnie. "My money went for everything that's not that important anymore. Hollywood just consumed me. I guess I let it. Lottie, I'm sorry. I'm so sorry for not telling you."

The sisters looked at each other for several moments. Lottie tried not to look at Winnie directly.

"Let's all of us go to the Road 40 Diner just like the old days. It's my treat. I have plenty of time on my hands. There's not much call for an older leading lady like me."

"Well, okay, let's go," said Gloria.

Winnie grabbed her handbag, walked to the front door, and then waited. Gloria and Rosa followed her. Rosa turned to Lottie.

"You're coming with us. Right? It would be nice if all of us went together to the diner."

Lottie shook her head and walked into the kitchen. Linda followed Lottie. Winnie looked at Gloria in despair.

"Well, I can't blame her for being angry," said Winnie.

"Lottie will cool down. I'm sure she will," said Gloria. "We all had a stressed-out night."

As the sisters got into Winnie's 1940 Cadillac sedan, Linda ran out the door toward them.

"Don't forget me!"

The Road 40 Diner was between Bergan's Ferry and River Falls. It was a little spendy there, but Winnie wanted a stiff drink, as only beer was served at the Doughboy Diner. The sisters, along with Linda, sat in a large booth near the back of the diner. Gloria, Linda, and Rosa were super busy in girl talk, but Winnie just looked down at the table. She didn't even touch the drink that she ordered.

The side door of the diner opened slowly. In the doorway stood Lottie. The lighting in the diner was dim, and the place was loaded with people. The girls were unaware of Lottie's presence as she slowly walked toward them. She stopped for a few moments as if she might change her mind. She then walked up to Winnie and tapped her on the shoulder. Winnie, startled, turned around.

"I would like to sit with you, Mom," said Lottie.

"You called me Mom."

Winnie broke out in tears. Lottie sat down and held Winnie's hand for several moments.

"There are some things that I can't change, Lottie. I'm going to do the best I can. Please be patient."

"I know," said Lottie. "You're not my sister anymore. Right?"

"You're right, Lottie. You are my daughter."

# CHAPTER 14

## *TRAINS, BOTTLES, AND BRUISES*

Mr. Diggs was the owner of a shoe shop in Bergan's Ferry. It was the only shoe repair place in town. Mr. Diggs at times shared the same crony table with Zach at the diner. Even though his quality of shoe repair was satisfactory, a few people preferred to take the seven-car ferry to River Falls, as the shoe prices were more reasonable and they also escaped Mr. Diggs' charming ways.

The front windows of his shoe shop always seemed to be in need of cleaning, and the entrance way was tacky looking. Inside the shop up front was a shoe rack. Men's white bucks and teenagers' saddle shoes were on display. There were oxfords and a few Florsheim shoes for the businessmen. They were five to eight dollars. The Red Wing steel-toed work shoes were popular but very expensive. They were twelve to fifteen dollars.

On the other side of the shop was an upright beverage cooler full of soda pop. The price was cheap, but the soda pop wasn't that great. Next to it was a round table with a couple of chairs. His wife made sandwiches and cookies for sale.

Last week, Mr. Diggs decided to take the ferry across the Copper River instead of the bridge that was twelve miles down the road. He had to pick up some supplies for his shop. The old ferry broke down and drifted downstream and ended up on a sandbar. He was three hours late for supper. No one missed him.

It was nine in the morning when Mark entered the shoe shop. He looked at the new black tennis shoes on the rack. Mr. Diggs gave him a harsh look.

"Hello kid. What do you want?"

"I can do some work for you if you can fix my shoes," said Mark.

"What can you do?" asked Mr. Diggs.

"I know how to clean windows and sweep floors. I can cut the grass. My dad showed me how to work a lawn mower one time. I saw that lawn mower in back."

"You strong enough to push that big lawn mower? Wait. You're that Indian kid. Right? There's no work here for you." Mark turned around and started to leave.

"Wait," said Mr. Diggs. He led Mark into the back storeroom where there were several boxes of old bottles.

"See all those bottles?" said Mr. Diggs.

"That's a lot of bottles. A whole bunch," said Mark.

"They're yours, kid. You can take them down to the grocery store and get some deposit money for them."

"I got my wagon, and my sister has a wagon," said Mark.

"Okay, that might work," replied Mr. Diggs. "Come back tomorrow. Tomorrow is Saturday. I'll be here at the store to let you in."

As Mark left the shop, Mr. Diggs called his wife up front and then laughed.

"So what's up with the Rainwater boy?" asked his wife.

"Looks like we'll get rid of all those old bottles," said Mr. Diggs.

"How's that?" asked his wife.

"That Rainwater kid will take them," replied Mr. Diggs.

"They're not worth anything," said his wife. "The stores won't take most of them for a return deposit."

"I know. That's his problem," replied Mr. Diggs.

Saturday afternoon, Sara walked up to Mark. "Where did Mommy go?" asked Sara.

"Mom left to see Dad at the hospital," answered Mark. "Mom said that we have to stay home. But we can't."

"What do you mean?" asked Sara.

"We have a bunch of bottles to pick up," replied Mark. "We can make some money. Dad said one time that you can turn in empty pop bottles and get two cents for each one. The shoe shop man has a whole bunch of bottles in his back room. We can use our wagons to pick them up, Sara."

"Where would we sell them, Mark?"

"Mr. Lewis at the grocery store would take them," replied Mark. "Uncle Bill did that one time. I asked Uncle Bill if they would take his empty whiskey bottles for money. He said that he wished they did."

Mark and Lottie pulled their old red Radio Flyer wagons down to the shoe shop.

"It's going take us a lot trips to get all these bottles to the grocery store," said Sara.

The children finished taking the bottles to the grocery store. They stacked the two dozen boxes of bottles against the side of the building.

"These bottles look so old," said Mark. "And there's still some pop in them. That's why some of these boxes were so heavy."

"We can come by Monday morning, said Sara. "Mr. Lewis can count them and then he can give us some money."

Mr. Lewis and his wife had the grocery store for about thirty years. They were having a hard time competing against the new Thriftway store in River Falls. They knew they couldn't go against a giant food chain like that, as their lease for their building was quite high. They seldom let anyone run a tab on groceries, as it was cash only, but they had a soft spot for the Rainwaters, and they also attended the same church at times.

The next day, Mark and Sara were with Mr. Lewis at the grocery store. Mr. Lewis picked up one of the bottles and then shook his head.

"Where did you get these bottles?" ask Mr. Lewis.

"The shoe shop man gave us these bottles," answered Mark.

Mr. Lewis pulled more of the bottles out of the boxes, as Lottie drove up. She got out and walked over to them.

"Good morning, Mrs. Rainwater."

"And a good morning to you, Mr. Lewis."

"What are you kids doing here?" asked Lottie. "You're not supposed to run off like you did yesterday without telling me."

"But we had to, Mom," replied Mark.

"So these are the pop bottles you talked about," said Lottie.

Lottie looked at some of the bottles.

"Sorry, but most of these bottles aren't worth anything, said Mr. Lewis. "They don't even make these brands anymore. Someone really got to these kids, Mrs. Rainwater."

Lottie picked up a couple of the bottles. "Some of these bottles are still full. Never been opened."

"I guess they couldn't sell them," replied Mr. Lewis.

"Kids, who gave you these bottles?" asked Lottie.

"It was the shoe shop by the ferry dock," said Mark. "He had the bottles in his back storeroom."

"We had to make a lot of trips to bring all these bottles to the store here," said Sara.

"I know, honey," said Lottie. "That was Mr. Diggs that did this to you. Mr. Lewis, one reason I stopped by was that we can't pay off the bill on the grocery tab just yet."

"Don't worry about it right now," said Mr. Lewis.

"Thank you so," said Lottie. "I'll pay you as soon as we can. There's not enough room in my car to take these bottles away. I'll have Bill come by early in the morning and take them away. Maybe he can use his dad's truck."

"That's fine, Mrs. Rainwater. Sorry I could only take in a few of these bottles.

How about two big Hershey candy bars with peanuts for the

four good bottles out of the bunch, kids?"

Lottie gave him a hug. "What's that for?" asked Mr. Lewis.

"Just because," replied Lottie.

Tuesday morning, Uncle Will stopped by the grocery store. He looked around and then walked into the store.

"Hello, Great Uncle Will. What can we do for you?" asked Mr. Lewis.

"I just happened to be nearby with my truck, so I thought I would pick up those worthless empty bottles for Lottie," said Uncle Will. "I can take them to the dump. I didn't see any of the bottles outside."

"Oh, your son didn't pick them up already?" asked Mr. Lewis.

"No, Bill has been out of town for the last two days."

"They're all gone," replied Mr. Lewis. "Someone did us a favor."

"Well that's sure strange, Mr. Lewis. That's okay. Less work for everyone. I know Lottie owes you some money. Here's ten dollars for now. Please put it toward their tab. I'll be back next week with a few more dollars. Just keep this between you and me."

"Thank you, I understand," replied Mr. Lewis.

Monday morning, Mr. Diggs was an hour late to open his shop, as his lights in his car were left on by someone. He had to jump-start the dead battery to get his car started. As he opened the front door of his shoe shop, he looked up at a wall of bottles.

"What?"

Mr. Diggs stepped back in amazement. Over ten times the bottles that the children took away two days before stood in the doorway and shop.

"How could this be?" said Mr. Diggs' wife. She squeezed her way past the boxes of bottles and into the shop.

"This place was locked," said his wife. "There must be over a hundred boxes. Where did all these bottles come from?"

\* \* \* \*

One of Mark's favorite places to sit was on a mound of dirt next to the tracks that was about fifty feet away from their house. From there, he had a commanding view of the rail yard and the sawmill across the way. Mark would raise his arm up and down to signal the train engineers to pull their steam whistle cords when they passed by. Even Sara liked sitting there with Mark at times. She envisioned herself hitching a ride to Hollywood to see all the movie stars. Lottie knew when Mark was on the mound, as there was coal dust on the bottom side of his pants.

Mark's favorite rail yard man was Mr. Mendoza. He was one of the men who worked in the rail switching yard. He was a big man from Mexico and had very dark brown skin. He spoke with a heavy accent. Mr. Mendoza and his family lived on railroad property in section housing. That was common in those days. These small houses were dark orange in color and were for the families of the railroad workers. When Mark's dad walked across the tracks to work, Mendoza always greeted him.

Mark's greatest event ever was when a huge Union Pacific steam locomotive came down the tracks to the rail yard. They were called Big Boys. It had sixteen nearly six-foot-high drive wheels, with four pilot wheels up front. The locomotive was over 132 feet long. It stopped at the farthest set of tracks across where Mark was sitting that day on the dirt mound. Steam escaped from the steam valves and ports. It was a massive display of machinery.

One of the engineers stepped down from the cab. He wore the typical blue-striped coveralls and the engineer cap. In his grasp was a large long-spouted oil can. He lubricated the fittings on various parts of the locomotive machinery. The other engineer stepped up into the coal tender behind the locomotive.

Mark jumped off the dirt mound and ran across the sets of tracks to see the locomotive.

Mark stood there in awe. There was the smell of machine oil, and steam engulfed parts of the engine section. One of the engineers walked over to Mark.

"You shouldn't be here, little boy. Does your mother know you're here in the rail yard?"

"Ah... No," said Mark.

"It's best you leave," said the engineer. "It's not safe here."

"But I wanted to see your giant locomotive," said Mark. "I've never see one like this before."

"Sorry. You can see it from over there," said the engineer.

The engineer walked Mark across the set of tracks to the other side. Mark got back up on the dirt mound and watched. The engineer boarded the locomotive and set it in motion. As the drive wheels turned, steam jetted out everywhere. The locomotive gained speed and left the rail yard heading north. Sara came up behind Mark and climbed up onto the dirt mound.

"Mark, we got to do something," said Sara. "We need to look for bottles so we can make some money. I've got these small gunnysacks that we can put the bottles in. Mommy said we can collect the bottles but we can't go across the tracks."

"Why do you always call our mom, Mommy? Only babies say that," said Mark.

"Because I want to," replied Sara. "And I'm not a baby. I'm as tall as you are."

"Never mind," replied Mark. "Uncle Bill said to look behind buildings where people work and along the railroad tracks. He said that they just toss the empty bottles out."

"Maybe down by the cement place," said Sara.

"And Uncle Bill said there's always a lot of empty bottle in back of the stores downtown in the alleys, said Mark.

As Mark and Sara walked down the side of the tracks, Blackie, their dog, followed behind them. Sara turned around.

"Go home, Blackie," shouted Sara.

Blackie stopped and then turned his attention to the pigeons that landed three tracks over. Blackie ran under the parked boxcars toward the pigeons as a train entered the rail yard.

"Blackie!" shouted Mark.

As Mark ran toward Blackie, he tripped and fell, hitting his knee on planks between the crossing rails. Blackie stopped as the pigeons took off, but the train was already bearing down on Blackie.

The train passed by and then stopped several yards later. Blackie was nowhere in sight. Mark held his knee as he lay on the ground. Sara ran up to him.

"I hit my knee," cried Mark. "Where's Blackie?"

"I don't know," answered Sara. "The trained stopped. I don't see him. I think he got run over."

As Sara tried to help Mark up, Mendoza the rail yard worker rushed over to them.

"What happened?" asked Mendoza.

"I fell and hit my knee."

"Let me carry you to your house," said Mendoza.

He picked up Mark and walked across the tracks to the Rainwaters' house and up to the front porch. Sara opened the screen door.

"Mommy, Mark is hurt real bad." Lottie quickly opened the screen door.

"What happened?" asked Lottie.

Mendoza carried Mark into the house and laid him down on the davenport.

"I guess he fell and hit his knee," said Mendoza. "I think it's banged up pretty bad, Lottie."

"He was running after Blackie, Mommy," said Sara.

"Honey, you're going to be okay," said Lottie.

"It hurts, Mom," said Mark.

"I know. It's going to get better," said Lottie.

"Mommy, I think Blackie got hit by the train," said Sara. "I think he's dead."

"Are you sure? Let's take care of your brother first, Sara," said Lottie as she gently raised his bloody pant leg.

"I think we better take him to the hospital," said Lottie.

Mark sat on the side of the hospital bed, and Lottie sat next to him. A large bandage was wrapped around his knee.

"He needs to be on crutches for about two weeks," said the doctor. "His knee really took a beating. The good thing is that your son doesn't have a fractured kneecap. You really have your hands full with your husband upstairs and now this. You look really tired. Is there anything I can do, Mrs. Rainwater?"

"I'm okay, doctor. Somehow we will get through this. Thanks for asking."

"The nurse will be back with the crutches in a few minutes," said the doctor.

As Lottie dozed off, she leaned to one side and then fell onto the bed. Minutes later, the nurse returned with the crutches.

"Ah... Your mother is asleep?"

"I think so," said Sara.

"Mom gets real tried sometimes," said Mark. "Uncle Bill is afraid that she might fall asleep when she drives the car."

"Oh...my," said the nurse. "Does she kinda sleep here and there?"

"Yeah. One time Mommy went to the other hospital to sleep," said Sara. "The bad kids at school called it the nut house." The nurse gave Sara and Mark a look.

* * * *

As the Rainwater family was at the hospital, the hobo, with

Blackie in his arms, lowered him onto the porch of their house.

"Just rest, my friend," said the hobo.

Blackie barked two times and then wagged his tail.

# CHAPTER 15

## *THE DINER'S NEW WAITRESS*

Lottie Rainwater parked next to the Chinese laundry on a Monday morning. This time, she didn't need a dress or to have her hair redone. The interview at the Doughboy Diner went much smoother than the last one at the firm. At least her hair didn't have blue and silver patches, and her makeup wasn't outlandish.

Mr. Wendal asked in the interview how many plates of food could she carry at one time. Lottie said one plate for sure. He also asked her if her hair was always that long. She said it was that long all day and night. Mr. Wendal just shook his head.

Lottie wasn't crazy about the waitress uniform that she had on. It was light gray with dark blue trim. The hat was dark blue as well as the apron. Lottie felt like she was in a West Point cadet military uniform. All she needed was some corporal stripes.

Lottie looked at her watch, and it was half past seven. The diner didn't open till seven a.m. She sat in the car for a few more minutes as she looked at the diner's menu. She was glad there weren't six dozen variations of breakfast to remember.

She thought about the part-time job she had over fifteen years ago at the diner's soda fountain booth. She was carefree and really didn't need the job back then. Today things were different. She had to do well for the two-day trial at the diner.

Lottie got out of her car and walked up State Street and then turned left on Main. As she walked up to the side door of the diner, out came Jim. He owned the plumbing repair shop in town.

"Hi, Lottie," said Jim.

"Good morning," replied Lottie.

"What brings you here in a waitress uniform?" asked Jim.

"I'm trying out for the waitress job. And you?"

"I just got done clearing a drain for them, Lottie. That new assistant manager is something else. His manners surely could be improved."

"I'll be back in an hour to get something to eat," said Jim.

"And please give me double butter for my pancakes."

"Of course I will," replied Lottie with a smile.

"Good luck, Lottie."

Lottie walked into the diner and hung her coat up. She recognized a lot of the people who were there that early Monday morning. Mr. Neilson waved at her as he was sitting down. Greta came through the kitchen swinging doors and walked up to Lottie.

"Hi Lottie. Good to see you. I heard that you'll be trying out for the job today."

"Sure am," replied Lottie.

"The manager just left again for the day for some odd reason," said Greta. "Just follow me around and observe how we take orders, carry the food, and all that. Toward the end of the day, I'll let you wait on a few tables. I'll be right along your side, Lottie. Don't worry about a thing."

"Thanks, Greta," said Lottie.

Greta was an older German lady in her late fifties who had worked there for twenty years. She could carry three plates of food at one time, and she knew the first names of most of the customers. Greta's hairstyle was a Heidi braid, and she often wore Bavarian dresses during the holidays.

Greta always waited on Uncle Will when he came in. Rosa said they got along too well. Gloria said it was none of her business. The waitresses all had the same opinion about Mr. Wendal. He was a jerk and didn't seem to make a lot of trips to the bathtub.

The second day was the real test for Lottie. Greta had that day off, and Lottie didn't know the other new waitress who was on duty with her. As Lottie tried to enter the side door, a young woman rushed out the door, bumping into her.

"I'm so sorry. Excuse me," said the young lady.

"That's okay," said Lottie.

"You're the new waitress?"

"Yes I am," replied Lottie.

"Good luck to you, ma'am. I had enough of that jerk face."

The young lady left in a hurry. Lottie went to the kitchen and sat off to the side at a small table. The grill was ablaze with bacon and hash browns. A large bowl of pancake batter was ready to go, and there were six pieces of dark rye ready to jump out of the toaster. To the left of the kitchen was a large double-door GE icebox.

In back, a little man was banging away with the washed pots and pans as he placed them on the rack. He stacked another tray of crystal-clear glasses. Ed, the dishwasher, could outwash anyone in the county. Everyone liked him, even though his singing wasn't that great. The coffee cups were red candy striped in color, and the plates were deep dished and could hold a ton of hash, eggs, and biscuits. The silverware was made in the state of New York.

One of the cooks stepped over and gave Lottie a cup of coffee. Lottie's hands shook a bit when she picked up the coffee.

"You're a nice lady. Try not to be nervous," said the cook.

"Thanks," replied Lottie. "The coffee tastes good."

Lottie hoped that Sheriff Taylor or Uncle Will would be in today. She knew with them around, Mr. Wendal might not give her a real hard time. They both were very protective of Lottie, and Uncle Bill would go to battle if he had to. Of course, she knew that they couldn't be there all the time. But it would be comforting with them around.

As Lottie took her first sip of coffee, Mr. Wendal came blasting through the kitchen door.

"First thing in the morning, you're sucking up all the coffee, lady?"

"Sir, My start time isn't for another ten minutes. I was just trying to collect myself," replied Lottie.

"Collect yourself out there, lady," said Mr. Wendal.

"My name is Lottie."

"Don't care," said Mr. Wendal. "Just go."

Lottie quickly put her apron on and went up front with her menu. To her surprise, in strolled the Wart sisters from the dress shop. They looked around. Erma had a smug look on her face.

All Lottie could see was fire. Lottie stepped back. The sisters walked around and then finally landed on a table. Sue sat down first. Erma pulled her chair way out from the table so she could fit herself in. She then looked over and gave Lottie a sinister smile. Right there, Lottie wanted to give her a black eye.

Reluctantly, Lottie walked over to their table, as it was her assigned section. She stood there in silence for a moment.

"Good morning," said Lottie, with a forced smile.

"Well, what do we have here?" said Sue.

"Looks like the lady thinks she's a waitress or something," said Erma. Sue laughed.

Lottie tried to maintain her smile. Lottie knew she needed this job and would just have to deal with it. One of the customers looked their way and didn't like what was going on.

"What would you ladies like to drink?" asked Lottie.

"We'll take some coffee with cream," said Sue. "And the cream better be fresh. The stupid waitress that just quit always brought us cream that curled in our coffee."

Lottie wished for a moment that those two would curdle in their coffin. "It will be fresh. Anything else, ladies?"

"That's all," said Erma.

"Yes, that's all," said Sue.

The sisters whispered to each other and then laughed. They quickly moved over to a large table nearby.

"This is the only large table we have," said Lottie.

"The customer is always right, waitress," said Erma.

Moments later, Lottie brought the sisters their coffee and then waited on the table next to them. Postman Joe sat at the table adjacent to the Wart sisters.

"Hi Lottie. You're a waitress?" asked Joe.

"Yes I am. This is my second day."

"Oh... How's your husband doing, Lottie?"

"John has been in a coma now for about five weeks. It's been rough, Joe."

"Well I hope he snaps out of the coma very soon," said Joe.

As Lottie left to get his order, the sisters started up a loud conversation.

"She thinks she's so pretty and tall," said Erma. "And that uniform is so tight on her. She's just teasing the heck out of him, I'm sure."

Joe looked toward them. He shook his head. "Ladies, tone it down a bit. Just be nice."

"Well, I guess you're an outspoken one," replied Erma.

"Yes I am, ladies," replied Joe.

Lottie brought Joe's order and started to leave his table.

"Waitress, we require service. Waitress!" said Sue in a loud voice.

"You best get over here, or we'll complain to the manager," said Erma.

By that time, a few more customers got wind of what was happening. They didn't like the Wart sisters' attitude. Lottie returned to the sisters' table.

"You forgot our pie," said Sue. "My sister ordered blackberry pie with ice cream. If you find the time, bring me the same."

"You didn't order any when I asked, ladies."

"Just bring it, waitress," demanded Erma.

Lottie looked at them cross-eyed and then stuck her tongue out at the sisters. She then left for the kitchen. Erma turned to a customer.

"Did you see that? No wonder her kid is a retard," said Erma.

"Give the waitress a break," said the customer. "You people are very rude. You deserved that."

Lottie got back into the kitchen and found a bowl. She filled it with soft ice cream. She then picked up a blackberry pie off the counter. The waitress came into the kitchen and approached Lottie.

"Are they going to get all that?" she asked.

"You bet they are. Just making sure I have enough," replied Lottie.

Lottie marched through the swinging doors of the kitchen and over to the Wart sisters' table. She stood there for a few moments with a cynical smile.

"I have your pie and ice cream, ladies. It's on the house," said Lottie. "Isn't that nice?"

"That much?" asked Erma.

Suddenly Lottie pushed the blackberry pie in Erma's face and dumped the bowl of ice cream on Sue's head.

"There you go, Lottie!" said a customer.

Lottie stood there for a few moments. She smiled as some of the customers applauded her.

"Thank you. Looks like I'm going to take a long break," said Lottie. She walked into the kitchen, and then Mr. Wendal turned to her.

"What's was going on out there?" asked Mr. Wendal.

"I'm sorry," said Lottie. "It seems that the Wart sisters didn't exactly say where they wanted the ice cream and pie."

Lottie grabbed her coat and walked out the side door.

# CHAPTER 16

## *THE CEMETERY*

Lottie walked onto the cemetery grounds just on the edge of town. The cemetery had a lot of history. In 1857, a wagon train came through en route to Coeur d'Alene, Idaho. Two people died when their covered wagon tipped over and slid down a hundred-foot embankment. The parents were buried along a large growth of young Ponderosa pine trees. They were the Bergan family. The surviving sons of the Bergan family stayed behind and decided to make a go of it. The Halverson family settled there a few weeks later. The two young men eventually married the Halverson's daughters. Many more families that came through joined them. Years later, the township became known as Bergan's Ferry.

Lottie walked up the pathway and stopped at the headstone of a young man who died in World War I. He was only twenty-two.

Lottie took one of the flowers in her hand and placed it in front of the small headstone. She made the sign of the cross and continued on.

She stopped in front of three headstones. She placed two flowers on each one of them and then stepped back. A tear rolled down the side of her cheek. She took a white handkerchief out of her pocket and dabbed her tears. She tried to say a prayer but had a hard time clearing her throat.

A tan-colored DeSoto stopped on the side road of the cemetery. Uncle Bill rolled down his window and sat there for a few minutes. Even though he seen a lot of death in his life from the two wars he was in, this was the last place he wanted to come to. He got out of the car and slowly walked down the path toward Lottie.

Lottie turned around and noticed him. She smiled as Bill walked up and stood next to her. He took his hat off and put his arm around her for a few moments.

"Gilbert went first," said Lottie. "You know, I considered him more than just a relative by marriage."

"I did too, Lottie."

"Then Mom and Uncle Lance went so quick," remarked Lottie.

"She treated me as if I was her firstborn."

Bill gave Lottie an odd look when she mentioned his dad. "Are you okay?" asked Bill.

"I'm much better than a couple of months ago," answered Lottie. "How about you?"

"I guess it's really getting to me. Gloria said I don't show much emotion at times. I don't mean to be that way. Sometimes I think there's something wrong with me because of that."

"I understand. No, you're okay, Bill."

"I just don't get why they all died together in such a short time," said Bill. "It's like this family was singled out."

"Don't say that, Bill. Father McDonald said that God will let some things happen for a reason. I just don't understand it either."

"Well, he might be right, Lottie. I sure don't know why."

"Let's sit over there," said Lottie.

They sat down on a bench under a large apple blossom tree.

"Bill, you know when you asked me one day if something was bothering me. Well, by now you must have heard about Winnie's confession, as I call it. Winnie also told us about Ingrid's affair. I hope I didn't speak out too soon."

"I figured Winnie would say something about that when all of you met at your house that night, Lottie. Now I know how you must have felt after you found out about being Winnie's daughter. I'm still upset about the truth not being told. Well, Winnie is still my sister. And I guess you're actually my niece now."

"Looks that way, Bill."

"But you can still call me Brother Bill if you like."

"Okay, Uncle Brother Bill."

"Works for me," said Bill with a big smile.

"A while back, you said to John that I was like kinfolk to you before you knew that I was actually related to the family. It was nice to say something like that, Bill. And your dad now is truly my Great Uncle Will. The new titles are a bit confusing."

"I can understand that," said Bill. "We're a lot alike. We never met our dads. I'm only two years older than you. Looks like I was born late in the game. Can you forgive Winnie?" asked Bill.

"I'm working on it," answered Lottie. "I just can't turn a switch and then everything is just fine."

"Yeah, I know what you mean, Lottie. It's not easy at times for any of us."

"I believe Great Uncle Will always loved you as if you were his true son, Bill."

Bill's eyes lit up.

"He always talked about you and was always worried sick when you were overseas."

"Thanks, Lottie. It is nice to hear that. It appears that Will did have some doubts if I was his son or not. I never felt completely connected to the family at times. Well, now I know."

"Bill, does anyone have an idea who your dad might be?"

"No, I don't believe so. Anyway, I told Will the other night that he will always be my dad. He gave me a hug and cried. That's the first time I've ever seen him cry. You know, he bought that Indian motorcycle back then for me as a coming-home present after the war. It was quite the surprise and very expensive."

"I didn't know that he paid for that," said Lottie.

"And you never want to be at his house after he has eaten hard-boiled eggs with pickles," Bill said.

"Say no more, Bill. I think I get the entire picture." They laughed.

"I was here a few weeks ago," said Bill. "Will didn't hear me wake up. He was on his knees in front of the graves. I just walked back to the car and waited a while. I came back a few minutes later after he got back up. We just stood there together for a long time. He has his faults, but in my eyes I will always consider him to be my dad. The kids said that you were here, Lottie. Why did you walk here? Did your car break down again?"

"It's only a fifteen-minute walk," replied Lottie. "Just wanted to save some gas."

"I heard that the job at the diner didn't go so good," said Bill with a grin.

"What's so funny, Bill? You came all this way to tell me that? Don't you have something else to do, like drink? I'm sorry. That's not fair." He smiled and gave Lottie's hand a squeeze.

"You don't have to apologize," said Bill. "I guess I deserve it at times, Lottie."

"Yes you do," said Lottie.

"I'm sorry things didn't work out for you at the diner. I just arrived there a few minutes after you left. The sheriff walked in just after I did and sat at a table next to me. Jim told us that the Wart sisters were sure a mess. Someone told Wendal that you were related to me. He came over to my table and started to shake his fist at me. The sheriff stood up and looked Wendal in the eyes and said that his handcuffs hanging from his gun belt would fit his wrists just fine. Wendal backed off, stood there for a moment, and then walked away talking to himself."

"Looks like I did cause quite the ruckus," said Lottie.

"Yes, ma'am, that was something," replied Bill. "You're the talk of the town, Lottie. You're famous. There's a rumor that your story ended up in the Coeur d'Alene news. Now that's big time."

"So what? I don't have a job," said Lottie. "I guess I got carried away at the diner. I really needed that job."

"You had a lot of help from those sisters, Lottie. Erma Wart is the worst one. Some people say that Sue can actually be nice most of the time when she's not with her sister."

Bill reached into his pocket and pulled out a twenty-dollar bill and handed it to Lottie. "It's just some part-time money from the gun shop."

"What are you doing, Bill? I can't take your money. That's a month's worth of booze money. I shouldn't have said that."

"Well, you wanted me to stop drinking and give life some serious thought, didn't you?"

"That's true. Thanks, Bill. You're the best. Are you ashamed to have someone like me in the family?"

"Are you ashamed to be with me because people say I'm a drunk? Now be honest."

"No," replied Lottie. "Besides, half the town wouldn't have anything to talk about if it weren't for our two families."

"You have a point there, Lottie."

# CHAPTER 17

## *A VISIT BY DR. ROSE*

Lottie was sitting in the hospital cafeteria having her third cup of coffee. Rosa said that Lottie drank too much coffee and that it's no wonder she's so nervous. Lottie just spent an hour with John upstairs early this morning. His wounds on his face were almost healed for the most part, but John was still in a coma. Lottie looked up at the cafeteria clock as she was expecting Dr. Rose. She would have met him at the diner, but she felt that she wore out her welcome for sure with Mr. Wendal.

In fact, no one sat at the Wart sisters' table for the rest of that day. Sheriff Taylor sat there the very next morning. He said that he just wanted to get an idea of what angle the pie came at Erma's face and so forth. People thought the sheriff was just kidding around when he said that. Uncle Will thought different.

Dr. Rose, coming off from highway 12, stopped at the only stoplight in Bergan's Ferry. He sat there for three minutes and realized that the light was never going to turn green. He didn't want to run the red light, as it would be his luck to be spotted by the police. He didn't have his driver's license, as he forgot his wallet at home. He turned right on a side street and circled around and arrived at the hospital in time. The doctor parked his worn-out Rambler sedan in the visiting parking area. After he turned the key to the off position, the engine sputtered, stopped, fired up again, and then stopped. He sat there for several moments and just tried to relax.

\* \* \* \*

Dr. Rose's early career was somewhat like that. It was hit and miss for a while. Years ago, after he got his degree, he decided to do something else. Since he never was mentally ill or had a nervous breakdown, how could he relate to patients in order to help them? All his knowledge was out of a book for the most part, and he never met anyone who was insane until his next job with the federal government. He got tired seeing the taxpayers' being money flushed down the commode every day, so after three years he quit. After that, he volunteered his services at a halfway house while he was looking for another job.

One day, Dr. Rose got inspired by a man at the shelter who was down on his luck. The man repeated a familiar saying: "I'm going to do the best I can with what I have to work with. I believe I can be of value to someone."

After that, Dr. Rose applied at the sanatorium. That was over ten years ago.

\* \* \* \*

When the doctor stepped out of the car, he noticed a pool of water under the radiator of the car. He opened the hood. He then closed the hood and shook his head.

"Hope my day ends better than it started," said the doctor to himself. A passerby gave him a funny look. As Dr. Rose entered the cafeteria, Lottie stood up and waved. The doctor joined her.

"It's good to see you, Lottie. It's crowded here. Either this cafeteria is too small or all the doctors and nurses are on break at the same time."

"You always have a sense of humor, Dr. Rose."

"I guess I do at times," replied the doctor.

"I was surprised that you make house calls, so to speak, Dr. Rose. And on a Saturday. Is this required by the sanatorium director?"

"No. Not at all," replied the doctor.

"I just felt that I should go a step further to ensure your recovery, Lottie. I'm not on the clock. I'm just here."

"Well, you're a real person, Doctor."

"I sure hope so," replied Dr. Rose.

"So, Dr. Rose, may I ask you how you've been?"

"Well, I forgot my wallet as I left home. The radiator in my car is leaking again, and the engine has seen its days. The stoplight in town here was stuck on red for the longest time."

"Sheriff Taylor declared that it is now a four-way stop," said Lottie. "It seems to work out fine." The doctor gave Lottie a puzzled look.

"Oh...well... Okay," replied the doctor. "I heard that your mother has set things straight about everything. I'm sure that was a relief."

"It sure was. We're working things out. I feel very hopeful. My mom is really trying hard in our new relationship."

"That's great, Lottie. As you know, your Aunt Rosa called me. She wanted me to see you. She's afraid that you might relapse."

"I suppose Rosa told you all about how my day was at the diner a while back."

"She did mention something about that," said the doctor.

"Yeah, it wasn't my best performance on a job, Doctor."

"I'm sorry, Lottie. We heard about it over in River Falls the next day. A lot of the people were on your side. Someone might have exaggerated about the ice cream and pie."

"That's accurate," said Lottie. "The pie was very fresh, and the ice cream was made the night before. I plastered the whole pie in one sister's face, and then I dumped the bowl of ice cream on top of the other sister's head."

Dr. Rose tried not to laugh. "Wow. That is something," said the doctor. "Anyway, Rosa believed you went a little overboard that day. And then you isolated yourself from everyone for a week. Rosa is concerned, and so is the whole family."

"I wish that she would've talked to me first, but I know she means well," said Lottie. "But then again, I wasn't answering the door. I was so embarrassed about what happened. I just didn't want to see anyone. We're broke as can be. I've been looking for a job. I guess the one interview and the job tryout at the diner really got to me. I just don't want to burden others with all my problems. Uncle Bill said I should accept more help."

"Would you feel left out or rejected if your loved ones refused your help if they were in need?" asked the doctor.

"I guess I would feel that way," replied Lottie. "Knowing me, I would probably force my help on them. You're right, Doctor.

But first, I need some advice about Bill, my uncle. He has a drinking problem. I support him as much as I can, and he's been to a couple of AA meetings. He's destroying himself, and I don't know why. Do you know anyone in AA who has been sober for a long time and can spend some time with him? He's really having a difficult time, Doctor."

"I know someone," replied Dr. Rose.

"You do?"

"Me," replied the doctor. "I've been a member of Alcoholics Anonymous for about ten years."

"You?" said Lottie. "But you're a professional and all that."

"That doesn't matter. Why not me? Alcoholism has no boundaries. None at all."

"I never thought about it that way," said Lottie.

"You can only do so much for Bill, Lottie. Here's my card. Feel free to help arrange for Bill and me to get together. I'll have plenty of time a week from now."

"Thank you, Dr. Rose. Oh, one more thing. Rosa asked me if you were single. She really didn't want me to ask you outright, but she really did."

"I understand, I think," replied Dr. Rose.

"You've met her before," said Lottie.

"Yes I have," replied the doctor. "She's very nice."

"Rosa works at the car lot just down the road," said Lottie. "They have some nice cars there, you know."

"And I'm still single. Actually I do need a car, Lottie. I'll check her out. I mean I'll check the cars out. But let's get back to you, Lottie."

"Well, okay," said Lottie.

After the visit with Lottie, Dr. Rose stopped by the gas station on his way out of town from the hospital. The good Texaco people topped off his radiator with water and added a quart of oil to his tired engine.

On his way back home, he seemed to be at ease with himself as he thought about his positive visit with Lottie. As a young man, he had been a loner and just concentrated on getting an education. He'd had only one girlfriend in his life, and then he found out after six months that she was already married.

After just passing the car dealership, the Rambler sedan shook as Dr. Rose quickly shifted down and jammed on the brakes, coming to a screeching halt. He then turned around on the two-lane road and drove into the dealership. He hesitated for a while and then walked into the dealership. Rosa noticed the doctor and walked up to him from her desk. She was all smiles.

"Hi, Dr. Rose," said Rosa. "What brings you to the dealership here?"

"Hi, Rosa. Lottie said I should come by and look at cars."

"I'm sure she did," said Rosa with a grin. "I'm not a salesman, but I'll be glad to show you around."

"That would be more than great," replied the doctor.

"I'm sorry. I really don't know your first name, Doctor."

"My first name is Randy."

"Randy and Rosa. That clicks with me." replied Rosa.

As Rosa showed him some of the cars, he stopped and looked at a 1950 Oldsmobile two-door hardtop.

"This car is really nice," said Dr. Rose.

"It has an automatic transmission," said Rosa. "It's not a gear jammer like your Rambler."

"I think this car is the one for me. May I be a little forward, Rosa?"

"You may, Dr. Randy."

"Could we have lunch together, Rosa?"

People said that Dr. Rose would become a part of the Lindstrom and Rainwater family very soon. He just didn't know it quite yet.

# CHAPTER 18

## *UNCLE BILL'S DESPERATION*

Uncle Bill sat on the side of his bed in his apartment looking at his framed Purple Heart. It took his thoughts back to a hillside in North Korea in 1953 during a battle when the Koreans attacked their position. The company commander and first sergeant were killed during the initial attack. Thirty-six men were left in his company out of 130.

Bill, the only platoon sergeant left, regrouped his men as darkness fell. The men were almost out of ammunition except for some ammunition belts for their remaining machine gun. Their annihilation was near. Bill devised a plan for his men to escape under the cover of darkness. Bill stayed behind simulating company activity through the night. The North Koreans thought that the remnants of his company were still there.

This gave his men time to retreat back to friendly lines that night. At dawn, the Koreans attacked. After the last machine gun ammunition belts were used up by Bill, the Koreans came in for the kill. Bill got a beat-up South Korean motorcycle started and was shot in the back as he left. He made it back to the rear lines.

The North Koreans retreated. US reinforcements retook the position the next day and collected their fallen comrades. Over eighty Koreans died at the hands of Sergeant William Lindstrom.

Bill was awarded a battlefield commission to first lieutenant and also received a Purple Heart. His injury was extensive. He was shipped back to the states for further treatment and then discharged. He was given a modest VA disability benefit. Bill continued to be wrapped in pain and nightmares of his ordeal.

* * * *

Bill reached for his Army Class A dress jacket that lay at the end of his bed. He checked to see if the crossed-rifle badges on the lapels were centered and the blue infantry shoulder braid on the right was still properly attached. The expert-rifle badge was on the left side of the jacket. The unit shoulder patch was razor sharp, as was his polished lieutenant bars. He took the Purple Heart medal out of the blue framed case and carefully pinned it on the jacket.

Bill stood up and stepped in front of a mirror in his bedroom. He carefully put on the jacket to complete his uniform. He stood there at attention for a few moments. His pants were perfectly creased, and the black stripe down each side of his pants legs displayed an officer's dress uniform. And for once he was clean shaven and standing tall.

He never dreamed as a boy that he would ever be wearing a uniform like that. The only uniform he could picture as a kid to wear was the Texaco uniform at the local gas station in town.

Bill's steps were unsteady as he slowly walked into the kitchen. He pulled the old rickety wooden chair away from the table. He carefully sat his six-foot frame down on the old chair and gently scooted the chair a bit forward.

On the table was a near-empty bottle of Jack Daniels. To his right was a 45 Colt handgun, one 45 caliber round, and a clip. Bill loaded the round into the clip and then inserted the clip into the 45. He pulled the slide back, and it was ready to fire. He slowly raised the gun upward toward the right side of his head. Bill hesitated for a few moments. The legs on the left side of his wooden chair suddenly snapped and gave way. The gun discharged. Bill was motionless on the floor. His Purple Heart was covered with blood.

The next morning, Lottie was walking down Main Street toward the Red Scarf Lounge. She planned to take Dr. Rose's advice concerning her other health issues. She was on her way to see a doctor friend of his in town. Unknown to her, Sheriff Taylor was taking long strides to catch up with her.

"Lottie!" She turned around and stopped.

"How can someone like you walk so darn fast?" asked the sheriff.

"Sheriff Taylor, how are you doing?"

"I tried to get ahold of you, but your phone must have been turned off, Lottie. I had Gloria come out to your place. She said you didn't answer the door."

"You were looking for me? What's going on?"

"You don't know?" said the sheriff. "Bill shot himself in the head yesterday."

She stood there stunned. "Shot himself. Oh my God," said Lottie.

Lottie became faint. The sheriff held on to her.

"Let's go into the lounge and sit down, Lottie. "You need to be off your feet for a while."

The sheriff held on to her as they walked into the lounge. We can sit here for a bit. Just try to relax. Bill will make it."

Lottie gave the sheriff a long look.

"How's Bill going to make it?" Asked Lottie. "He just shot his brains out."

"No. The bullet just grazed the side of his head, Lottie. The doctors said that he's stable. I sat with him for a few minutes last night. He's was sitting up in bed and complaining about the bad coffee. Bill just looks like heck right now, Lottie. He's one tough nut. Just calm down. We'll see him tonight."

"What caused him to do this?" asked Lottie. "Things seemed to be better with him since he made a few AA meetings."

"I don't know, Lottie. The tenant across the hallway heard the

116

gunshot and rushed over to his door. The tenant opened the door, and there was Bill sprawled out on the floor. He was wearing his Army uniform, complete with all the ribbons. The tenant said he looked dead as can be and then some."

"It seems when it rains, it pours on our families. When will it stop, Sheriff?"

"I know. It sure seems that way, Lottie. I wish I had some answers."

"Time goes so fast," said Lottie. "It seems like it was just yesterday when Bill and I did so many things together as kids years ago. I was the only tomboy among all the girls. We also built a tree house in the woods. And then we would go to the post office on Sundays when the office was closed. We drew mustaches and eye glasses on the criminals shown on the paper wanted posters in the lobby. I was the better artist of course," said Lottie.

"So you and Bill were part of the civil disobedience bunch back then?"

"Yeah I guess," replied Lottie. "Bill was so active and outgoing. In fact, he introduced John to me for the first time and said that John was for sure the one for me. I didn't know that at the time. And what are we going to do about John? He's still not any better."

"I don't know, Lottie. All we can do is pray for him."

"I know Bill is still in pain from his war injury. He's been through a lot," said Lottie. "Something must have snapped in Bill's head not to live anymore. Being in the Pacific during the Second World War and then Korea just drained him. I wonder why he had his Army uniform on when he was so determined to leave this earth?"

"I believe the uniform showed what he was all about all his life," replied the sheriff. "It was the extension of him. It showed his accomplishments, his drive, and I guess his loyalty."

"I think you're right," replied Lottie. "He was always there for everyone. Let's see Bill right now." She wavered as she tried to stand up. The sheriff held her arm.

"Lottie, we should sit here for a few more minutes. Perhaps you need to eat a little something. Looks like we're not getting waited on. I'll go to the bar and have them cook up some eggs and toast for us."

Lottie nodded and then sat back down. As the sheriff was at the bar, he noticed a man sitting in the back room. He was partially bent over with a full bottle of whiskey in front of him. He had a blood soaked bandage around the side of his head with a brown canvas hat pressed down over his head.

"Is that Bill?" thought the sheriff.

The sheriff stepped a little closer, then quickly walked back to their table.

"Lottie, guess who's sitting in the back room there?"

"Please, I don't want to guess, Sheriff. Just tell me who it is."

"It's Bill, Lottie. He's sitting back there."

"He's supposed to be in the hospital," said Lottie. "Are you sure it's him?"

"Well there are not many men running around town today with a big bloody bandage wrapped around their head," replied the sheriff.

"I'll take a look," replied Lottie.

"Okay, you will see," said the sheriff.

Lottie got up and slowly walked over to the back room. Lottie looked back at the sheriff and nodded. She went over to Bill and stood there for a few moments. His eyes were closed.

"Bill, it's me."

Lottie sat down at the small table with him. Bill raised his head and looked at her.

"Lottie," said Bill.

"Bill, you don't look so good. What are you doing out of the hospital?"

"I'm okay," replied Bill. "I don't need to be there. It's not that bad. The bullet just tore some scalp off my head and gave me a super headache."

"Yeah, I guess. And you're clean shaven," said Lottie.

"Well, I thought I would clean up my act." Bill tried to laugh. Lottie shook her head.

"Bill, it's not funny."

Bill's eyes closed from time to time. She grabbed his hands and held on tightly.

"Why did you try to kill yourself?. Say something," said Lottie.

"My head hurts, really bad, Lottie."

"Really now," said Lottie.

"I botched the job," said Bill. "As I was about to put the barrel of the gun squarely against my forehead, two of chair legs gave way. I guess my right arm dropped down, pulling the gun away and upward. The bullet just scraped the top side of my head."

"Bill, why?" asked Lottie.

"I didn't want to live anymore knowing that someday I'll be paralyzed. The bullet is still lodged close to my spine. If the bullet moves just a hair, I won't be able to move a muscle. I'll be eating my lunch through a straw at the nursing home. I couldn't handle something like that."

"So the bullet wasn't removed at the field hospital in Korea?" asked Lottie.

"No, they didn't want to take the chance," replied Bill. "A hospital here in the states was the best bet for me, but it looks like that might not happen at all."

"You know what? I don't even have an urge to open this bottle of whiskey," remarked Bill.

Sheriff Taylor walked over and joined them. "We need to get him back to the hospital," said the sheriff.

"I'm fine," said Bill.

"You're stubborn, just like your niece," said the sheriff.

"The sheriff is right, Bill," said Lottie. "Bill... Uncle Bill."

"Oh, I shot someone," said Bill.

"Oh God," said the sheriff. "I really don't want to hear this, Bill."

"The bullet from my 45 went right through the ceiling and got the cat upstairs that was sleeping on the floor," said Bill. "The cat's keister just got nicked. So Chuck upstairs isn't real happy with me. I don't blame him."

"Bill, promise me one thing," said Lottie. "Don't shoot yourself again."

"You mean like dead?" answered Bill.

"Bill, I'm not kidding."

"Yes, ma'am. No bullets or booze."

"Okay," replied Lottie.

"Lottie, please do one thing for me right now," asked Bill.

"I will. Anything."

"Stop squeezing my hands," said Bill. "They're numb. Please let go of them, Lottie."

"Oh, okay," replied Lottie.

# CHAPTER 19

## *UNCLE BILL AND SUE*

Uncle Bill sat down on a bench just outside the post office near the flower pots. He carefully opened a government-marked envelope and looked it over for a few moments. Out from the post office came Sue Wart. She spotted Bill and walked over to him.

"Bill. Bill Lindstrom. Is that you?" asked Sue.

"So far, I am," replied Bill. "Sue from the women's clothing store? You look different."

"My hair is quite different now, and I'm wearing clothes from the fifties, not the thirties," said Sue. "And I'm not following the advice of my sister anymore. I guess I'm trying to be a modern woman of today."

"Well, you look great," said Bill. "Here, have a seat, Sue."

"Thank you, Bill. It has been a while since I've seen you."

"It sure has, Sue. I look different right now. This modern headband is called a big bandage. It's not too stylish, but it does keep my head together."

"You're so funny, Bill. I heard about your accident. I'm glad you made it through all this. I really am."

"Yeah, I guess the whole town has heard about it by now. That wasn't my best day, Sue. Not going to do that again."

"Hopefully your letter is of good news," remarked Sue.

"I believe so," said Bill. "Very good news. It's from the Veterans Administration concerning my war injury. I was shot in the back while I was in Korea. The bullet is still lodged close to my spine. The VA said that there's a new procedure for my type of injury that can be done in a Boise hospital and that my request for this operation has been approved. They will be sending me a notice very soon to arrange for the first appointment."

"That's wonderful, Bill. I didn't know that you were wounded."

"And the crazy thing about this is that I was denied a review of my injury four months ago. I was so upset over their decision that I sent the VA a letter telling them where they could go. And I was also busy, I guess, trying to blow my brains out. I don't know how this happened."

"Someone is looking out for you, Bill."

"I believe so. How have you been, Sue?"

"Well, business could be better."

"Let's go to the diner for some coffee, Sue." Bill held his hand out to her.

"Sure," replied Sue. "It would be my pleasure."

* * * *

Lottie was parked across the street from the Doughboy Diner. As she shifted the Ford into gear, she stopped and noticed Uncle Bill and Sue walking down the sidewalk toward the diner. As her eyes were fixed on them, her car rolled back and hit the car behind her.

"Oh, what now?" said Lottie.

Lottie looked into her rear view mirror and saw Sheriff Taylor in his police cruiser behind her. She went forward a few feet and turned the engine off. The sheriff got out of his police cruiser and looked at his front bumper. Lottie got out and walked up to him.

"Why am I not surprised that you hit my car, Lottie? The top bumper bar is scratched and bent. I just had it replaced last week, and you're illegally parked to boot. You seem to disregard the laws of this town and county."

"It's not my fault. You sneaked up behind me in your car."

"You rolled back into me," said the sheriff.

"It's still not my fault, Sheriff."

"I've given this family a lot of breaks," said the sheriff. "But now I must..."

"Look! There's Uncle Bill and that Wart sister across the street. They're walking so close together that it looks like they're joined at the hip as they stroll down the sidewalk."

"Did you see that?" asked Lottie.

"I've got eyes, Lottie. Those two together? What are they up to?"

"They shouldn't be together," said Lottie. "Let's go in the side door and sneak up to a table behind them and listen in."

"I really have better things to do, Lottie. But as a lawman, I can't be listening in on people's private conversations. We can sit a few tables over and just observe. Right?"

"Well, okay," said Lottie. "Let's wait a few minutes after they settle down at a table."

Bill and Sue were sitting at his favorite table in the corner of the diner.

"I was just thinking about us sitting together, Bill. My sister and I may not be real favorites among the Rainwaters and your family right now. Lottie would really have a cow if she saw us sitting together."

"Grinning, that's for sure, Sue."

"We were rude to Lottie on her second day of work at the diner here," said Sue. "It was really our fault, now that I think of it. I'm sure you heard all about it."

"Yup, I sure did, and then some," replied Bill. "Lottie was a little extreme on her delivery of the ice cream and pie."

"She was," said Sue. "It's funny now, but it wasn't then. I must level with you, Bill. It was Erma that sprayed Lottie that day with her car. And we both were rude the time when Lottie was shopping for her dress. We're just not good people. Not at all. I'm sorry, Bill."

A tear formed in Sue's eye. She shook her head.

"Hey, it's okay," said Bill. "You know our two families are not quite all there. My Dad digs holes all around looking for the Indian treasures. Lottie ends up in the sanatorium, and I tried to blow my brains out. My sister finally let the truth out about Lottie's birth just lately. When my mother died, she told me on her death bed about her affair from years ago concerning my birth. And my older brother is a crook. I think all us could use some real fixin'."

"Bill, someone is behind us. I hope it's not who I think it is."

Bill turned around. "It's Lottie and Sheriff Taylor," said Bill to Sue. I'm in trouble now."

Lottie looked over at Sue with a scornful glare in her eyes.

"Lottie, calm down," said the sheriff. "We're busted. Let's not make a scene. You shouldn't even be in here."

"Hi, Miss Wart," said the sheriff. "Good to see you again,

Bill. We're just leaving. Right, Lottie?" Lottie and the sheriff got up and left out the side door.

"Well, we got through that," said Sue.

"So far, we did," replied Bill. "Anyway, my mom had an affair before Lottie was adopted into the family. So I'm that baby."

"So Great Uncle Will isn't your dad?"

"No, he isn't. But I will always refer to Will as my dad. He's a little bent out of shape right now, but he's still a great man."

"My sister Erma is afraid of him. When he came in our shop last month, he screamed at Erma concerning his tab. She was afraid he might go psycho with that shovel of his that he carries all around town."

"Dad is quite harmless. And Lottie isn't really my sister. You know Winnie, the actress in our family?"

"Yes," replied Sue. "She's a pretty woman."

"Lottie is actually Winnie's daughter," said Bill. "So Lottie is really my niece. She found this out on her own just before she went to the sanatorium. My sister just admitted this to all of us the other day. Lottie was devastated. Of course, I was blown away for the both of us."

"Oh my," replied Sue. "And I thought my whole family was so complicated."

"Lottie's dad died in Europe before she was born," remarked Bill. "So neither one of us knew our dads."

"I'm so sorry for the deaths and everything else," said Sue.

"Thank you," said Bill. "It's been a rough year."

"Bill, guess what? I'm Erma's sister only through adoption."

"I didn't know that," said Bill. "We have something in common."

"I was a baby when the Wart family adopted me," said Sue. "I don't know who my parents were, so I know how you feel. Erma is a few years older than I, and she's so old fashioned. We inherited the shop a few years ago. Anyway, Erma feels so self-conscious about all the warts on her face that she demanded I put at least two imitation warts on my face. I'm told that the family's last name fits Erma's face." Bill tried not to laugh.

"I don't see your fake warts," said Bill.

"Not part of my makeup anymore."

"Lottie is under a lot of stress, said Bill. "John, her husband, is still in the hospital. To make things even worse, the family is dead broke and their house is in foreclosure."

"All we knew was that Lottie was in the sanatorium, Bill. Looks like all of us had some turmoil in our life. There's something that I wanted to know for some time about Sheriff Taylor, Bill. Evidently your dad knows the sheriff quite well. Are they at odds with each other at times?"

"In fact, they're close friends," said Bill.

"They are?" said Sue.

"It's just their way of kidding around," replied Bill. "Once in a while, they will have a real serious talk."

"Sheriff Taylor seems a little odd, and no one knows where he came from," said Sue. "He's only been in town here for less than twenty years, but people treat him as they've known him all their lives. Just like some people call your dad Great Uncle Will and they aren't really related to him."

"My dad was able to connect with people. He started the bank many years ago and was very close to a lot of them. He did a lot for this town. But when he had his accident, he was never the same. Now some people think he's crazy, and my two brothers back then didn't help things any. A lot of folks who knew him well still greet him as if he was really their uncle."

"Anyway, a customer told me about Sheriff Taylor saving her friend's uncle one day, Bill. I guess he was working on his car in the barn one morning," said Sue. "The makeshift jack stand collapsed partway and pinned her Uncle Henry under the car."

"That's what I heard," said Bill.

"He was close to death," said Sue. "Her uncle could tell it was Sheriff Taylor's police cruiser, as it's the only car around that has an odd humming noise from the engine. He didn't actually see the sheriff directly, as he blacked out from time to time. But it must have been the sheriff who grabbed the axle hub, lifted it up with one hand, and then pulled him out from under the car. Five minutes later the ambulance arrived, and the sheriff was already gone. Henry said that it would have taken at least three or four men to lift that corner of the car up and to pull him out."

"That's quite the story," replied Bill.

"Henry said that the sheriff visited him in the hospital and didn't admit that he saved his life or was even there," said Sue.

"Well, Sheriff Taylor is a different kind of man, Sue. Lottie told me a story that happened about eight years ago. Three men got kicked out of the Red Scarf Lounge and ended up in the rear parking lot breaking car windows. An employee heard the noise and went back to the storeroom. This is what is crazy, Sue. The worker opened the back door a crack and saw the sheriff standing in front of one man down on the ground, and the other two men looked like they were thrown up against the building. They were all out cold. He cuffed them together and marched them down the street to the jail."

"That sounds like the sheriff," remarked Sue. "How can that be? He was at least fifty years old back then and surely not the biggest man around."

"I don't know," replied Bill. "The sheriff deputies told my dad one time that Sheriff Taylor is some kind of superman. I assumed they were just joking around. I'm going to get with my dad very soon. I think he knows more about the sheriff than we think. He does stumble through his job at times but seems to do okay. The sheriff is a forthright man and seems to be very protective of our two families."

"I heard him say one time that he's a hard-core lawman," said Sue. "He's quite serious about his job."

"He's a classic," remarked Bill. "Sue, I just remembered something. My thinking still isn't real clear yet from my head injury, but weren't you in my English and math class in high school? And one time you made a banana peanut butter sandwich for my lunch?"

"I was in your class, and I did make you that special sandwich, Bill. I guess I had a crush on you."

"Really?" replied Bill.

Sue nodded with a smile. She held Bill's hand for a moment.

"There's a town dance next week, Sue. It's on a Friday night. Would you consider going with me? If you don't mind the big bandage around my head."

"Of course I would, Bill. Not to change the subject, but I hope

Lottie will forgive me and my sister."

"She will get over it," said Bill. "She's a caring lady and is good at forgiving people. I'll push her in that direction."

Sue stood up to leave. She leaned over and gave Bill a kiss on his forehead. There was silence for several moments.

"I might have moved a little too soon," said Sue. "I'm sorry."

"No, I'm fine," said Bill. "I really am."

A few feet from his table, she turned around and smiled. Bill gave her a wink as she left.

Bill sat there for a while thinking about what happened. He wasn't much interested in girls as a boy. Bill ended up being involved in two wars and never really had a chance to think about a relationship. He knew that Lottie would be talking to him very soon about Sue's presence with him at the diner. Little did Lottie know that Sue one day would be very important in Uncle Bill's life.

# CHAPTER 20

## *BACKYARD SURPRISE*

A worn-out-looking county utility truck slowed down near the Rainwaters' house. As it stopped abruptly, a shovel flew off the truck and landed in the street. The driver, an older utility worker, got out and took one glance at the shovel. He then walked up to the Rainwaters' porch and knocked on the door. The other utility worker got out of the truck, picked up the shovel, and placed it back on the truck bed.

"This is too early in the morning" thought Lottie. She went to the front door and slowly opened it.

"Good morning. Hey, is the bank sending people out in county work clothes now to snoop around my house and yard again?"

"No I'm not from the bank, ma'am," said the worker. The other worker joined them.

"We're from the county utility department," said the older worker with the dented safety hat. "There's our utility truck over there." Lottie opened the screen door and looked down the street.

"I'm Ray, and this is my new helper."

"I'm Mathew. Pleased to meet you, ma'am."

"Ray, Do I know you from somewhere?" asked Lottie.

"No, I don't think so, ma'am."

"I didn't mean to be rude when you first came to the door," said Lottie. "What can I do for you?"

"This is 411 South Willow road, ma'am?" asked Ray.

"Yes it is."

"We need permission to go on your property," said Ray. "An

old section of the water pipe needs to be taken out. The area in question is in back of your house. I believe the county line ends in the middle of your back property. One side is the county, and the other side is the city."

"No wonder I get confused walking across the yard back there," said Lottie.

"I don't get it," said Ray.

"Go ahead and dig all you want. I don't care. It won't matter now," said Lottie.

"What was that?" asked Ray.

"Oh nothing, Ray. Feel free to do the work out there."

The workers walked to the backyard and looked around for a few minutes.

"So you're on loan to us from River Falls," said Ray to Mathew.

"Yes I am. I've only been with them for a few days."

"Well I hope you're up to it," said Ray. "There's lots of rock in the ground here. We don't have a backhoe to dig out the pipe. The shovels are all we got."

"What happened to the backhoe, Ray?"

"Someone got it stuck in a deep hole across town," replied Ray. "They haven't been able to pull it out for two weeks."

"Well, it's going to take us a long time to do this job, Ray."

"I believe so," said Ray. "That's okay. We'll just work a little harder. I overheard that their home is in foreclosure. I hate it when things like that happen to people. Wish there was something I could do for them."

"I feel the same way," said Mathew.

"I'll go back to the truck and pull out the plans for the lines in this area." Lottie walked over to Mathew from the back porch.

"It's going to get hot today," remarked Lottie. "I'm going to have some cold ice water for you guys."

"Thank you," said Mathew. "You have a lot of yard here."

"It's about three acres, but how do you know where this pipe is at?" asked Lottie.

"Ray is getting the plans right now. We should be able to pinpoint the location of that water pipe."

As Lottie left, Ray returned with a wooden case. He pulled the plans out and looked at them for a few moments.

"I should have gotten the newer plans," said Ray. "These are kinda old."

Mathew looked at the plans and shook his head. "They're hard to read, Ray. The paper is so faded in places."

"You worry too much, Mathew."

Ray spread the plans out on the ground. "You're right. These are hard to read."

Ray grabbed his 100-foot tape measure and made some measurements across the yard and then from the house. After finding the boundary marker on the east side of the house, Ray made another measurement and marked the spot with two stakes.

"This is it," said Ray. "I guess we're ready."

"Great," said Mathew. "I'll get the shovels."

"No need to, Mathew. I'll get them. I need to get my smokes out of the truck anyway. Be right back."

Mathew walked around the area that was staked for a few moments.

As Ray left for the truck, Mathew picked up the plans, looked at them, and then put them back into the case. He moved the stakes eight feet over and stepped back a ways. Ray returned to the backyard and lit up a cigarette.

"Can't beat these Lucky Strikes," said Ray. "Want one?"

"No thanks," replied Mathew. "I don't smoke."

Hours later, Ray and Mathew stood on the side of the hole that they dug. They were muddy and their shirts were stained with sweat.

Fred Rubio

"Well, we haven't hit any pipes," said Ray. "The hole is about six or seven feet wide and over five feet deep. Still not any signs of a pipe or anything. I don't get it."

"Let's get back to the shop," said Ray. "My knee is really killing me. It's getting late. I'm going to talk to Mrs. Rainwater about this hole," said Ray.

"I'm just going to skim a little more dirt off the sides of this hole, Ray. I'll be there in a few minutes."

Ray walked up to the porch where Lottie was sitting. "Would you men like some more ice water?" asked Lottie.

"No, ma'am. We're done for the day, Mrs. Rainwater. We couldn't locate that pipe for some reason. We won't be able to come back for two or three days. Should we fence the hole off? It's kinda deep."

"No. I'll just tell my kids to stay away from the hole."

"Well, okay," said Ray. Ray returned to the utility truck and sat inside. Mathew joined him.

"Well, did you get dirty enough today?"

"I sure did, Ray."

Ray took his hard hat off and leaned against the seat back of the truck. He held his head for a few moments. "This just isn't a good day for me," remarked Ray.

"Are you okay?" asked Mathew.

"I'm okay. Just a headache."

"That a pretty good dent in your hard hat," said Mathew.

"Yeah, it's a doozy," replied Ray. "I was at the county warehouse after part of the roof collapsed from a heavy snowfall. I just got on the scene. I was only there a minute, and something told me to put my hard hat on. Two seconds later, part of a beam came down right on my head. If I didn't have my hard hat on that soon, I would have been a goner. I was lucky."

"Perhaps it wasn't luck," said Mathew.

132

"How so?" asked Ray.

"Do you go to church?" asked Mathew.

"Not now. I just lost faith in some things. I knew of the Rainwaters through a past acquaintance of mine. He died in Korea. He was Mrs. Rainwaters' brother-in-law."

"That's a shame," said Mathew.

"Gilbert was a good man, Mathew. We both hit it off pretty good at one of those hobby conventions when he was on leave. Now he's gone just like that. His interest was in model airplanes like me. Can you imagine me trying to build a model airplane with these huge hands? I belong to the Army National Guard unit, so we also shared our military experience. Gilbert and I were going to get together when he came back home to retire. I don't know why I'm telling you all this."

"No problem. I understand," said Mathew.

"Gilbert was killed in Korea," said Ray. "It's not fair at all that he left this world so soon. I met Gloria, his wife. She's a nice woman. It's been lonely for me. My wife died two years ago. I just don't know if there's a God anymore. Maybe I'm giving up too soon on everything. I don't know."

"I'm sorry to hear that about your wife, Ray. Who knows? You might even meet someone very soon."

"How's that?"

"Just a thought," replied Mathew. "Perhaps you can go back to church. You might find answers to a few things."

"Well, I'll give it another try," said Ray. "Hey, my head. I think my headache is gone. It doesn't just stop like that. They usually last a day or two."

The next day, Sara and Mark were in the backyard. "I'm still having a hard time with these crutches, Sara. I think they're too big for me."

"No they ain't," said Sara. "The nurse said these are for children, and they've been adjusted the right way. You aren't using them right."

"How do you know? I only see old people on crutches," replied Mark. "And if you know so much, why did the workmen dig that big hole?"

"The old workman said that they might have to dig straight down to China to find the bad water pipe," said Sara. "That's where all the Chinese people live. Right?"

"I really don't know how far down China is, Sara. Maybe we can ask Great Uncle Will. He knows everything," said Mark, as he slowly edged his way toward the hole.

"We can't go there, Mark. It's off limits."

"I'm just going closer to see how deep the hole is, Sara."

"I'm going to tell," said Sara. "Yes I will."

"Don't be a tattletale," said Mark.

As Mark leaned over to look down, the one end of his crutch slipped. He lost his balance and tumbled into the hole. Sara ran to the edge of the hole.

"Mark, are you hurt?"

"I don't think so."

Sara, down on her knees, grabbed Mark's outstretched hand and pulled with all her might.

"Oh, you're too heavy," said Sara. As Sara let go of Mark's hand, he slid back down the hole.

"Sara, get me out of here before Mom sees me down here."

"You're in big trouble now. You're all covered with mud. You're going to get a spanking."

Sara ran into the woodshed and up to the kitchen door.

"Mommy, come quick!"

Lottie opened the kitchen door. "What's going on out there?" asked Lottie.

"Mark fell in that hole! I told him not to get too close to it," said

134

Sara.

Lottie rushed out of the kitchen and to the backyard where Mark was. Sara followed her. Lottie got down on her knees at the edge of the hole.

"Honey, are you hurt?"

"I'm okay, Mom."

"I told you kids not to go close to this hole." Lottie reached down to Mark.

"I'll pull you out. Here, grab my hand."

As Lottie reached down and grabbed Mark's hand, the dirt below her knees broke away. She fell headfirst in the hole and laid there sprawled out in the mud next to Mark.

"Mommy!"

"I'm okay, Sara. Now we're both covered with mud. Sara, call Gloria and... Never mind. Our phone is turned off," said Lottie.

"Mark, I'm going to lift you up as high as I can. With the help of Sara, I'm sure I can get you up and out of this hole. Look. What's that?"

"Look at what?" asked Mark.

"There's something sticking out of the side of the hole there next to you," said Lottie.

Lottie got down on her knees and loosened the dirt around a small burlap bag that was partially exposed. She pulled it out and pried open the draw string.

"These seem to be old coins or something," remarked Lottie. Some of the coins fell out as she handed the bag to Sara. "Take this bag. Be careful."

Lottie picked up the loose coins and rubbed one of them. Gold coins?" Lottie stood up and lifted her arms into the air and screamed.

"Oh sweet Jesus. We're rich! We hit pay dirt!"

"With the help of Mark, Lottie climbed out of the hole. She

grabbed the burlap bag.

"Kids, don't go anywhere. I'm on my way to the bank. I have to get there before they close."

Lottie ran to the house, grabbed her handbag, and got into her car. Mark looked around.

"Mommy said we can't go anywhere," said Sara.

"I can't go anywhere," said Mark. "I'm still in this hole."

Lottie tried to start the car. The engine turned over slowly and then finally started.

A short distance from the house, the old Ford sputtered and then stopped. Lottie tried to start the car again, but nothing happened.

"I bet I'm out of gas," thought Lottie.

Lottie got out of the car and walked along the road. Her handbag was hard to carry with the weight of the coins in it. She switched shoulders after a bit. A few minutes later, she came to the dealership where Rosa worked.

Lottie stood there in the driveway for a few moments, looked around, and then walked up the driveway into the dealership. Rosa saw Lottie at the front door and walked up to her. Rosa gave her a look over.

"Hi, Rosa."

"You're all muddy," remarked Rosa. "You look like you fell in a ditch or something."

"I kinda did fall in a ditch."

"Well, sure looks like you did, Lottie. And what do you have in your handbag? Bricks? Are you okay? You need to wash the mud off your face and hands. And quit getting so dirty."

"I'm fine, Rosa. I don't have the time to explain. I want to look at one of the cars up front," said Lottie.

"The keys are in them," said Rosa.

Lottie quickly walked out and sat in the car parked by the front door. Rosa followed her.

"This is a pretty nice Oldsmobile," remarked Lottie.

"They will really get uptight if they see you sitting in these cars with your dirty clothes, Lottie."

Lottie took the keys from above the sun visor and started the car. She leaned back in the seat for a few moments.

"What are you doing, Lottie? You can't afford bread, let alone a newer car."

"I'm just going to test drive it. I'll fill you in later."

"You can't drive this one. Dr. Rose just bought this car, Lottie." Lottie started the car and moved forward.

"I'll be right back, Rosa."

"There's no plates on the car, Lottie. Stop!" Lottie drove down the driveway and turned onto the highway leading to town. The lot boy, at the other end of the dealership, saw Rosa running after the Oldsmobile as it left the dealership at a high rate of speed. He then rushed into the shop and picked up the phone.

"Operator, connect me to the police department."

Lottie drove down Main Street and failed to stop at the stoplight that didn't work. She continued on and parked in front of the bank. She got out of the car and walked into the bank and stopped at the secretary's desk.

"I'm here to see my Uncle Zach."

"He's gone for the day," said the secretary. "I'm too busy to talk to you. And you look awful."

"Just trying to match your looks, dear," replied Lottie.

As Mr. Perkins, the bank manager, was just leaving his desk, she rushed up to him and placed her handbag on his desk.

"Hi, Lottie. I haven't seen you for a while. How is John doing?"

"He's still in a coma."

"I was hoping that there would be some improvement, said Mr. Perkins. Ah... Are you okay? You're kinda..."

Lottie took the burlap bag out of her handbag and emptied

some of the coins on his desk. "What's all this?" asked Mr. Perkins.

"We found them after the utility department dug a hole in our backyard," answered Lottie. "They were looking for a broken pipe. Just credit these coins to our account. They must be worth something. We can't lose our house!"

"The foreclosure proceedings went into effect on your home a week ago, Lottie. I'm sorry. Plus I don't have any idea what these are or what they're worth. They seem to be gold pieces. But orders are orders. Your uncle is hell bent on taking the house. Now there's no stopping the foreclosure."

"Great Uncle Will would have helped us," said Lottie.

"That's true, Lottie. I wish he still owned the bank."

As Lottie walked past the secretary's desk to leave, the secretary looked up and gave Lottie a cold-eyed look.

"Looks like you will be chasing the bus out of town real soon when you lose your home," remarked the secretary.

Lottie stepped back over to her desk. She pulled the wig off the secretary's head, exposing her short gray hair.

"You're going to be chasing your fake hair down the street, missy," said Lottie.

Lottie stepped outside and threw the wig up in the air. The wind blew the wig several feet down the street. Screaming, the secretary ran out the door chasing her wig.

Sheriff Taylor was sitting in his police cruiser in front of the police station. His deputy ran out of the station and up to him.

"I just got a call, Sheriff! There's a white stolen Oldsmobile going down Main Street. Should we take two cars?"

"Don't need to, Deputy. I'll handle this one by myself. Just man the station."

The sheriff checked his revolver to see if it was loaded. He searched through all his pockets and found two bullets. He loaded the revolver and placed it back in his holster.

The sheriff left the police station and drove down Main Street with his lights flashing and siren on. He slowed down for a garbage truck that stopped near the bank. The truck partially blocked the sheriff's view.

Mr. Perkins stood in front of the bank and tried to get Lottie's attention as she drove away. Moments later, the truck moved, letting the sheriff through. The sheriff pulled up and stopped near Mr. Perkins.

"I'll get that car thief and bank robber," shouted the sheriff as he pulled away from the curb.

"Wait! You don't understand," Sheriff.

Sheriff Taylor caught up with Lottie just outside the city limits.

Lottie pulled over to the side of the road and shut the engine off. Sheriff Taylor got out of his car and boldly walked over to her. As the sheriff grasped the handle of his 38 Special revolver, the holster came loose and fell to the ground. He quickly picked it up. Lottie's head was bent down as she gripped the steering wheel.

"Lady, please look at me," asked the sheriff. "The law is standing in front of you. You're under arrest for stealing a car, driving a vehicle with no plates, and probably bank robbery. Lady, look at me, please."

Lottie raised her head and looked up at Sheriff Taylor.

"It's you. I should have known. Can't you keep out of trouble?"

"I'm on a test drive. Rosa knows all about it."

"You can't afford this car," said the sheriff. "You can't even afford to breath the air. Why are you all covered in mud? You're a mess."

"Sheriff, you're the third person today to tell me that I'm a mess. My car is out of gas. It's sitting between the house and the dealership. I had to go to the bank. Our house is officially in foreclosure, and there's nothing I can do to change that."

"I know, Lottie. Well, I'll pick up some gas and get your car going. Okay?"

"Thanks. Winnie always said you were very kind."

"Now you're getting me off track again, Lottie. I'm supposed to see your driver's license. That's a state requirement upon a traffic stop."

"My license expired two weeks ago," said Lottie. "I didn't have the stupid two bucks to renew it." Her eyes teared.

"Hey, things will get better. I'm sure of it," said the sheriff.

"Rosa said that you failed your eye exam in River Falls for your driver's license."

"Well, it's in the works, Lottie. Ah, I better go and get that gas," said the sheriff.

"Oh no!" shouted Lottie. "Mark is still in the hole."

Lottie started the car and took off, throwing dust and loose gravel all over the sheriff and his car.

"That woman just may be a little off," said the sheriff.

Lottie sat in her rocking chair on the front porch. Mark was out of the hole, and the kids were cleaned up, fed, and in bed. A beautiful Idaho sunset was in the making, and a gentle warm wind was blowing in from the west. She still had her muddy dress on, and her hair was still a mess. Lottie was half asleep, and at this point she probably didn't give a hoot.

# CHAPTER 21

## *THE HOUSE AND AGENT BEN*

Lottie had a hard time accepting the fact that they had only a few days left before they had to be out. Their house stood on three acres with pine trees and forage grass. The old house was their palace in the rough and located in the right place for them. The center of town was within walking distance from their house, and the sawmill was just across the railroad tracks.

They had the best view of the hillside and peaks. The sage-covered hills, on the west side of the valley, glistened when hit by the morning sun. On a clear winter night, the snow-capped peaks of Carter's Ridge shone brightly from the moonlight. People say that Sam Carter went up to the ridge decades ago looking for the legendary Nez Perce Indian treasure. Sam Carter never made it back, but his old mule did.

Lottie didn't mind going to the woodshed to use the toilet. When they were first married, they lived in a boarding house and shared a bathroom with nine other people. When John lived on the reservation, he shared an outhouse that leaked when it rained.

The logging trucks made a lot of noise during the day with their engines roaring, but it was a delight for Mark. He also loved watching the trains and the railroad workers in the rail yard. The family got use to the Midnight Express that roared down the tracks. The whole house shook and rattled for about four minutes.

During a heavy rainstorm, Mark was the rain captain of the woodshed. He placed pans on the floor to catch the dripping water from the old roof. Lottie wouldn't miss the cold air coming through the edges of their wood-framed windows, but she would miss the beautiful bushes and trees that one could see through all those old windows from within.

She stepped into the kitchen and looked at the side of the door frame where she penciled in the heights of Mark and Sara as they grew. The dark blue spot in the corner of the kitchen floor was still visible from when Sara accidentally dropped a bottle of ink. Lottie walked into the living room and gazed at the old rustic wood stove. She remembered cooking on that stove when the power was out. They were simple meals.

The first night, Lottie made toasted cheese sandwiches with franks. The second night, it was baked beans and franks. The third night was navy beans and hot dogs.

She wasn't ready to take down the pictures or roll up the rugs just yet. She walked up the stairs and stopped when her right foot rested on the one squeaky step of the staircase. She sat down and looked up at the stained-glass window above the staircase. It was like a prism when the sun's rays entered the window.

Lottie knew when the kids were on their way down the staircase at night to the toilet. One of them would always land on the step that squeaked. And on their way back from the woodshed, they always stopped in the kitchen and looked for snacks.

On some mornings, one could hear the prairie grouse that walked back and forth across the roof. At times, Lottie would be out back sitting out on the porch when the kids took their afternoon nap. Two large ravens often perched on the porch railing and talked back and forth to each other while looking at Lottie. She always gave them something to eat. The ravens never tried to pry the clothes pins off the clothes lines or intimidate the rabbits in the cages. The ravens were always on good behavior when visiting the Rainwaters.

Animals seemed to be attracted to the Rainwaters' house.

Perhaps they saw comfort and security there. Even Blackie welcomed them.

Lottie didn't know what to do with the rabbits. She was sure that Sara and Mark wanted to keep all forty-two of them. And John would be upset if they were given away. Uncle Will agreed to take in the rabbits, and Uncle Bill would set their pens up. They weren't sure where they would get that much feed.

But it was still hard for her and the kids to take. As she got up from the staircase, she heard a knock at the front door. Lottie realized now that the house was really just a house and not her family. She slowly walked down the staircase and to the front door. Lottie opened the door, and there stood Mr. Perkins from the bank and a younger man in a sport jacket and tie.

"Mr. Perkins, I didn't expect to see you just yet," said Lottie.

"I'm sorry, Lottie, that we came unannounced," said Mr. Perkins.

"It's okay. The kids are over at my sister's house, and I just came back from the hospital. No problem."

"This is Agent Ben from a financial bank investigation branch out of Boise. This is Lottie Rainwater, Agent Ben."

"It's nice to meet you," said the agent. "I've heard a lot about you. May we have a word with you?"

"Well, okay," replied Lottie. "We're not in more trouble are we, Mr. Perkins?"

"Not at all. We just need to ask you a few questions."

"Please come in and have a seat at the living room table," said Lottie. "I'll get some coffee. Be right back." As they sat, Agent Ben looked around for a few moments.

"So you've known the Rainwater family for some time?" remarked Agent Ben.

"About thirty some years, and I've known the Lindstrom family about as long, Ben. I was a young man back then with just one year of college. Great Uncle Will gave me a chance, and I've been at the bank ever since. He was very good to me. I respect him very much."

"That's a long time," replied Agent Ben.

"The Rainwaters are good people," said Mr. Perkins. "They're going through some real tough times."

Lottie came out of the kitchen and placed the coffee cups on the table. She poured the coffee and then sat down.

"Your faces are so sober," said Lottie. "Did someone else die that I don't know about?"

"No, nothing like that, Mrs. Rainwater," said Agent Ben.

"Good, and you can just call me Lottie. No need to be formal around this house."

"This coffee is good," remarked Mr. Perkins. "Hot and strong."

"Glad you like the coffee," said Lottie.

"It's great," said Agent Ben.

"My secretary at the bank is still shell-shocked from a couple of days ago," remarked Mr. Perkins. "She hasn't been able to make coffee or anything else."

"How's that?" asked Agent Ben.

"Well, her wig was pulled off her head, and then that person threw it out in the street," replied Mr. Perkins. "It got caught up in the wind and lodged around a radio antenna of a passing car. She's in River Falls trying to find another hairpiece. She was very upset."

"That's quite the story," said Agent Ben. "I thought I'd heard just about everything in my line of work." Mr. Perkins gave Lottie a long look.

"After Uncle Lance's death, Lottie, Mr. Perkins contacted our branch in Boise, as he felt that there was something odd going on at the bank and a few other things. We'll be investigating Zach and all the bank records. We may be talking to Will Lindstrom as well."

"What's going on?" asked Lottie.

"We can't say right now, Lottie," said Agent Ben. "But it's real important that you tell no one of our visit or anything about what you found in the hole out back." She nodded.

"It's my understanding that Zach and Lance Lindstrom were your two uncles and that Will Lindstrom is your father by adoption," said Agent Ben.

"Yes, that's true," replied Lottie. "I was adopted by the Lindstroms when I was a baby. I just found out that I'm the daughter of one of the Lindstrom sisters. Winnie, their oldest sister, is my mother. So I'm actually the niece of Great Uncle Will. That is a long story in itself."

"I understand," said Agent Ben.

"Bill just found out that my Great Uncle Will isn't his dad," said Lottie. "So a lot has been going on in our two families."

"That must have been a real tough go for you and Bill," replied Mr. Perkins.

"Who in the family do you think has been the closest to Zach and Lance?" asked Agent Ben.

"I'm not sure," replied Lottie. "Winnie, their oldest sister, has been gone for the most part chasing her acting career. Gloria was away most of the time, as her husband was in the service. Rosa, the second-oldest sister, never connected very well with them. And Great Uncle Will sure wasn't close to Zach and Lance anymore after they got 100 percent controlling interest of the bank after his accident."

"Great Uncle Will refused to fight the takeover," remarked Mr. Perkins. "He just gave up, Agent Ben. That was about eight years ago."

"Great Uncle Will never did say much about anything," said Lottie. "But when he did, he seemed to confide in Bill and me more so than the rest of the family. I'm not sure why. Those two brothers never attended our family gatherings. They just kept to themselves, and Uncle Zach seemed to be always off to some distant place looking for odd-like treasures. Uncle Lance was busy running the bank. Some people didn't trust him. This was such a close family except for those two."

"So you believe in what you've seen and heard to be true," said Agent Ben.

"Yes I do," replied Lottie. "Everything."

"Did either one of them favor you more than anyone else, Lottie?" asked Agent Ben.

"Well, perhaps Uncle Zach," replied Lottie. "When he did speak to me, he was courteous. One time, I took care of him for several days after his first heart attack. I went there every day and tended to him. He told me one time that I was good for the family. Uncle Zach rarely spoke to any one of us after his brother died. Sheriff Taylor said that they were sure the oddest two of the bunch and should have been in the jail next door. You're sure asking me a lot of questions."

"I know we are," said Mr. Perkins. "We have our reasons."

"We're real curious about the burlap sack that you found," said Agent Ben. "Lottie, do you still have those coins in the house here?"

"Yes I do. I'll get them for you."

Lottie got up and went into the kitchen. After a few moments, she returned and placed the small burlap sack on the table. Agent Ben took a few of the coins out and looked at them.

"Very interesting," said Agent Ben.

"I hid them in a large cookie jar in the kitchen, Agent Ben. My kids won't peak in there, as they know that it's going to be a long time till they see any cookies anywhere, the way things are going. What are we going to do? These old coins or whatever they are just might be worth something. We need the money, Agent Ben. My husband has been in the hospital for weeks. So I have more problems than just this house. Believe me."

"I'm sorry to hear that," said Agent Ben. "Please, just be patient, Lottie."

"The bank isn't too sorry. I don't mean you, Mr. Perkins," said Lottie. "I know that you were you just taking orders. Anyway, we found these coins by accident. The utility people came by two days ago and left a deep hole out there. They failed to locate the pipe. I told my kids not to go near the hole. Mark, my oldest, took a nosedive right into the hole."

"A nosedive?" said Agent Ben.

"I mean that Mark fell in the hole. I also fell in the hole trying to pull my boy out. That's when we happened to see the burlap sack sticking out the side of the hole."

"Her Uncle Zach owned this house before he sold it to the Rainwaters," said Mr. Perkins. "And now he's legally taken it back."

"Well, so much for family ties," said Agent Ben. "That's unfortunate that a family can't work things out. Lottie, is there any particular reason why your Uncle Zach would want this house back?" asked Agent Ben.

"Well, we're behind on the payments," answered Lottie.

"No. I mean something other than that," replied Agent Ben.

"I have no idea, Agent Ben. We do have some acreage. Perhaps the railroad would have some need of this property."

"I would like to send one of my men out later in the day to see if there's anything else buried there," said Agent Ben.

"Sure," replied Lottie. "What about this sack of coins?"

"Just put them back in the cookie jar for safekeeping," said Mr. Perkins. "Well, we must be going, Lottie."

"Mr. Perkins, is there any way you could help us? Anything?" asked Lottie.

"At this point, I'm not really sure, Lottie."

"I know," said Lottie. "My lips are triple sealed."

"Well, we must be on our way," said Mr. Perkins.

"I'll show you out, gentlemen." Agent Ben and Mr. Perkins got into the black sedan.

"Lottie, thanks for the coffee," said Agent Ben.

Lottie stepped over to the passenger side of their car. "I'm sorry. I didn't quite hear you, Agent Ben."

"Thanks for the strong coffee. That's the way your Uncle Zach likes his coffee."

Lottie had a puzzled look on her face as they drove away. She walked back into the house. She grabbed her coffee and walked out on the back porch and sat down in an old wicker chair. It was a quiet day. The log trucks didn't run on Saturdays, and the mill was running just five days a week. There was a little chill in the air for being a summer morning. Lottie wrapped her shawl a little tighter around her. Lottie now accepted the fact that there wasn't any help on the horizon for them. So now it was up to God.

To Lottie's surprise, the two large ravens, which often visited the Rainwaters, circled the house and then landed on the porch railing right in front of her. The one raven held a slice of bread in its beak and then dropped it on the porch railing right in front of Lottie.

The other raven held a cookie in its beak and dropped it on the railing next to the slice of bread. The ravens looked at Lottie as if they were waiting for her to do something. The ravens lightly ruffled their feathers for a moment and then remained silent. Lottie slowly reached out and picked up the bread and the cookie and held them in her hands.

"Thank you. You're one of God's wonderful creations."

The ravens uttered a few loud sounds and then took off, heading east toward Carter's Ridge. Lottie looked at the piece of bread and the cookie. It reminded her of the Book of Kings in the Old Testament where the raven brought food to Elijah.

"No one is going to believe this. They brought us something to eat."

# CHAPTER 22

## *GREAT UNCLE WILL'S PREMONITION*

Lottie was on highway 12 three miles out of Bergan's Ferry. She slowed down and made a right turn onto a well-kept gravel road leading up to Great Uncle Will's house.

The two-story ranch house was built in 1895. An old split-rail fence surrounded the front of the property. The house had a red brick chimney on the side leading up through the edge of the cedar shake roof. His 1942 Packard was parked in the breezeway. A rustic-looking barn stood in back with rough-cut red cedar siding.

A large stand of pine trees stood behind the house. The summit of Carter's Ridge could be seen from the driveway. Lottie parked in front of the breezeway and sat in the car for several moments. This was her first home when she was a baby. Now thirty some years later, it appeared that this was going to be her home again.

Lottie got out of the car and walked up to the door inside the breezeway. She knocked lightly a few times and then walked into the kitchen.

"There's only one person who snores like that," thought Lottie.

She walked into the living room and found Uncle Will sound asleep on the couch with an old army wool blanket draped across him.

"Great Uncle Will. I'm here. I'm here."

Uncle Will woke up and tried to grab his glasses that were on the coffee table beside him.

"Ah. I don't need these glasses to tell who you are." He got up and slowly walked over to Lottie.

"It's good to see you, Lottie. Give me a hug." She gave him a hug and then stepped back.

"Did you sleep in your clothes again? I can tell that you did."

"Looks like I did, Lottie. See, I'm already dressed for the new day. Take your coat off and stay a while. We have a lot to talk about your move, and there's also another very important matter I need to discuss with you."

"Thank you," said Lottie. "I would have brought something, but there isn't much left in the house."

"I don't have any coffee going. How about some orange juice?"

"Sounds good," replied Lottie.

Lottie folded up his blanket and placed it at the end of the couch and sat down. Uncle Will returned with the glasses of juice and gave one to Lottie. He sat down next to her and held the glass of juice out toward her.

"Prost. To better days," Uncle Will said, as they clicked their glasses together. Lottie took a swallow and then set the glass down.

"This really bites," said Lottie. "This is stronger than my coffee. What's in it?"

"I must have put a little too much vodka in it," said Uncle Will. "No wonder I went out so quick last night. I took this bottle way from Bill a while back. I thought I would sample some of it. I hear that the deadline to move out is coming up in just a few days."

"We have about four days, and then we have to be out of the house," said Lottie. "Gloria and Linda are going to help me pack most of our things very shortly. We got some empty boxes from the market and feed store."

"We can use my truck to haul your furniture over here to the house," said Uncle Will. "Bill and a friend who knew Gilbert are going to help."

"Are you sure about all this?" asked Lottie. "We have a lot of stuff. And the kids can be noisy at times."

"Of course I am," answered Uncle Will. "I have this big house, and it's just me living in it. Besides, I could use a good cook."

"Am I hired?" asked Lottie with a grin.

"Of course," said Uncle Will. "You and John can stay in my room upstairs. The kids can sleep in the other room, and the third room up there can be used to store a lot of your stuff. We also have plenty of room in the barn for things. It's pretty weather tight."

"Where are you going to sleep?" asked Lottie.

"You're sitting on it, Lottie. I don't sleep upstairs anymore since Ingrid died. Those stairs are just too much for me. I got the bathroom down here, and you can use the one upstairs. It's been a long time since you kids slept in this house."

"As I recall, Lance and Zach slept in the one room," remarked Lottie. "Gloria and Winnie slept with me right across the way. I always liked the top rack of the bunk bed. Rosa always complained about my snoring, and I complained about her hogging the bathroom. Winnie had the big bed by herself, as she was the oldest."

"I remember when Lance and Zach would sit on the floor up there and play Monopoly when they were small, Lottie. They said that they were training to be big bankers like me. They were so innocent back then. Remember when I taught you how to play solitaire? You were a quick learner."

"I sure do," answered Lottie. "We would be up there with the cards spread across the bed. Ingrid would come to the staircase and scream, 'You better not be up there teaching her how to play those stupid cards.' She didn't want you to corrupt my mind with those cards. I still play solitaire. John said that it's a white man's game." They laughed.

"How is John doing, Lottie?"

"About the same. In front of the kids I try not to act worried about anything, but sometimes I just break down and cry. It's hard on the kids."

"I know, Lottie."

"When you said that John and I would sleep in your room, I started to think "What if John doesn't make it?""

"Hey, don't say that, Lottie. John is a strong man, and a whole lot of people are praying for the family. You must believe that."

"I know people are," replied Lottie.

"Take another drink of my orange juice. This juice shall set you free," said Uncle Will with a smile.

"That's not in scripture," said Lottie with a grin.

"Yeah, I know. I wish I could've done something so that you didn't have to give up the house, but I was flat out of that much cash. I tried to get a lien on this place to stir up some cash but was turned down by Anderson's Mortgage in town, Lottie. I knew the manager's dad for years and did him a lot of favors. But he's dead, and the son pretended that he didn't know me."

"I understand," said Lottie. "We don't have a dime to share with you when we move in, you know."

"That's not a problem with me, Lottie. Don't feel bad about that. I finally got a buyer for some of my timber. I hope to sell a few acres next month. And I just sold that old coin collection of mine. It brought me a few dollars. So we're okay."

"I wish you didn't sell your coin collection."

"No reason to take it to heaven, Lottie. God doesn't need it."

"That's very true."

"I did have several old Spanish coins in that collection, but they were nowhere to be found," remarked Uncle Will.

"Did Mr. Perkins tell you what we found in the hole in the backyard?" asked Lottie.

"Yes he did. Kinda odd isn't it. Some of my coins were missing, but now coins turn up in the hole in your backyard and maybe much more concerning the bank. Something stinks in Denmark. I just know it."

"I think you're right," said Lottie.

"So don't worry about a thing," said Uncle Will. "It will be a delight to have you and the family here as long as you want."

"Thanks so much. You're a lifesaver," replied Lottie. "Looks like you're keeping Old Red out of the weather. The barn door was partway open when I drove up. Hard to miss that bright red paint job."

"I guess I forgot to close the door all the way," said Uncle Will. "After I had that old Mack Truck restored, I wanted to keep it in pristine condition. It brings back a lot of memories. You know I always liked trucks. Maybe that's why I became a truck driver at such an early age. Back in the day, there was no power steering or power brakes on those old trucks. Plus you had to have a strong leg to work that clutch. I was pretty big for a kid. I lied about my age when I got hired part time at a trucking company in Boise."

"Did your dad send you to college at that time?" asked Lottie.

"Yes he did. He paid half of my tuition. I ended up getting a two-year degree. It took a while, as I was already married to Ingrid and Winnie was just born. I was so young and doing so much."

"Mom was such a pretty woman," remarked Lottie. "I heard that she always had a crush on you in school."

"That she did. I wasn't sure why she got interested in me in my senior year in high school."

"You were tall and handsome," said Lottie.

"That's what some people said," replied Uncle Will. "She was my first girlfriend. I guess I might have married her for her looks back then. You know how young men are. I'm sure you remember the time Lottie that I told her in a roundabout way, when I was quite upset, that I married her for her looks only. You know how that turned out for me."

"How could I forget?" replied Lottie. "You ended up eating at our place for a while."

"Later, I inherited some money from my Uncle Jim. With the help of my uncle's influential friend, I opened up the bank. I had a lot of help. That sure was a long time ago. I spent too much time at the bank."

"The depression didn't help any," said Lottie.

"That's for sure, Lottie. I just wasn't a drinker or a party goer like Ingrid was. But she was a great mother. I loved her for that. Of course I wasn't happy with all the deceit. I hope Bill can pull out of his drinking nightmare. Bill is as addicted to booze as I was addicted to work when I was his age."

"I have a real personal question to ask you."

"Another question, Lottie? You're going to owe me a nice baked apple pie."

"Did you ever have a hunch that Bill wasn't your son?"

"Yeah, I guess I did. Sheriff Taylor overheard Winnie and Ingrid talking one day. After a while, he put two and two together. I heard a rumor back then that someone saw Ingrid in River Falls with another man. I sensed that Winnie was keeping something from us."

"So did Bill," remarked Lottie.

"You have a dimple on your cheek. So does Winnie exactly in the same location. I didn't think that was coincidental. And Winnie always spent more time with you on her visits than her sisters. Not that she didn't love them."

"Bill thinks the world of you," said Lottie.

"I'm blessed that he does. I was determined to love Bill whether he was my real son or not. What's even better is that you ended up being a blood relative of mine through this whole mess."

"Lance and Zach said one time that they didn't want to be tied down to a family," said Uncle Will. "I never raised them to think that way, Lottie. Lance was engaged one time to a nice lady, but when she talked about having children... Well, Lance ended that relationship."

"Will you ever forgive them?" asked Lottie.

"I'm working on it. It's not easy."

"I know what you mean," said Lottie.

"I talked to your mom the other day. Winnie is excited about the relationship she's having with you. She's trying her best."

"I know. I think it's going to work out," replied Lottie.

"Lottie, in the past years you probably figured out that some of the townsfolk think I'm crazy for digging everywhere. I guess I do look odd walking around wearing that old dark blue suit and that top hat with the shovel over my shoulder. I know that I may be off at times. Rosa's new squeeze said it's best if you know that you're goofy than not to know at all. At times, Lottie, I just don't give a hoot. Does that make any sense, Lottie? Am I goofy?"

"You mean digging for the Nez Perce Gold?" asked Lottie. "I'm sure I'm the last one you should ask. You're not the only one that might be a little off. Here I exploded on the Wart sisters that day, and Bill tried to blow his brains out." They laughed. "You still get those headaches from the accident?"

"Sometimes I do. And at times I feel that I'm in a fog or something. I really have to focus when I'm playing checkers with that slick Sheriff Taylor," said Uncle Will with a big grin.

"Are we the only two families in town that are messed up?"

"Oh I don't think so, Lottie. I think we're just quite open about it."

"We sure are," replied Lottie.

"We will get our redemption," said Uncle Will. "I just know it."

"What do you mean?" asked Lottie.

"You will see, Lottie. My redemption will be the finding of the Nez Perce treasure. When I find it, the doubters won't think I'm so crazy. Your redemption will come too. And it will happen very soon, Lottie."

"You know Sheriff Taylor better than anyone in town," said Lottie. "I think he isn't telling us everything."

"Lottie, you're just like Bill. You always have questions about everything. But that's okay."

"I know."

"Did you know that the sheriff always considered our two families as being like family to him, Lottie?"

"I knew he was always looking out for us. He's a good man," replied Lottie. "My mom said that the sheriff was an orphan as a child. He never knew his parents. She said that his birth is on record, but the dates don't seem to jibe. He applied to be a police officer in Boise way back when. No one recalls what he did before that. The story goes that he had an old diploma signed by the commandant of the Boise Police Academy."

"I don't know, Lottie. He must have gone through some kind of training to become a policeman."

"How did my mom know all this?" asked Lottie. "The sheriff never talks to anyone about his past. Don't say anything to him about what I said. Now things are starting to go together."

Uncle Will gave Lottie a funny look. He took another sip of his orange juice and burped.

"Well, he gets the job done, Lottie. The bad guys don't stay very long in this town. You were somewhat of a tomboy when you were a kid, and a tall lanky girl at that, with a lot of spunk. It was like you were trying to prove something. Rosa said you were a gutsy kid. But underneath all that it seemed you were a little fearful at times. I just hope that wasn't any doing by me or Ingrid."

"Not at all. You know when I was a small girl, I heard a lot of people referring to you as Great Uncle Will who weren't even related to you. You were always a powerful figure. So at times, I called you that too. I'm not sure how you took that. I'm like Bill. I consider you to be my dad."

"That was never an issue with me, Lottie. It's fine. Either title will work. Just don't call me late for dinner. Mr. Perkins dropped by yesterday after he and Agent Ben talked to you, Lottie. He had a few things to say. There's going to be a meeting at the bank this coming Wednesday at twelve noon."

"Who will be there?" asked Lottie.

"Sheriff Taylor and Mr. Perkins will be there. Agent Ben and a few other people will also attend. Your Uncle Zach will be the center of attraction, so to speak. It's going to be a real hot meeting."

"Are you going to be there?" asked Lottie.

"No. I'm not part of that bank anymore, as you know. They wouldn't even consider any statement that I would put in writing. I made a point a while back not to step foot in front of Zach or Lance again. I know that's harsh. I'm not proud of it. So I need you to be at that meeting."

"Me at the meeting?" said Lottie. "Why me?"

"You know Zach better than you think you do, Lottie."

"And I have my reasons not to be there," said Lottie.

Lottie realized that she raised her voice at the man she loved so much. She sat closer to him.

"I'm sorry I raised my voice at you," said Lottie.

She started to cry.

"That's okay. You're still the gutsy lady that I've known since you were a baby. I know you can do this."

"I'm crying my eyeballs out, and you say that I'm a gutsy lady?"

"That's what I said, Lottie."

"So you want me to just walk right into the meeting and just sit down like I own the place?"

"Yes ma'am. That's it."

"They won't let me stay there and listen in."

"Yes they will," replied Uncle Will. "Sheriff Taylor will be there. I've talked to him already."

"You know I think dearly of Sheriff Taylor, but sometimes he can't even find the keys to his police cruiser. One time, he lost his revolver for a day or two."

"Believe me, Lottie. Don't underestimate Sheriff Taylor. He's extremely capable when he wants to be."

"What if they ask me what I'm doing there? I wouldn't know what to say except that the bank is taking our house!"

"Just say that you are representing Will Lindstrom, that you're there on his behalf. I know what I'm doing. Lottie. Pay close attention to your uncle's actions at the meeting. Do you believe me?"

Lottie looked at him for several moments and then kissed him on his forehead.

"I believe you, Dad."

# CHAPTER 23

## *LANCE'S DOWNFALL*

Linda made a turn off of Willow Road and parked alongside the Rainwaters' house. As Linda got out of the car, Lottie walked up to her from the backyard.

"Hi, Linda. I wasn't expecting you here today."

"I thought I would come out and see if you needed any help. I'm going to miss coming here on Saturdays," said Linda as she looked around the yard. "I really felt like I was doing something very worthwhile."

"Yes you were," said Lottie. "It was great for us girls and everyone else to get together and make meals for the people who came here. There was plenty of room here to set everything up and just far enough from the center of town to have some privacy for the guests."

"It was the perfect place," remarked Linda.

"So there won't be a breakfast at another location?"

"I don't know," answered Lottie, shaking her head. "I guess you have your driver's license now?"

"Not quite. I failed the test yesterday."

"Does your mom know that?"

"Not exactly, Lottie."

"Well she either knows or doesn't know. I can tell if you're fibbing because your eyes usually twitch when you do." Linda smiled and shook her head.

"Okay. I'm busted. Take me to jail."

"I can't. I could use your help," said Lottie.

159

Linda was Gloria's only child. She started to learn how to cook at an early age and was deep into her school studies, unlike some teenagers back then. She also liked tagging along with Lottie and her kids. Linda was very much like her. Linda didn't like to accept help, and her tongue was a little sharp at times. Gloria said one time that she felt like scolding them both together, as they were so much alike.

They sat at the kitchen table for several moments in silence.

"This may be the last time we'll be sitting in this house, Linda."

"It sure looks that way, Lottie. There's a lot of great memories in this place."

"I think it's going to be hot today," said Lottie. "We should get going while it's still somewhat cool up in the attic. There's a lot of stuff we have to carry down from there. What's in the sack that you brought in?"

"Some coffee," said Linda, as she reached into the sack on the floor.

"You brought coffee? You're a lifesaver, Linda. I'll make the coffee before we get started. Oh, before I forget, how are you doing?"

"What do you mean?" asked Linda.

"Great Uncle Will said he spoke to you the other day. He felt that something was bothering you."

"How would he know?"

"He's a little unsettled at times, but he knows more than one thinks. Come on, you can tell me, Linda."

"I asked Mom the other day if she would ever get married again," said Linda. "She indicated that she might one day. How could she say something like that? Dad has only been gone a year!"

"Your dad didn't want her to be alone for the rest of her life, Linda. In fact, your dad told Rosa one time that he wanted her to marry again if he didn't make it back from Korea."

"He said that?" Linda asked.

"Yes he did," replied Lottie. "Your mom will always love Gilbert no matter what."

"I miss Dad so much." She gave Linda a hug.

"I know you do, honey," said Lottie. "There was something I needed to do today. Oh, I know. Great Uncle Will wanted me to attend a meeting at the bank at noon. I don't want to go, but I kinda said that I would."

"Why does he want you there?" asked Linda.

"He wanted me to experience the first part of my redemption. I have no clue what he meant. He was pretty insistent that I be there."

As Lottie started to open the can of coffee, she looked up at the kitchen clock.

"I'd best go to that meeting. Your Aunt Winnie gave me a nice business suit a while back. I never did wear it. I would look somewhat business like in that outfit. Here, finish opening this. Be right back." Lottie returned with the business suit on.

"That was a quick change, Lottie. Navy blue really looks good on you."

Lottie looked at the can of coffee and then became ecstatic as she lifted the coffee can in the air.

"This is it!" said Lottie.

"Is what?" asked Linda.

"Linda, it's the coffee! I know it now. Take me to the bank. We have to go right now. You can drive me in my car. I'm too nervous to drive. Sure thing, it's the coffee. Agent Ben was right on the money!"

"Lottie, you're not going crazy. I mean I don't get what you're saying."

"You think I'm going nuts again," said Lottie. "This will be all over in a short time. We'll get even."

Linda parked in front of the bank. "Here we are. It's almost twelve," said Linda.

"This won't take long. Just stay parked here." Lottie stepped out of the car and then turned to her.

"Oh, my handbag, Linda." She handed Lottie her handbag.

"What's in there? It's so heavy."

"Nothing. Just wait, Linda."

Lottie walked briskly into the bank and approached the secretary.

"Oh it's you," said the secretary as she quickly scooted her chair back.

"I'm here to attend the meeting in the back office. I'm not here to pull your hair off again," said Lottie.

"I sure hope not, Mrs. Rainwater."

"I'm also sorry about last week," said Lottie. "I was a little intense. We're having a very hard time."

"Sorry for being so mean to you that day, Mrs. Rainwater. My views of you have changed after Mr. Perkins filled me in on what was really going on, and I didn't know that your husband was ill. Your uncle really steered me wrong about you and everyone else. Please don't say anything about our conversation. I think he's dangerous."

As the secretary stood up, Lottie stepped around the desk and gave her a hug.

"Hope we get through all this," said Lottie.

"Thanks, Mrs. Rainwater. This way, please."

Lottie followed her to the back office, and then she opened the door for Lottie.

"Thank you, ma'am," said Lottie.

Lottie paused for a moment at the doorway. She then walked in and stood there defiantly before them.

Her uncle was sitting at the end of a long, wide oak table. Sheriff Taylor sat on one side of the table and had a bottle of root beer in front of him. His deputy sat next to him. Agent Ben sat across from Sheriff Taylor with three other men from the county, and Mr. Perkins sat next to the sheriff's deputy with a notepad in front of him.

Uncle Zach, with a long, cold stare, looked Lottie up and down.

"What is that woman doing back here in my office and at this meeting?" said Uncle Zach. "Woman, go home. We don't want you here."

"What home? I won't have a home to go to in a few days," said Lottie.

Uncle Zach stood up. "Get out!" Sheriff Taylor stood up and grabbed Zach's arm.

"Sit down, Mr. Lindstrom. I mean now," said the sheriff. He sat down with an enraged look.

"Perkins, you set this whole thing up. I bet you did. You're fired."

"It will be a pleasure not to work for you anymore. You're a little man compared to Great Uncle Will."

Sheriff Taylor took a swallow of his root beer as he smiled after hearing Mr. Perkins' remark.

"Mrs. Rainwater, please have a seat," said Agent Ben.

"Thank you, sir," said Lottie.

"You people were here for two days turning everything upside down," said Uncle Zach. "What's going on here?"

Uncle Zach shook his head as he grabbed his cup of coffee. He drank half of it and then slammed it down on the table. Lottie looked at Uncle Zach's coffee cup and then at Agent Ben.

Lottie smiled. Agent Ben looked at her and then nodded.

"Mrs. Rainwater has something to say," said Agent Ben. She stood up.

"Gentlemen, I have a story to tell," said Lottie. "Please be patient with me."

"Now what?" said Uncle Zach. "Is it story time now?"

"Let her go on," said Agent Ben.

"The Uncle Zach that I knew never drank coffee. It made him sick as a dog. I saw you drink half of that coffee right down, Uncle."

One of the men sitting across the table looked at Zach's coffee cup and then at Agent Ben. Uncle Zach looked at his coffee cup and back at Lottie. He became restless as Lottie continued on.

"Uncle Zach served in the Army during the First World War, and during that time, he got a tattoo on the back side of his left wrist," said Lottie. "It said '3rd Flight Squadron,' with a propeller and bayonet under the logo. As kids, we thought it was neat when Uncle Zach would flex his wrist. The bayonet and the propeller would move back and forth."

Uncle Zach looked down at his arm as she spoke. "Uncle, show us your left wrist," said Lottie.

"I don't have to be a part of this circus. I own this bank," said Uncle Zach.

"Raise your sleeve up, Mr. Lindstrom," said Agent Ben. "Raise your sleeve."

Reluctantly, Uncle Zach slowly raised his sleeve.

"Bingo," said Sheriff Taylor. "His wrist is clean as can be. Not even a scratch."

"So it looks like we have Lance sitting here instead of Zach," said Mr. Perkins. "Great Uncle Will was right all along. You impersonated your brother Zach after his death. I knew there was something wrong, but I just couldn't place it. Lottie really came through on this one." Lottie sat down. She had a smile on her face.

"Thank you, Mr. Perkins," said Lottie.

"I'd like to add one more thing," said Mr. Perkins. "We found some real interesting things in the hole behind Lottie's house. The house that Zach once owned."

"What do you have to say for yourself, Mr. Lindstrom?" asked Agent Ben.

"Are you going to believe this woman? She was in the same nut house that my old man was in not too long ago. The whole family is mistaken about a bogus tattoo just to unseat me from this bank. My crazy old man is just trying to get back at me."

"Your story doesn't hold any water," said Sheriff Taylor. "I've seen Zach's tattoo once before."

"A person also came forward and said that you paid those men to beat up John Rainwater," said Mr. Perkins. "Evidently, you wanted to erase any income coming into the Rainwaters' household in order to hasten the foreclosure of their house. There's something on their property that you wanted to find."

Lottie looked intensely at her uncle. Uncle Lance dropped his head for several moments and then looked up with a subdued look.

"That brother of mine was always off looking for gold and those worthless artifacts. When he came back from the war, he pretended that he was a war hero. He was nothing but a clerk at an Army airfield. He buried his money because he didn't trust anyone. He even took some gold coins from our crazy dad. He wasn't any saint by far."

Uncle Lance slid out a 44 revolver from the table drawer in front of him. He smiled as he waived it back and forth.

"Lance, easy with that big gun! It doesn't have to be like this," said Sheriff Taylor.

"Please, put the gun down," said Agent Ben.

"Uncle Lance slid the gun across the table to Lottie. She picked up the gun and stood up. She held the gun with both hands and pointed it directly at her uncle.

"Go ahead, get even, Lottie!"

"Uncle, you always hated my husband."

"I don't have anything to live for. Go ahead, shoot me! Then we both can go to hell," said Uncle Lance with a cynical smile. All eyes were on Lottie.

"Lottie, put it down. He's not worth it!" said the sheriff. She lowered the gun.

"I knew you didn't have the guts," said Uncle Lance. You're weak like that lame Indian that you married."

Uncle Lance let out a sick laugh. Lottie suddenly raised the revolver. Her hands shaking, she pulled the trigger. The cuckoo clock on the wall, above Uncle Lance's head, exploded. Everyone ducked for cover. Lottie pulled the trigger again and blasted the window out next to the cuckoo clock. Uncle Lance fainted. Lottie placed the gun on the table. She stood there in complete calm. The deputy quickly stepped over and grabbed the gun.

"I guess no one dozed off during this meeting, Agent Ben. What are your wishes with this imposter?" asked Sheriff Taylor.

"Have your deputy take Lance to the county jail in River Falls as soon as possible."

"Lottie, thank God you aimed high or you just hate cuckoo clocks," said the sheriff. "Please come with me. We have to go next door. Nothing personal."

"I'm not going next door," answered Lottie.

Linda was parked in an alley just down from the bank. She sat there crouched down in the seat. Uncle Will was walking down Fourth Street and then stopped at the entrance of the alley after he saw Lottie's car. He walked up to the car and looked in.

"Is that you, Linda?" She cautiously raised her head.

"Why are you parked here with Lottie's car?"

"Quick, get in the car, Great Uncle Will. Keep down. They might be looking for me. Please take your top hat off. It's sticking up too high."

"Who will see us, Linda girl?"

"The police," answered Linda. "I heard gunshots when I was parked in front of the bank waiting for Lottie. I think she robbed the bank. They're going to think I was the getaway driver. And who knows what else happened. Maybe there's dead people in there!"

Uncle Will looked around and then took Linda's hand. "Just slow down, Linda. Just start from the beginning."

"Okay. I was at Lottie's house, and she remembered that she had to go the bank meeting. She went crazy over the coffee. She was too nervous to drive, so I drove her here. Lottie wanted me to park right in front of the bank and wait for her until she came out. She had something heavy in her handbag. It was probably a gun," remarked Linda.

"What gun?" asked Uncle Will."

"I'm sure I heard two gunshots. It must have been her. Lottie said at the house that she wanted to get even."

"And then what, Linda?"

"A few minutes later, I saw Sheriff Taylor taking Lottie out of the bank by the arm and into the jail. I took off and drove in the alley here."

"It was supposed to be just a meeting, Linda. I didn't know that she kept a gun around. Maybe my gun is still in my desk at the bank. I believe it's still loaded."

"What are we going to do?" asked Linda.

Uncle Will looked at her and then sat there motionless for several moments with a glazed look in his eyes.

"I know what I have to do," said Uncle Will. "Sheriff Taylor won't be real happy with me when I get done."

"When you get that look on your face, I know something strange is going to happen, Great Uncle Will."

"My car is at the gas station. It won't be ready yet. Please take me home so I can get Big Red. I'm going on a mission."

"That big truck?" asked Linda. "No disrespect, Great Uncle Will, but you're not going to lose it again, are you? Promise you won't do anything weird."

"I can't do that. I might break my promise. I wouldn't want to do that to you," replied Uncle Will with a smile.

Lottie was in one of the three jail cells sitting on a cot with a distraught look on her face. Sheriff Taylor stood outside of the cell with his arms crossed.

"So you threw me in the slammer," said Lottie. "Winnie sure is going to be upset with you."

"I had no choice, Lottie. You needed to cool down. I'm sure she will understand. Well, maybe she might."

"Oh, she will be upset with you. Where's my handbag?"

"It's on the office desk up front. What were you doing with a sack of old coins in your handbag?"

"I was going to give them to Mr. Perkins for safekeeping. Can I go now, sheriff?"

"You're going to be here for a while, Lottie."

"I was just sitting here thinking how terrible you are for locking me up here in this dingy-looking place. I'm not a criminal."

"You think I'm terrible? You just tried to put two big holes in your Uncle Lance!"

"I just wanted to scare him," said Lottie.

"You also scared every person in that room," said the sheriff.

"Sheriff, don't I get one phone call?"

"Do you mean someone will call you, or do you mean that I have to let you call someone?" said the sheriff. "My phone line won't reach back here. Maybe I can find an extension. I'll be back in a few minutes. I have to make a phone call and fill out a report."

Sheriff Taylor sat in his broken-down chair and propped his feet up on his desk as he spoke to the county prosecutor.

"So my deputies just got there with Mr. Lindstrom. Actually, her observation of him at the meeting helped us greatly to identify who he really was. Yes, she did shoot up the place. No, she was just trying to scare her uncle. I might charge her for unlawful discharging of a firearm in the city limits. The Rainwater family has been through a lot. Now tell me all about that fishing trip you took last week."

\* \* \* \*

Lottie paced up and down in the jail cell. She looked up at the cell window and then opened it. "Bars everywhere," said Lottie. As she sat down, she heard a roar outside the cell window.

"Sounds like his big truck," thought Lottie.

Uncle Will got out of the truck and dragged a cable up the window of the jail.

"Lottie! Are you in there?"

"I can't quite see you. I'm in here!" said Lottie. "Is that you, Great Uncle Will?"

"Did you shoot anyone or rob the bank?"

"Nothing like that!" answered Lottie. "I killed the cuckoo clock. That's all I did. What are you doing in the alley with your truck?"

Uncle Will strung the large cable around the window bars of the cell.

"Great Uncle Will, what's going on?"

"No one is going to keep you in jail. When I'm done, just scramble out the window. Linda is parked just down the alley."

"No! Don't do what I think you're going to do!" shouted Lottie.

"Get clear of the window!" shouted Uncle Will.

Lottie stepped back from the window and crouched down on the cot. Uncle Will got back in the truck and shifted the transmission into first gear. As he gunned the engine, the truck lurched forward and pulled a large part of the wall out with the window in it. He dragged part of the jail wall behind him and turned onto Fourth Street and then headed out of town.

"Did we just have an earthquake?" thought the sheriff.

The sheriff wrestled to put his boots on, opened the office door, and then rushed to the back of the jail.

There sat Lottie covered in dust.

"It's all your fault for putting me back here," said Lottie.

"What happened? Where's my wall!" asked the sheriff.

"I don't know. You didn't ask me if I was okay, Sheriff Taylor."

The sheriff unlocked the cell door and walked up to the hole and looked out. He sat down on the cot across from her.

"It seems like if there's trouble brewing around here, you're always connected somehow," said the sheriff. "Even when you and Bill were kids, you guys were always into something. I'm going to add this to your list of crimes."

"I didn't plan this," said Lottie. Lottie stood up and tried to brush the dust off her clothes.

"Where are you going?" asked the sheriff.

"I have to get home and try to make dinner for the kids. I have things to do," said Lottie. "Besides, this cell is a mess."

"The shooter has things to do," said the sheriff. "I need a break. This is too much for one day. Don't bother to lock up. Just let yourself out. I'm going down to the diner to have something to eat."

The sheriff left the cell area talking to himself. Lottie stepped through the huge hole and walked down the alley. She stopped and turned around. She stood there for a moment.

"Great Uncle Will, what did you do now?"

# CHAPTER 24

## *THE REDEMPTION*

Lottie sat at a large desk with a desk lamp in front of her with a three-tier wood file tray off to the right. Ledgers were sprawled out on her desk. Two pencils and a green Parker ink pen straddled the ledgers. She was wearing the navy blue business suit that she wore at the bank meeting a while back. Since then, she had it cleaned and pressed. She had a look of calmness.

Lottie's eyesight was never that great when she had fine print in front of her. The newspaper print would give her fits. She wished that she had her glasses on when they signed for the mortgage on their house six years ago. She missed the extra fine print that stated after one year, the monthly payments would increase thirty percent. Mr. Perkins had his hands tied on that matter. Brother Lance made sure of that.

Lottie made sure this time that she had on her new thin-framed secretary glasses. No more mistakes could be made. She leaned back in her wood swivel chair and closed her eyes. Lottie painfully recalled the night that the hospital called about John. Then there were the Wart sisters from the dress shop. The job interviews weren't her best performances. The day at the diner just seemed to cap everything off, and then the countdown of the days before they had to leave the house for the last time. Lottie dozed off for a minute or two. When she awoke, Uncle Bill was sitting in front of her grinning from ear to ear.

"Wake up, lady," said Bill. "Where's everyone?"

"Oh, I must have dozed off again. We're actually closed till

171

Monday. How did you get in, Bill?"

"The door was unlocked," answered Bill.

"Looks like I better do a better job of keeping this place more secure when I'm alone here," said Lottie. "Being right next to the police station isn't a guarantee that nothing will happen."

"So how does it feel to be the big boss lady of this bank?"

"It still seems like a dream, Bill. It's not official yet, but I'm allowed to put my name on the letterhead and exercise some other duties as owner. It's been quite the crazy ride. Hard to believe isn't it."

"I'm sure Will is pleased over all this," said Bill. "He talked about total redemption for all of us."

"What do you mean redemption?" asked Lottie.

"He said his redemption would be that he would surely find the Nez Perce treasure and that yours was coming soon. Inheriting this bank may be the redemption."

"I think this could be, Bill. Just a while back the bank was taking our house, and now I'm taking the bank. Who would ever have guessed?"

"I just got back from the clinic in Boise," said Bill. "Rosa filled me in on some things this morning. I was shocked. She said that you shot the place up and then the sheriff threw you in the slammer. Then you were busted out of jail. I missed all the excitement! It was like the old Western days. The word around town is that you're the pie-throwing, gun-slinging lady." He laughed.

"How did they know what happened at the bank meeting, Bill?"

"I don't know."

"I hoped that I wouldn't create any more episodes of my life around here," said Lottie. "Don't need another title, and the sheriff isn't happy with me. He thinks I know who destroyed the jail."

"I know for sure who it was, Lottie."

"Don't say it, Bill. We don't know a thing."

"I'll just buy the sheriff a root beer, and that will settle him down, said Bill. Rosa said that you acquired the bank, but she didn't exactly say how you did. This really is the story of the century for this town."

"This is going to be a long story, Bill. You heard about Mark falling in the hole in the backyard when he was on his crutches. That was the hole the utility people dug looking for the broken water pipe. We found those coins in that hole by accident."

"That worked out well in the end," said Bill.

"The next day, we were visited by Mr. Perkins and Agent Ben. Your dad convinced me to attend a meeting at the bank. There I noticed that Uncle Zach was drinking coffee. He hated coffee, and I also uncovered that there wasn't a tattoo on his wrist."

"That's what Rosa said, Lottie. I remember now that Uncle Zach would become quite ill if he drank coffee. You're quite the detective. So at the meeting was when you shot the whole place up with that big 44 revolver?"

"Well, I kinda did. But no one got hurt, Bill. The only thing that happened was that I blasted the cuckoo clock to pieces and shot out the window next to the clock. Uncle Lance also fainted. They thought he was dead at first."

"You sure shook up everyone in that office, Lottie."

"I sure did. After further digging, they found more gold coins and money. I believe it was part of your dad's coin collection. They also found some very sensitive forms and records of transactions."

"Those old Spanish gold coins are worth a lot of money," said Bill. "I believe Uncle Zach owned that house for many years just before it was sold to you."

"Yes he did," replied Lottie. "So the rumor that he buried some of his personal wealth in the ground was true. There was also a rumor that the Nez Perce treasure might be buried on our land. Maybe that's why John was drawn to this house."

"It's no wonder my brother Lance wanted your house back."

"The authentic will wasn't found till two days after the meeting here in the bank," said Lottie. "His will was found in a safe deposit box right here in the bank. Uncle Lance never knew it was there. Evidently he drew up a phony will giving him full control of the bank and all personal wealth that belonged to Uncle Zach."

"Who would have known?" said Bill. "They were identical twins, dressed alike at times, and their handwriting was identical. And here we thought that Uncle Lance's trickery had stopped a long time ago."

"Rosa just found out that Dr. Rose was on the panel back then during your dad's incompetency hearing at the sanatorium. Dr. Rose was the only one who didn't go along with the sanatorium's decision to commit your dad. When I was at the sanatorium, the doctor didn't mention anything about that to me. I guess it wasn't important at the time. Get this, Bill. Uncle Zach also blackmailed his own brother. What do you think about that?"

"Why am I not surprised?" said Bill.

"He had evidence on paper how Uncle Lance cheated two customers out of their money," said Lottie. "He convinced him to give up his interest in the bank. He signed over everything over to Uncle Zach to keep from going to jail. I wonder if Uncle Lance was responsible for his death, Bill? I trusted him the least."

"He had heart trouble for the last several years, replied Bill. I'm not surprised he died when he did. And the booze didn't help him any. I'm told he was even drinking during his lunch break. So how did you get involved in the bank?"

"In the will, I was given 100 percent controlling interest of the bank, Bill."

"Why did he choose you? Lottie? Not that I disapprove. I'm very glad you got the bank."

"I'm not sure, Bill. I did take care of him one time for several days after he had his heart attack a year ago. Winnie said he favored me the most."

"Maybe he appreciated you more than you thought, Lottie."

"Evidently he did. His will also stated that his personal monies would be split up among the brothers and sisters," said Lottie. "We have a copy for you to read."

"I'm surprised Uncle Zach did that," said Bill. "But how about Will? It was his bank." Lottie shook her head.

"That's the sad part," said Lottie. "I told him after the reading that I would turn the entire bank over to him. He thanked me for the offer but refused. He said that the family should have some share in the bank but that I should retain controlling interest. Your dad volunteered to be the chairman, so to speak, without pay. All of us plan to split everything anyway with him. I said that he could have his office back for as long as he wanted it. In fact, he can have the bank back if he ever changes his mind."

"That made him happy, didn't it?" said Bill.

"It did, but he's not happy about his cuckoo clock being blown away," said Lottie. "I guess it was a gift from Greta at the diner."

"You sure do deserve the controlling interest in this bank, as you're the one who exposed Lance. You're our hero, Lottie."

"I think I had some help from God and our angel on that one," remarked Lottie. "After the reading of the will, I haven't been able to get ahold of your dad. Do you know where he is?"

"I went to the house this morning, Lottie. He wasn't there. His special shovel was gone. I think he's hiding out. And I think I know where. How was the real will found?"

"After Uncle Lance's admission, it led people to believe that the will was a fake. The secretary came forward and explained that the authentic will was hidden in the bank and Uncle Zach never told her where. She was instructed that only upon his death would she reveal this to Mr. Perkins. Evidently Uncle Zach knew his days were numbered because of his health."

"Looks like Uncle Zach wanted to leave us a riddle to solve," remarked Bill. "Mom said he was always a jokester when he was a kid."

"Uncle Lance found out about the conversation between Uncle Zach and the secretary back then concerning the will," replied Lottie. "He himself was unable to find the original will. After Lance assumed the identity of Zach, he kept a tight rein on her. She was afraid of him. Anyway, they believed that the secretary really didn't know much more than that."

"There was a safe deposit box in the bank that was never used, as it had a defective lock, Bill. A note was taped on the box that it was unlockable. Evidently it was never repaired."

"So everyone knew about the defective box," said Bill. "And here it was in front of everyone."

"Sheriff Taylor was in the bank while Mr. Perkins and the other men looked for the will," said Lottie. "The sheriff said if he was going to hide something, he would hide it in plain view. He walked around the bank for a while and then turned his attention to the safe deposit boxes. He walked right up to the defective deposit box. He removed the note on the face of the deposit box and pulled it out. There was the will."

"How did he know that?" asked Bill.

"You and I talked about Sheriff Taylor before, Bill. He seems to always show up at the right time to help people. I don't think that was luck on the sheriff's part when he picked that deposit box."

"I heard one time that you said the sheriff was an angel. Is that true, Lottie?"

"I might have. The kids seem to see angels all the time. Sara said that even Blackie can tell if one is an angel. If they can, why can't we? But you know how kids are, Bill."

"I bet you do believe that the sheriff is an angel, Lottie."

"I didn't exactly say that, Bill. Well, okay, I think he's our angel.

I told you about the two ravens that brought bread to me."

"That's hard to explain away," said Bill. "Maybe an angel from heaven sent the two ravens to you as a sign of support. Maybe it's some kind of a message."

"I believe so, Bill. Mr. Perkins and a lawyer are helping us with all the forms necessary for the changeover and approval that the banking commission requires. I will have to get a license or two for my new job. I need you to work here at the bank, Bill. It would be a great job for you."

"Me?" asked Bill.

"You could use a job, Bill. Didn't you complete a two-year business course in River Falls a while back? And you're good with people."

"I would have to shave every day and wear a coat and tie."

"You did that in the service for years when you weren't shooting people. You worked in Army personnel for a time. Right?"

"I'm not sure if I could be at a desk all day. But maybe one has to keep you from shooting up the place," said Bill with a chuckle.

"Wait a minute, young Uncle. You're the one who shot off that 45 in your apartment and almost killed yourself."

"I guess neither one of us has been real stable lately. But no one is perfect," replied Bill with a grin.

"We'll get Rosa to watch us both, Bill. She could work here. She has loan experience at the dealership. He has been so helpful. I hope to give him a raise real soon. What will people in this town think about me being in this position?"

"A lot of people will be happy for you, Lottie. Are you still going to live in the same house?" asked Bill.

"Of course I am. I don't need a new house to show the town that I'm going to have a little money now. We're going to fix just a few things on the house for now. We need to pay off the sanatorium and the hospital as soon as we can."

"You're not going to be wearing that blue outfit every day, are you, Lottie?"

"I will have to rely on Sue Wart to help me out on that one, Bill. I'm sure they will let me run a tab now. I don't think most people know yet what really happened in the last three weeks. We kinda skipped over this. We have to find your dad. You said you might know where he's at. I know he's not with Gloria or Rosa. Not even the sheriff knows his whereabouts. And he seems to know everything that goes on in this town."

"I bet he's staying with Greta from the diner who has a crush on him," said Bill. "I believe she has a small boarding house. I don't know where that's at. But why is he doing that?"

"Perhaps he's afraid that Sheriff Taylor is going to arrest him for destroying part of the jail," said Lottie.

"I didn't even think about that," replied Bill. "I'm sure the sheriff wants some answers."

"The mayor and city council are giving the sheriff a lot of heat to find out who did this, Bill. The repair bill for the jail will be quite extensive."

"Will has something going on. Does the sheriff have any proof that Will busted you out?"

"I don't believe so," replied Lottie. "It's been a long day. We need some coffee. I'm going to get some at the diner."

"Weren't you barred from the diner after you destroyed the Wart sisters that day?"

"Yes, but I'm now sixty percent owner of that diner, so I control the lease. Thanks to Uncle Zach. Mr. Wendal doesn't know it yet." She smiled as she did a curtsey and left.

Uncle Bill sat there in amazement. He got up and sat at one of the padded office chairs behind a desk. He turned the swivel chair from side to side and looked around.

"Is this for me?" Bill thought.

He always liked adventure. As kids, Lottie and Bill played in the woods pretending they were in Africa exploring a new continent. The Army provided him the travel and thrill of being on the edge. But he was tired of the hardships and death among his fellow soldiers. Could he be content just to stay in one spot for the rest of his life?

After a few minutes, Lottie returned with the coffee.

Bill stepped over and joined her at her desk.

"I think this is the thing for me to do, Lottie. I need to settle down and stay on the road of sobriety. I should have been the one to get coffee if you're going to be my boss. We all need to treat this as a serious venture with no special favors just because we're family."

"You're right, Bill. Rosa will make sure that happens. She's a stickler on things like that, but that's good."

"Lottie, we should take down that old shed in back and use that space to rent out or something. It's overgrown with bushes."

"See? You're already an asset to this bank," said Lottie. "I'm not sure if it's on our property or not. I noticed a small truck and a couple Chinese fellows hanging around in the alley back there at times. It's a little hard to see through the bushes from here. I think they're connected to the small warehouse across the way."

"What do you think will happen to Lance?" asked Bill. "I don't think any of us really want to press charges against him, but we may have to. He's going to have to face the prosecutor in reference to the banking issues, his impersonation of Zach, and instigating the beating of John."

"He's no doubt going to prison," replied Lottie. "I think forgiveness is going to take some time for us, Bill."

"Did you hear that, Bill?"

"Hear what, Lottie?"

"I think I hear voices."

"Are you okay, Lottie?" Bill tried not to laugh.

"Well maybe I'm just wore out from all this. But you know when I'm here alone, it's real quiet. I swear that I can hear voices, and there's the odd noises at times."

"It's probably from the jail on the other side of the wall," said Bill. "And maybe it's the street noise. There's no insulation in these old walls like the new buildings they build now days."

"I suppose so," replied Lottie. "I haven't had much rest for a long time, Bill. I hope we don't get any more surprises down the road. 1953 has been quite the year for all of us. Let's lock up and go to the hospital and visit John."

"Great. We can go in my car, Lottie."

"I just wish John would come out of his coma," said Lottie. "I would gladly trade all this for his recovery." Lottie started to cry.

"I know you would. John is going to make it, Lottie."

# CHAPTER 25

## *GREAT UNCLE WILL'S QUEST*

Sheriff Taylor walked out of the police station, stood there for a few moments, and then sat down on a bench outside the bank. He was in deep thought as he sat there. He was hesitant to walk into the bank and approach Lottie concerning the jailbreak. Over the years, he developed a special relationship with the Rainwater and Lindstrom families. He didn't want to weaken or lose that relationship by insisting that Lottie disclose who it was that damaged the jail.

But it was the sheriff's duty as an officer of the law to launch an investigation. He wasn't sure what he would do if he found out who the lawbreaker was. In the back of his mind, he knew that it was his friend and that many hearts would be broken if Uncle Will was arrested, convicted, and spent time in prison. The city council and the mayor wanted results right now.

Sheriff Taylor hoped for a way out of this. He thought about turning in his badge if the investigation were to implicate Uncle Will. For the most part his job was done in Bergan's Ferry, but the sheriff would miss his friend. They seemed to like arguing over a checker game or a game of gin rummy. They loved the same people, and they had something else in common that was unknown to all.

Sheriff Taylor got up and stepped into the bank. He was greeted by the secretary with the new wig.

"Good morning, Sheriff Taylor."

"And a good morning to you," he replied.

"I'm wearing my new hair. I feel younger already," said the

secretary. "My new boss paid for it. She's the greatest."

"Yes she is, and you look...ah...great," said the sheriff. "I'm here to see the owner of this bank."

Lottie looked up from her desk in back and smiled as the sheriff walked up to her.

"Good morning, Sheriff Taylor. What brings you by the bank at the bottom of the morning? Isn't this the time you're usually at the diner having your scrambled eggs?"

"Well I have some heavy official business to attend to this morning."

"And where is that?" asked Lottie.

"It looks like my official business is right here in the bank with you."

"Please, have a seat," said Lottie with a solemn face.

"Thanks, Lottie."

The sheriff looked around for a while and leaned back a bit in the plush bank chair.

"Still a light crew?" asked the sheriff.

"We won't be fully operational till next week."

"A lot of changes are being made around here, Lottie. I always wanted to know how it felt to sit in one of these fancy bank chairs. My chair next door is a real rag."

"You're across the street at the diner half of the time," said Lottie. "Would it really matter?"

"I guess not. I'm impressed, Lottie. You've come a long way from a pie-throwing mom to an owner of this old bank and then some."

"Yes I have. Before I forget, I would like to thank you for finding that will. I still would like to know how you figured that out, Sheriff. Was it divine intervention? Perhaps your angel power?"

"I don't quite follow you there. But I've been a lawman for a number of years. In my line of work, one's investigation skills becomes sharper and sharper as the years go by. Very little gets by me, Lottie."

"I can see that. So what can I do for you today?"

"I dropped by your uncle's place yesterday. He wasn't home. Do you know where he's at, Lottie?"

"No I don't. I was hoping you might tell me. On Thursdays, you and Great Uncle Will usually played checkers."

"When I was at his place, there were mounds and mounds of dirt piled up in back of the house," said the sheriff. "I guess he's digging around his place looking for the Indian treasures. I walked over to the barn. The door was just open a crack. I didn't go in, as I don't have a search warrant. I peeked through the crack in the door and noticed that there wasn't any chain attached to the hitch on the back end of his truck. The truck looked nice and clean."

"Was there supposed to be one?" asked Lottie.

"We found part of the jail wall just outside of town. It was off to the side of the road. The chain was still attached to the window bars. Part of the chain broke off, so the remains of the chain were still hooked to the truck as he was heading down the road."

"So you're saying a man was driving a vehicle that was dragging part of the jail wall down the road. And it had to be a truck?"

"Did I imply that it was a man, Lottie? It had to be a very large truck or something. We both know who busted you out of jail."

"We do?" replied Lottie.

"Lottie, I have a big gaping hole in the back of my jail. I had to put several pieces of plywood from the mill to cover it up. Now I have to tell the undesirables I put back there not to remove the plywood and escape. I might have to hide all the handsaws in town!"

"You're quite serious about all of this, aren't you, Sheriff?" He lowered his head for several moments.

Lottie realized that the sheriff was serious and that he was between a rock and a hard spot. This time, she couldn't talk her way out of this or change the subject. She didn't want the sheriff to be hurt in any way, as she always considered him a father-like image to her. He looked back up at her and shook his head.

"I'm just trying to do my job, Lottie. The mayor and city council are coming down hard on me. They want me to catch the person who did this. You know the city is always strapped for money. It's going to cost at least six hundred bucks to repair the damages to the jail. And we're not even talking about the cost of the trial for the lawbreaker."

"Who do you think did this?" asked Lottie.

"It's obvious, Lottie. I just can't come out and say it."

"Sheriff, you're reluctant to call out the name that you think busted me out of jail. You want me to disclose a name. Don't you?"

"Well, I don't know," replied the sheriff.

"Technically, I wasn't busted out," said Lottie. "Yes the jail was damaged, but you're the one who implied I could leave."

"You're trying to really twist things," said the sheriff.

"Did anyone see my uncle drive down the center of town in a huge red Mack Truck pulling a giant piece of cement behind it?"

"Well, no one reported to me that they saw anything like that," said the sheriff. "Everyone is so tight-lipped."

"Why is that?" asked Lottie. "Let me tell you why. Even though some people think he's crazy, many people are thankful for what he's done for this town over the years."

Lottie didn't know that the sheriff didn't even ask anyone in town if they saw Uncle Will in his truck that day. And he hoped no one on the city council or the mayor's office saw anything.

"So you have no proof," said Lottie.

"No I don't. As I said, no one came forward. Not one soul."

"I'll show the town that I'm a lot like Great Uncle Will. I will donate the money to repair the jail. Will this gesture end this investigation? I will even throw in a new chair for you just like the one you're sitting on."

"And a chair like this?" asked the sheriff. "This case is closed. Great Uncle Will always said that you were a very compassionate woman, even though you're a little..."

"You implied one time that I was like a daughter to you."

"I'm not sure what I said. Lottie. Besides, I may have to put you or someone else in the two families in jail again for something down the road."

"Oh, that's very reassuring," said Lottie.

The sheriff leaned over and pulled a step stool over to him. He placed his feet on the stool and leaned back.

"I'm glad the official business is over," said the sheriff.

"Are you comfortable?" asked Lottie.

"Yes, very much so."

"I'm going to have the secretary get us some coffee and rolls for us since you missed your breakfast, Sheriff. And then I'll close early. We can just sit and talk about the old days."

\*\*\*\*

"Thanks for making room at the boarding house for me the last few days, Greta."

"You've been at this dig for weeks. Are you sure you're at the right location, Will?"

"That's what my map says," answered Uncle Will.

"I don't want to know where," remarked Greta. "Just surprise me when you do find it, Will. But I have one question. Where did you get the map from? It looks so old."

"Mr. Cole, the dentist, gave this map to me a few weeks ago, Greta. He got it years ago from an elderly disgruntled Indian medicine man on the reservation who needed dental work. I believe this map is authentic. I can feel it in my bones. We're close. Got to go. My men are waiting for me at the dig this morning."

\* \* \* \*

Uncle Will walked down the alley and up to the old shed behind the bank. As he entered the shed, he turned around.

"What are you kids doing here this morning?" "Sara and I are spying on you," answered Mark. "Spying? How long have you guys been doing this?" "For a little while, Great Uncle Will," said Mark.

"Did you tell anyone about me going into this shed?"

"No. Nobody," answered Sara.

"Aunt Gloria saw you here before," said Mark. "She said you might be digging for the Indian treasure. Aunt Gloria said she would take us to the movies in River Falls if we don't tell anyone about this big secret."

"And she's going to buy us popcorn," said Sara.

"So she's keeping all this a secret?" Mark nodded. "My Gloria girl always was good at keeping secrets, big and small. Well, we shall see."

"Does your mom know?" asked Uncle Will.

"Nope, just Aunt Gloria and us," said Mark. "But what's the ladder for going into the ground?"

"Down there is the big tunnel we've been digging," answered Uncle Will. "You know what? The city wants to smash down my bank and put a library in its place. And then put in a big parking lot next to it. They can't do that! We don't need a new library. No one reads books anymore. People are going to watch those new televisions all day."

"Want to work for me, kids?"

"Yes we will," said Sara.

"Stay here and guard the entrance. If anybody comes near this shed, just let me know. I'll need to get down there. Those Chinese workers don't like being down there without me. They think it's a haunted place or something."

"Okay," said Mark.

Uncle Will climbed down the ladder and into the tunnel. He crouched down as he walked to the end of the tunnel. At the end of the tunnel, poles were placed holding up some of the old floor beams of the bank. Oil lamps hung from the supporting poles. Sacks of dirt lined the tunnel, ready to be hauled away. Uncle Will looked at his map and then quickly folded it and placed it in his side pocket.

"This is it!" said Uncle Will. "Men, we're close! Today is the day!"

Uncle Will pointed to exactly where they should be digging. The men dug away. Suddenly a wall of dirt fell and exposed a rotted log wall. As the men struck the log wall with their picks it collapsed, exposing a small tomb-like room. Dust-covered leather bags were stacked on the floor. Antlers, bows, and spears lined the inner walls. A wooden chest was half sunken in the dirt.

"This is the real mother lode," said Uncle Will.

Two men unearthed the chest with their shovels and stepped aside. Uncle Will gave his crew the thumbs up and knelt down over the chest. The men laid down their picks and shovels. Uncle Will was entranced as he knelt there. He pried opened the lid and carefully lifted a heavily wrapped object out of the chest. With his hands shaking, he unwrapped the covering. There before him was the golden mask of the Nez Perce Sun God. He rested the mask on his lap. The reflection of light off the mask was almost blinding.

\* \* \* \*

"Thanks for the rolls, Lottie. They were delicious. It's great to sit here and relax. And not to worry about bullets flying all around in this bank. It's so quiet and peaceful."

"I'm glad you're at ease now, Sheriff Taylor."

"In fact, two new deputies assigned to the River Falls department will be following me around next week. They can't wait."

"Why is that?" asked Lottie.

"The judge wants his two nephews to be lawmen just like me, Lottie. That's a tall order for those two to fill."

"Just like you? Exactly like you?" asked Lottie.

"Do I detect a little sarcasm there, Lottie? Did you know the jail and the bank here are the two oldest buildings in the state? If these old floors could talk, there would be a lot of stories to be told. I noticed that the floor creaked badly when I walked up to your desk. You might want to get an expert to check out the old floor supports. Did I just hear voices?"

"Voices?" said Lottie.

Lottie looked down toward the floor and then listened for a few moments. She shook her head.

"Is there something wrong, Lottie?"

\* \* \* \*

Uncle Will pulled the linen cloth away from the mask. He got up on one knee and then stood up the rest of the way. He held the mask over his face, turned around, and faced the Chinese workers.

Uncle Will started to chant loudly, moving his head back and forth as he walked forward.

Uncle Will's chanting and the brilliant reflection of the gold mask horrified the Chinese workers. As they ran away from Uncle Will, two of the men collided against each other and bumped into one of the poles supporting the floor beams above. The pole shifted to the side, and part of the bank floor started to drop.

\* \* \* \*

The coffee cups on the table trembled for a few moments, and then the bank's floor in front of Lottie's desk broke up and caved in. Lottie jumped away from her desk as the sheriff fell off his chair. The desk slid to one side, and the sheriff's chair fell into the hole. He struggled to keep from sliding into the hole.

"Looks like hell just opened up!" yelled the sheriff.

Lottie, on hands and knees, crawled to the edge of the hole and looked down. The men below pulled the debris off Uncle Will and helped him to his feet.

"Here it is!" yelled Uncle Will.

"You found it! Oh, Lord. It's true! Are you okay?"

"I'm okay, Lottie."

The sheriff got partway up and looked into the hole. Mark and Sara came running into the bank.

"Did Great Uncle Will find the treasure?" asked Mark.

"He sure did," said Sheriff Taylor.

"Is he a hero, Sheriff Taylor?" asked Sara.

"I don't know, honey. You kids step back. The rest of this floor just might cave in. Now step back."

\* \* \* \*

Uncle Will was sitting on the bench in front of the bank with his suit jacket across his lap. His left lower arm was wrapped with a bandage, and a large Band-Aid was above his right eye. Bill was sitting next to him.

189

A crowd gathered in front of the bank. The sheriff, standing next to Lottie, turned to the crowd of people.

"Everything is under control," said the sheriff. "Your law enforcement is at work. Don't ask me any questions, people. I don't know a thing."

"We do," said a man in the crowd. "Great Uncle Will was right all along. He said the mask was buried here somewhere. He's our town hero. He just put Bergan's Ferry on the map."

The sheriff turned to Lottie. "Now Great Uncle Will is going to be a celebrity," said the sheriff. "Lottie, you know this is a federal offense. Your uncle just destroyed part of this bank. Are you going to press charges against him?"

Lottie tried to keep a serious face as she spoke. "You can't be serious. No, I'm not pressing charges. It was fine with me for him to dig anywhere he wanted to. And he probably found termites as well."

"But did he have a permit?" asked the sheriff. "Did he?" The sheriff looked around at everyone and shook his head.

"Sometimes I just can't believe what I see or hear." Lottie put her arms around the sheriff.

"Please calm down. You know we think the world of you. You're our favorite sheriff."

"Of course you do," said the sheriff. "You're the only two families in town who hit my police cruiser, shot up the bank, and caved in the bank's floor. And let's not forget about my police station that got destroyed by someone. All in three or four weeks!"

"Sheriff, I feel bad about all this," said Uncle Will. "I'll spend some time today in jail. Tonight you can order some Chinese food for me, Sheriff. I like the egg rolls. And the diner makes a great scramble in the morning. All on the taxpayers' money. Right?"

"Well, Great Uncle Will must have broken some law today, or he probably will next week," said the sheriff. "I'll put him in jail for now just to ensure public safety. I'm sure I'm going to hear about this. The jail is open, Great Uncle Will. Just use the cell on the right. I'll be across the street at the diner. I need a rest and a shot of root beer or something."

Lottie sat with Uncle Will in the jail cell. She placed a blanket over his lap. He still held on to the gold Sun God mask with both hands.

"You're not going to sleep here tonight with this mask in your arms, are you? You look awfully tired and a little beat up."

"I believe Bill and Mr. Perkins will be here shortly to put this mask in the bank safe," said Uncle Will.

"Was there anything else in the chest?" asked Lottie.

"Bill said there were several large pouches of gold nuggets, old Spanish gold coins, jade jewelry, and many other priceless Indian artifacts, Lottie. It's a real mother lode. All the gold nuggets and coins are going in the safe as well. And as we speak, my Chinese friends are securing the tunnel. Yup, I finally found the Nez Perce treasure. God has been good to me. Now this town won't think I'm so crazy."

"I agree," said Lottie. "No one will say a word if you go home to your place."

"I just plan to stay the night and part of the morning."

"You just want the sheriff to feel bad about all this," said Lottie. He laughed.

"Oh he deserves it at times," said Uncle Will. "I'll make it up to him someday and let him win a game or two."

"Sometimes I think you toy with the sheriff. And at times, you know exactly what you're doing."

"Well one has to be good at something, Lottie."

"You damaged your own bank, you know."

"How's that?" asked Uncle Will.

"I listed you as part owner of the bank a while back," said Lottie. "It was approved by the state banking commission. For some reason, they acted quickly. Not even on a technicality can one come forward and lodge a complaint against you."

"Does the sheriff know this?" Lottie.

"I don't know."

Lottie kissed Uncle Will on the forehead and stepped out of the cell to leave.

"Lottie, thanks for doing that. Lottie, one more thing."

She stopped and turned to him.

"I almost forgot. Bill said there was a very interesting old map in the chest! It might be a treasure map."

"I didn't hear that," replied Lottie.

An hour later, Sheriff Taylor came back to the jail carrying two plates and four large cartons of hot Chinese food. He entered Uncle Will's cell.

"I came as quick as I could," said the sheriff.

"Here's your plate and two boxes of Chinese, to include the egg rolls, and I have mine," said the sheriff. "Mind if I join you?"

"Of course, you can dine with me, Sheriff. What would you have done if someone came forward and disclosed the name of the one who tried to break Lottie out of your jail?"

"I would have convinced that person not to say a word about their claim and that I had it handled," remarked the sheriff. "Can't always believe what witnesses say. And then I would have convinced Lottie to pay for the damages or at least have an anonymous donor to pay up, if you get my drift. As you know, no one came forward and Lottie volunteered to pay for the damages. She gets me going at times, but she's quite the lady."

"You're a real friend", remarked Uncle Will. "Do you have the checkerboard and cards in the office?" asked Uncle Will.

"Sure, and this time I'm going to watch you real close. Do you really have another map?" asked the sheriff.

"Sure do."

"You know I always carry a shovel in my patrol car. We could work together. Right?"

"Why not?" answered Uncle Will.

# CHAPTER 26

## *THE LITTLE AVENGER*

Mark and Sara still picked blackberries and sold them to the diner's bakery and to old Gus across the railroad tracks. The bakery made berry-filled rolls and berry pies. Gus made blackberry wine for sale. Sara and Mark found blackberries along the railroad tracks, and another good spot was along the road that went to nowhere. They wouldn't pick berries past the old Johnson house, as Sara was afraid of the coyotes. They would get twenty cents for a bucket of blackberries and twenty-five cents for the boysenberries. Some people couldn't tell the difference between the two types of berries.

Gus was an old man who lived in a shack across the tracks. He worked for the Union Pacific railroad and then became mostly blind before he retired. They allowed him to live there rent-free. Part of the shack rested on the edge of the river. It was home for Gus.

No one could figure out how Gus made the wine, being blind and all that. Trains rarely used the rail yard on Sundays, so people drove across the tracks and bought wine from him. He sold it by the glass or by the bottle.

The town of Bergan's Ferry had a blue law. No alcohol could be sold on Sundays. So once a year, the police would raid his shack and confiscate all the wine. Sheriff Taylor would stand there while his deputies poured out the wine out into river. The sheriff thought it was a waste of his time, as it wasn't like old Gus was a big-time operator.

The city wanted to tear down his shack, as it was sliding little by little into the river. But they couldn't do a thing, as it was on railroad property. The city really wanted to shut down his wine business, as he wasn't collecting taxes on the wine he sold.

The kids liked selling berries to Gus, as he paid them well and always had a story to tell about his railroad days. They also made extra money by helping him wash out the wine jugs and for other chores they did for him.

One day Lottie was sitting on the front porch and noticed an ambulance in front of Gus's shack. Three or four railroad workers were near his front door. After an hour, the ambulance left and the family never saw old Gus again.

One crazed hobo said that the night before he died, Gus was visited by an angel. The kids said that they saw a blue light shining through the shack's window that night. No one believed the hobo or the kids. The shack finally broke up and slid into the river three days later. Nothing was left where the shack stood except for some broken pieces of glass from a wine jug. No one knew if Gus had any relatives in the area. He was buried by the city with a marker on his grave. The kids placed pansies on his grave every so often. Pansies were Gus's favorite flowers. He was about sixty-five years old.

\*\*\*\*

Mark and Sara walked down the alley and entered the back door of the diner early in the morning. They waited for several moments, and then Mr. Wendal approached them.

"Hi, Mr. Wendal," said Mark. "We have two buckets of berries for you. We just picked them yesterday."

Mr. Wendal looked at the berries and then reached into his pocket. He pulled some change and counted off forty cents and handed it to Mark.

"I shouldn't even do business with you kids after what your

lunatic mother did a while back," said Mr. Wendal. "I need a small bucket of boysenberries for tomorrow."

"Just a small bucket?" asked Mark.

"It's a special order for the Wart sisters," replied Mr. Wendal.

"Okay," said Mark.

Mark and Sara were at the kitchen table that evening. "Mom, what does lunatic mean?" asked Sara.

"It means like a crazy person," answered Lottie. "Why?"

"We delivered blackberries to Mr. Wendal today," said Sara. "He said you were a lunatic. So that was a bad word. Right, Mommy?"

"Yes it was, Sara. But that's okay. He's just a very rude man."

"We have boysenberries for the bakery tomorrow," said Mark.

"You didn't go too far up that road, did you?" asked Lottie.

"No. We didn't go past the old Johnson house," answered Mark.

"The boysenberries are for the Wart sisters," said Sara.

"The Wart sisters? There're the ones who were so rude to me in the diner a while back," said Lottie. "They seem to like their berry rolls."

\*\*\*\*

Mr. Wendal was in the bakery, the back part of the diner. He looked over at the kids as they came that morning.

"So you got the boysenberries. Are these berries fresh? They better be," said Wendal.

"We always have fresh berries," replied Mark "We just picked them yesterday afternoon. And we washed them already."

Mr. Wendal walked over to the table and poured the berries into the mixing machine along with the batter.

"Is that for the Wart sisters?" asked Mark.

"Yeah it is," answered Mr. Wendal. "What are you still doing here? Why don't you leave?"

"You didn't give us any money," answered Mark.

Mr. Wendal reached into his pocket and gave Mark a dime and then laughed.

"We always get more for these berries," said Mark.

"That's all I'm going to pay. The other manager pays way too much."

They took the money and started to leave. Mark turned around.

"My mom won't be happy about this," said Mark. "Our Aunt Rosa said our mom owns this building and we're bank people now."

"I'm going to tell our Great Uncle Will to come to your place and drag your house down the road with his big truck!" said Sara.

Mr. Wendal gave the kids a glum look and then quickly walked out of the bakery to the front of the diner. As Mark and Sara left out the back door of the bakery, Mark noticed an opened can of black paint on a work bench. Near the bench was an unfinished sign.

"Sara, I'm going to use some of this black paint."

"What?" said Sara.

"What's going on, Mark?"

"The Wart sisters are rude people. Right?" said Mark.

"Yeah that's right," answered Sara.

"Wait here," said Mark.

Mark took the can of paint and entered the back door of the bakery. He looked around and then walked up to the mixer. As it was churning the dough and the berries, he poured some of the black paint into the mixer. He quickly left and ran out the back door and placed the can back on the work bench.

"Let's go, Sara. Come on."

"What did you do in there with the paint?" asked Sara.

"I'll tell you when we get home," said Mark. They ran down the alley and then onto Fourth Street.

\* \* \* \*

Lottie was at her desk in back of the bank. It had been two weeks since Uncle Will discovered the Nez Perce treasure. He was busy with reporters from everywhere. Lottie had to hire an extra secretary to handle all the calls coming in. Dozens of pictures were taken of Uncle Will holding the mask. Bags of mail were stacked in his office. The Nez Perce Indian council made him an honorary member of the tribe. They also made a headdress for him and said that he also could have his pick of their horses.

Uncle Will asked them if they could give him a goat to eat down the weeds around his place instead of a horse. They honored his wish.

Uncle Will's cuckoo clock was replaced, and a new window was installed. His 44 revolver was placed back in his desk drawer, but Uncle Will carried the bullets around in his pocket. Not that he thought Lottie would pick up the gun again. The workers just finished up on repairs of the office floor and supporting floor beams.

Lottie looked back at one of the family's struggles. She remembered so vividly being on the other side of the counter pleading for more time and a change in their mortgage contract on the house.

Now she was on the other side of the counter.

The bank was the next struggle. Over the years, Lance and Zach drained much of the bank's assets. Luckily many of the leases and partial ownership of property and buildings were still controlled by the bank. Hard cash for emergencies would be hard to come by for a while. But her main struggle for John's recovery wasn't over.

As Lottie was ready to make a phone call, the Wart sisters entered the bank. Erma Wart looked around for a few moments, but this time she didn't have a smirk on her face. Lottie clearly remembered the day when the Wart sisters walked into the diner. This time she was in control of things, not the sisters. Lottie was also determined to be on her best behavior.

The sisters approached Mr. Perkins. Erma eyeballed Lottie as she stood there with Sue.

"Mr. Perkins, we would like to talk to you concerning a business loan," said Erma.

"I can't at this moment, ladies. I have a client who will be here shortly. I'm so sorry but I could have Mrs. Rainwater assist you."

"We require someone who's more than a clerk," said Erma. "Who do you have that could help us, Mr. Perkins?" Lottie got up from her desk and stepped forward a few feet.

"I should let you sisters know that Mrs. Rainwater is my boss and owner of this bank," said Mr. Perkins.

A worried look came over Erma's face. "So it's true," said Erma. "Maybe we should leave, Sue."

"Ladies, what can I do for you?" asked Lottie.

"We would like to apply for a business loan," said Sue.

"Please, have a seat at my desk."

Lottie pulled up two chairs for them. The sisters seemed to be uncomfortable as they sat there.

"Before we start, we have something to say," said Sue. "We apologize for our treatment of you at the diner a while back and..."

"You're not apologizing for me too, are you?" asked Erma.

"We were out of line," said Sue. "It was a humbling experience when you dumped all that pie and ice cream on us. It really got our attention. I don't know about my sister, but I'm ready for an attitude change. Your Uncle Bill has been a lot of help to me." Erma gave Sue a look and then shook her head.

"We've been under a lot of pressure lately and have been losing business," said Erma. "We need to bring in a fresher line of clothing."

"And our store needs some updating," said Sue. "It's hard for us to come in here and ask for a loan."

"I guess I could say that I give credit or run a tab for only my good customers," replied Lottie. "But I won't say that. And I wasn't quite myself that day either. I'm sorry for that day at the diner."

Lottie noticed dark stains on Erma's lip and on her dress. A dark stained white paper sack was resting on Sue's lap. Sue noticed Lottie looking at the sack.

"Would you like one of these boysenberry filled rolls?" asked Sue. "They're half-baked. They're good that way. We have two left. Oh my. I think we ate a few too many."

"The two sisters are half-baked," Lottie thought.

"No thank you," answered Lottie.

As the sisters completed their loan application, they became ill.

"I'm not feeling so well," remarked Erma. "Something didn't go down right after we ate these rolls."

"That sticky taste is still in my mouth," said Sue. "Oh...my stomach."

"I'm going to get sick," said Erma.

Erma grabbed her mouth and ran toward the door. Sue followed her. Mr. Perkins looked up and then walked over to Lottie.

"They sure left in a hurry. What did you do to those ladies this time, Lottie?"

"Not a thing" answered Lottie. "I was quite cordial with them. Your last appointment of the day didn't show up. You didn't by chance pond off the Wart sisters on me?"

"Well that did give you a chance to toy with them a bit,"

answered Mr. Perkins.

Mark brought some boysenberries to the bakery early this morning. He did have a funny story about the berries. I'm sure he had nothing to do with this."

Mr. Perkins gave Lottie an odd look. "Are you sure of that, Lottie?"

# CHAPTER 27

## *THEIR REWARDS*

In the past few years, the Rainwaters were confronted by creditors. Their increased mortgage payment didn't help any. Then John lost hours at work, and things began to slide quickly. After a visit, a collector sat down with Lottie and prayed. Days later, someone paid off Mark's hospital bill. To this day, they don't know who the kind soul was. There were a lot of people like that in Bergan's Ferry.

Lottie took on a responsibility that she thought she would never have. Now she was the creditor and knew how it was to be the one in need and was determined to follow Uncle Will's righteous policies.

Lottie was now inclined to believe Sara and Mark that someone, perhaps an angel, was responsible for their rescue. But the family needed John to be rescued from his coma.

Lottie didn't look like a bank lady in her Ford sedan that morning as she parked in front of Mr. Diggs' shoe shop. She sat in the car for a moment thinking how she was going to approach him. He wasn't exactly her idol after he conned Mark into taking those worthless bottles that day. As Lottie got out of her car, she noticed the stacked boxes of bottles against the wall of the shoe shop.

Lottie stood at the counter with a confident smile. Mrs. Diggs was at the counter. She had a hard time looking Lottie squarely in the eyes.

"Mrs. Rainwater, what can I do for you?"

"Good morning. Is your husband available, Mrs. Diggs?" She

nodded. Mr. Diggs came up to the counter and stood there with a smirk on his face. He was a large man who always needed a shave. They weren't quite the match, as his wife was a pretty woman.

"Oh, it's you," said Mr. Diggs with a harsh voice.

"Do you know why I'm here, sir?"

"I know why. It's not my fault that your kid doesn't know what bottles have a return deposit."

"Of course, it's not your fault that you took advantage of a little boy," said Lottie. "Your lease is up for renewal. Here's your new lease papers from the bank. Please take a look at them."

Lottie handed the papers to him.

Mr. Diggs took them and slammed them on the counter. Mrs. Diggs picked up the papers. Her husband came around the counter and stood in front of Lottie.

"Who do you think you are coming in here acting like the big Indian chief of this town?" said Mr. Diggs. "I'm a lot bigger than you are."

"Nelson, please calm down. You're being stupid," said his wife.

"You're a bully," said Lottie, as she stepped closer to him. I should come back here with my Uncle Bill. He's almost as big as you are and fought in two wars. He would like to practice on you. And then there's Sheriff Taylor. One call from me would bring him here, and you would get a pistol whipping till Christmas. Then there's my Great Uncle Will, who you think is crazy. Who knows what he would do."

"Look at these papers," she said to her husband. He looked at the papers for a few moments, and then his face turned pale. He shook his head and then stepped back around the counter.

"You probably noticed the heading on the first page," said Lottie. "As you can see, it shows that I'm the head Indian chief of the bank."

He laid the papers down on the counter. Despair was written

all over his face.

"Also, there's boxes of bottles outside against the building," said Lottie. "It's against the city ordnance and your lease."

"There's so many of them," said Mrs. Diggs.

"Not my problem," said Lottie. "Just remove them, or I will close down this building. You will have three days to clean it up. I will bring Sheriff Taylor with me the fourth day to see if you complied. Is that clear, Mr. Diggs?"

"Yes, ma'am."

"And I almost forgot. Your lease renewal is also pending upon your attitude. Have a very nice day," said Lottie with a smile.

That afternoon, Lottie walked into Mr. Chu's Laundry. There were only a few people in town who disliked Mr. Chu because he was Asian. Lance was one of them. Mr. Chu always kept his storefront, clean and his shop was well kept. She walked into the laundry and up to the counter.

"Mrs. Rainwater, how are you?"

"I'm fine. Much better than before, Mr. Chu. I'm so sorry that I didn't return this dress you lent me a while back. So many things have happened since then."

"That's okay," replied Mr. Chu. Mr. Chu took a dress off the rack. "See here. This is your dress from last time. It's been cleaned and pressed. We trade."

"Thank you, Mr. Chu."

"Is it true? You the new bank owner?" asked Mr. Chu. "That's true," replied Lottie. "Everything happened so fast." "That's very good, said Mr. Chu. "When you left that day, we were worried about you. We happy for you."

"You're very kind, Mr. Chu. I would like to make a change in your monthly lease payments. There was a mistake made."

"Change? Mistake?" said Mr. Chu.

"Yes. My Uncle Lance, who owned the bank at one time, charged you too much on your lease. So your lease payment will be lower."

"Lower?" Mr. Chu was dumbfounded. He gave Lottie a hug. "Thanks so much!"

"Looks like I'm not the only hugger in town," said Lottie.

"My pleasure, Mrs. Rainwater. Oh. Sorry for that day when our young daughter did your hair. She thought she did a good job. I didn't think so. Interview okay that day?"

"I believe I made an everlasting impression on Mr. Green," replied Lottie.

The next day, Lottie arrived at Mr. Lewis' grocery store across town. Lottie sat in the car for several moments. She was embarrassed to come say as she hadn't paid anything on her grocery tab for a while, but she did have good news for them.

Lottie recalled, when she was a child, Ingrid would take her to the grocery store for a treat. In the store was a small soda fountain. The milk shakes back then didn't have preservatives or artificial flavoring, and the milk was wholesome. They were the best.

While Lottie was drinking her milk shake, Ingrid would sit there and have a beer or two. Lottie couldn't always finish her milk shake, so Ingrid would pour the rest of her beer into Lottie's glass and drink it down. This also helped kill the smell of beer on Ingrid's breath.

Lottie got out of her car, grabbed her paperwork, and entered the grocery store. She noticed that the old soda fountain was gone. Mrs. Lewis approached her with open arms.

"Mrs. Rainwater, we were so worried about you."

"I'm fine," said Lottie. Mr. Lewis joined them.

"We heard so many rumors," said Mr. Lewis. "Someone said you were in jail. Then another person said Bill was in the hospital with a head injury. And let's not forget about Great Uncle Will."

"I was in jail for just a few hours. That's a story in itself, and Bill is out of the hospital. He's fine. And Great Uncle Will is famous, as you all know by now."

"He sure is famous, replied Mr. Lewis. "He's our hero."

"I guess our families have been busy. I would like to pay my bill in full. I'm sorry I waited so long. How much do I owe you?"

"Mr. Lewis went behind the counter and looked at his record of charges.

"It comes to thirty-five dollars and some odd cents. Oh, thirty-five dollars even." She placed two twenties on the counter.

"Please keep the difference, Mr. Lewis."

"That's five dollars. Are you sure?"

"I insist," said Lottie. "And thank you so much for giving us the credit. What happened to the soda fountain that was here? I always loved sitting there with my mom years ago."

"It's at the used equipment store. We regret doing that now," remarked Mr. Lewis.

"How about the other gossip?" asked Mrs. Lewis "Is it true that your uncle is in jail? Or should I say the real Uncle Lance?"

"That's true, and I think for a long time," replied Lottie.

"So what will happen to the bank?" asked Mr. Lewis.

"I inherited the bank from my deceased Uncle Zach. So it looks like I'm in the banking business."

"You've accomplished a lot," said Mrs. Lewis.

"I think it was God's accomplishments, not mine. I've made some changes in your lease payments. Here are the new lease papers. The changes are on the second page, I believe. I hope it meets your approval."

"We were hoping the lease payments wouldn't go up," replied Mr. Lewis. "I guess we'll have to manage."

Lottie sat down on a chair near the counter. Her face was flushed. After reading the second page, Mr. Lewis looked at Lottie with a puzzled face.

"Our lease is lower?" said Mr. Lewis. "What did we do to deserve this? We're just a small store. We don't have any connections and the like, Mrs. Rainwater."

"Well you do now. Please, just call me Lottie."

"Thank you, Lottie," said Mr. Lewis.

"Now we can make some improvements to attract business," replied Mrs. Lewis. "That new Thriftway store in River Falls is giving us a lot of competition."

"And maybe we can get that soda fountain back," replied Lottie.

"You could? How?" asked Mrs. Lewis.

"I'll have my Uncle Bill work on that."

"Thanks again. Are you feeling okay?" asked Mrs. Lewis.

"I'm just a little light-headed," answered Lottie. "I skipped breakfast this morning. That's probably why. I'll just sit here a while."

Lottie suddenly slumped over in her chair. Mrs. Lewis held on to her until the ambulance arrived.

Sheriff Taylor and Bill were in the hospital waiting room waiting on word of Lottie's condition.

"I was the only one the hospital was able to contact," said Bill. "Luckily I got ahold of you and Gloria. I left word at the diner for my dad. Hopefully everyone else will get the word."

"Sheriff, would you like some water from the cooler?"

"That cooler water doesn't do it for me right now, Bill. One would think that a pop machine would've been installed somewhere. I sure could go for a root beer. Hope that water will work for you."

"Smiling, Bill said, "I'm good. I'm getting use to drinking water and pop. You don't drink liquor, Sheriff?"

"Nope. I just never had the urge for the stuff."

"I'm worried about Lottie," said Bill. "She's been burning the candle at both ends trying to learn the banking business."

"Lottie is driven, Bill. One day she insisted that I teach her how to shoot. She still practices once in a while with one of Bill's guns. I guess she's still somewhat of a tomboy."

"But she missed twice when she shot at Lance at the bank."

"Bill, she could've easily nailed him twice in the noggin if she wanted to."

"I forgot about Lottie learning how to shoot," said Bill. "I'm glad I wasn't dead center on my target that day.

Lottie was always headstrong and had a hard time with her health since she was a kid. She never looked ill but at times she would be bedridden for a day or two. No one knew what the problem was."

"Here I am, the so-called big sheriff of this town and county, and I can't do a thing for either one of them. Nothing."

Dr. Allen entered the waiting room and sat across from the sheriff and Uncle Bill. He looked over his charts for a few moments.

He was an older, short man in his early sixties. He was plainly dressed and wore the typical lab coat. It is said that he was a young Army doctor who spent time in the last days of World War I.

The doctor had a large scar across the side of his neck where a bullet almost ended his life. In that short time, he saw so much destruction of life that he swore he was leaving the doctor's profession when he came back to the states from the war. He'd been at the Bergan's Ferry hospital ever since.

"How is she doing, Dr. Allen?" asked Bill.

"Nothing real serious that we can see. The nurse is doing some lab work on her now. I believe she has some immune problems. She's been pushing herself too much. And with her husband still in a coma... Well, it's just a lot for her to handle. It would be a lot for anyone. She's wearing herself out."

"We've tried our best to slow her down, Doctor," said Bill.

"As I recall, Lottie always had that problem since she was a young girl," said the doctor. "She needs at least three days' bed rest and three good meals a day. She told me in a polite way that she didn't need a doctor to tell her how to run her life. She's a stubborn lady. Is she always this way?

"That she is, Doctor," said Uncle Bill.

"I believe she can go home tomorrow afternoon depending on the lab reports," said the doctor.

"So she's going to be okay, Dr. Allen?" asked Uncle Bill.

"I believe so, Bill. Someone must stay with her to make sure she complies with my orders. So who would that be?"

"Gloria and Rosa can take care of her," replied Uncle Bill.

"But will she listen to them?" asked the doctor.

"She will listen to me," said Sheriff Taylor. "I'm not just a lawman, but I do consider Lottie somewhat like a daughter to me."

"And the sheriff also locked her up in the jail not too long ago," remarked Bill with a smile.

The doctor gave the sheriff a look and then laughed. "I heard about that. The Wart sisters in the diner were my favorite event. Nothing surprises me anymore when it comes to the Rainwater or Lindstrom families. You can see her for a few minutes. Bill, please don't shoot yourself again."

# CHAPTER 28

## *THE GOOD DEEDS*

After a bad dream, Lottie was up for an hour and then returned to bed. She dreamed that she was trying to find her way home but seemed to move in slow motion as she walked. It was difficult for her to understand the directions given to her from people around her. Every turn was the wrong turn. Far off in the distance she could see John and the house, but as she got closer everything became distorted and seemed farther away.

Lottie hated to think what kinds of dreams John might be having. She had the luxury of waking up, but not her John. She just wanted him to make it home to her and the family.

Rosa came back into the room and sat on the bed next to her. She held Lottie's hand.

"How's my niece, doing?" asked Rosa.

"I'm feeling better. If you weren't watching me so close, I could sneak out the window and do something interesting instead of being stranded in this bed."

"You know this is for your own good," said Rosa.

"I know. How's the bank doing?" asked Lottie.

"Well I just completed another car loan for a customer," replied Rosa. "The loan experience at the dealership over the years has really been an asset. Mr. Perkins is doing a great job getting us trained."

"And how about the new teller?" asked Lottie.

"She's doing fine. She has a good head for numbers and seems to works well with the customers. I think she has an eye for Bill. I told him that there won't be any office romances. And I said that I was still his big sister."

Lottie laughed and poked her. "Rosa, so you're the romance police. Right?"

"Of course I am. Linda will be by this morning and will stay the night with you and the kids. Do we have to close the window and nail it shut so you don't sneak out like you did once before when you were a sick young kid?"

"I promise not to run away, Rosa."

"Tonight I'll stop by the hospital to see John, Lottie."

Rosa kissed her on the forehead and left the room. Lottie fell asleep and then was awakened by some chatter outside her opened window next to her bed. The two ravens were perched on the window sill. They ruffled their feathers, and then they were silent. Lottie got up, picked up a slice of toast from the plate on her nightstand, and placed it on the window sill.

"Now I'm able to give you something to eat."

She woke up some time later and wondered if the ravens at the window were just a dream. The slice of toast on the plate was gone.

Sara and Mark rushed into Lottie's bedroom room and jumped on the bed.

"Hey, take it easy. It's early in the morning."

"It's not that early, Mom," said Mark. "It's lunchtime."

"I fell asleep again that long? That's a first for me. So tell me what's going on."

"We picked a bunch of berries yesterday afternoon," said Sara.

"I picked most of them, Sara," replied Mark.

"No you didn't, and..."

"Now don't argue, kids. Okay? You know that you don't have to pick berries. I know you always liked doing that. I'm getting some money from the bank now. Next month, we will start paying on the hospital bills and all that. We are going to make it.

Uncle Bill is going to try to get the rabbit business going again on the weekends."

"We still want to help out," said Sara.

"Well, okay," replied Lottie. "And don't spend it all at the five and dime store. Better yet, you bring me the money and we'll put some of it in your piggy bank."

"Do we have to?" asked Mark.

"Yes," said Lottie.

"We saw the two ravens today," said Mark.

"So they did come by," replied Lottie.

"We went with Linda this morning to town while you were asleep," said Mark. "When Linda was in the market, we saw Sheriff Taylor's police car parked in front of the church."

"We went inside and spied on him," said Sara. "He didn't have his big gun with him, and he wasn't wearing his hat."

"I told you kids not to play in the church. That's God's house, not a playroom."

"The sheriff was kneeling," said Sara. "Then he stood up and raised his arms."

"Did he know you kids were there?"

"No," answered Mark. "We hid behind the seats in back. A light came through a big window, and then his hair turned to gold.

We couldn't understand what he was saying. It sounded funny. Linda said maybe it was pig latin."

"The sheriff looked really tall," said Sara.

"That's a wild story," said Lottie. "That was the sun shining through the window on his hair, and he was just praying out loud. Linda was kidding you about him talking in pig latin. You talked about seeing angels before. Is the sheriff your angel?"

"Sheriff Taylor is not our angel," said Sara.

"Why is that, Sara?" asked Lottie.

"He's really old," replied Sara. "He can't fly that far from heaven to here anymore. But we're not real sure yet about the sheriff. He could be the other angel."

"I'll think about all this," said Lottie.

She thought about what the kids experienced that day in the church. A lot of things just didn't add up too well concerning Sheriff Taylor. He had often been seen sitting on a bench in the park as the morning sun came up.

The sheriff's police cruiser was rarely seen at the park. His apartment was on the other side of town. His ankle injury from the train conductor days still plagued him, so it would have been a long walk for him back to his apartment. He said one time that heaven will have free taxi service.

Very little was known about the sheriff before he came to Bergan's Ferry. The sheriff seldom needed his deputies to assist him in making an arrest. He always seemed to be in the area at the right time when people needed his assistance. Lottie wondered also if his awkward style and absentminded ways were just a cover- up of who he really was. Winnie rarely shared with anyone the conversations she had with the sheriff. Uncle Will never mentioned the sheriff's past life either.

Lottie was on her way to hand in person a foreclosure notice to the Brown family. They lived on Waller Road just out of town. She was going to send Rosa out to serve the notice, but Lottie felt compelled to do this herself. She got out of the car and walked up to the door and knocked lightly. Lottie waited for several moments, and then Mrs. Brown opened the door.

"Hello, Mrs. Rainwater."

"Good morning, Mrs. Brown."

"Please come in. I guess I was expecting someone from the bank. I heard that you're the new owner of the bank. I'm actually glad to see that."

"Yes I am. Unfortunately I'm here to give you the final notice of foreclosure on your house. I wish I was here under different circumstances. Is your husband available?"

"No, he's at the mill." They sat down on the sofa. Lottie handed the papers to her.

"I'm lost for words," said Mrs. Brown. "I shouldn't be surprised about all this. I try not to think about all this, but it's hard not to. She glanced through the papers.

"When do we have to move out?"

Lottie was uneasy as she sat there. She knew how it was to be in that position, but she also had a responsibility to the bank.

"When do we have to move out? Mrs. Rainwater..."

"I'm sorry. In fourteen days," answered Lottie.

"My husband David is only working part time. He hopes to get a better job with the Forest Service. It's tough to get a job when one is over forty."

"I see that there's a creek running through your property," said Lottie. "Is it Halverson's Creek?"

"Yes it is," answered Mrs. Brown. "It's full of fish and has the cleanest cold water around. It runs straight through our four-acre lot. At one time, my husband was going to start a small business here."

"There must be a better way," said Lottie. "I'll have

Mr. Perkins check further into this. I'm going to grant you an extension on the move-out date. Just hold tight for now."

"We would appreciate it so much," said Mrs. Brown. "I almost forgot. My Uncle Henry wanted to know how his guardian angel is doing? He hasn't seen the sheriff around lately."

"Sheriff Taylor is doing fine," said Lottie. "Old Henry is your uncle? Well, this is a small world. I'm sure my Great Uncle Will knows him."

"Yes he is. Henry believes that Sheriff Taylor was his angel that day when he was pinned under the car in his shop."

"That's very interesting," replied Lottie.

Lottie walked out the door and then tuned to her. "Your husband's first name sounds familiar," said Lottie. "Was he the witness who testified against the men who beat my husband up that night at the mill?"

"Yes he was. A man really pressured my husband not to say anything, but my David stood up against his threats."

"I just had a change of thought, Mrs. Brown. Maybe you can keep the house. Yes, I will make it happen."

"Bless you, Mrs. Rainwater! You're for sure our angel."

"No, I think someone else is," said Lottie.

On her way back from the Browns' house, Lottie felt the rear tire hit something as she came down the hill and slowed down for the railroad tracks.

As she got out and walked to the rear of the car, the old Ford rolled forward and stopped partway on the tracks. A train in the distance sounded its whistle.

"Oh my God. I've got to move this car!"

Lottie tried to open the driver's door, but it was stuck. She ran to the other side of the tracks and then turned around.

"I can't believe it!"

Sheriff Taylor, in his police cruiser, pushed her car across the tracks. A few seconds later, the train roared by. Lottie leaned up against her car.

"This is just too much," she said.

The sheriff got out of his car and rushed over to her. "Are you okay?" Lottie nodded.

The sheriff opened her car door and applied the emergency brake. "Now your car won't roll. And it's best to put the transmission in gear."

"Oh I'm losing it," said Lottie. "I stopped back there, and I didn't even think of all that for some reason."

"That was a close one, Lottie. Why did you stop?"

"I thought there was something wrong with my tires in back. Wait... How did you open my door so easy? It was stuck. I couldn't open it."

"I just pulled a little harder, Lottie. I'm trained to handle emergencies like this. You should know that."

"In any case, thanks Sheriff. You could have been hit by that train. I guess your front bumper is scratched up again."

"Of course it is. Any time you're around me, things happen. Why don't you sit in the car and relax. I'll check out the back tires."

The sheriff walked back and knelt down and looked at the right rear tire.

"Yup, it's shot. A piece of metal went right through it. I'll find the jack and get the car jacked up. Hopefully your spare is aired up."

As the sheriff jacked up the car, a stranger walked by and then stopped.

"Car trouble?" asked the stranger.

"Just a bad tire," said the sheriff.

"Need any help?" asked the stranger.

"I have it handled, sir. Thanks anyway."

The stranger continued down the street. Lottie sat there in the car for a while thinking that maybe she should've taken up her Uncle Will's offer to help her get a little newer car. Five minutes later, Lottie felt the back end of the car drop. She turned around.

"You're not done yet, are you?" asked Lottie.

The sheriff closed the trunk and walked up to Lottie. She gave the sheriff a look.

"It's finished, and the tire and the jack are in the trunk, Lottie."

"Who was that man who stopped to talk to you?"

"I don't know, Lottie."

"You changed that tire awfully quick, Sheriff. I helped John change a tire before, and it takes a lot longer than that. Look at you.

You didn't even get dirty."

"As I said before, Lottie, I'm skilled in many areas."

"And you surely are. There you stand before me, Sheriff. You're the angel! That's why you never got together with Winnie." He was taken by Lottie's remarks.

"You don't smoke, cuss, drink, or spit," said Lottie. "You always act like you're awkward or absentminded."

"Lottie, I think you're a little off. I mean mistaken."

"How about the time when Henry was pinned under his car?" remarked Lottie. A smile slowly formed on the sheriff's face. "And then that night when you took care of those three men behind the tavern. There's plenty more stories, Sheriff. And now you appeared out of nowhere just in time to push my car across the railroad tracks."

Sheriff Taylor was lost for words.

"You know that we love you for doing all these things for us and the town."

He placed his hands over his ears. "Can't hear you. No time to listen. Got lawman stuff to do!" The sheriff quickly got into his car.

"Please wait! shouted Lottie. "I won't say anything! I can keep a secret. My lips are tripled sealed." The sheriff quickly drove away.

Lottie thought, "I think I'm the only one who scared an angel away."

# CHAPTER 29

## *LOTTIE AND WINNIE*

Lottie was at the diner sitting at a table near the bakery. It was still hard for her to imagine that weeks ago she was barred from the diner because of her pie and ice cream fight with the two Wart sisters. Some of the customers waved at Lottie as she sat there. They were her fans that day when she was a struggling waitress.

Now Lottie was looked up to by a lot of the townsfolk. Many people felt that it was proper she ended up following in the footsteps of her Uncle Will. One person said that they were very much alike, as Lottie and her uncle were both in the sanatorium and the banking business. But now that didn't seem to bother most people in Bergan's Ferry. Some of them were extra nice because they needed a loan. Lottie sat there before waiting on Winnie to arrive. In the past, Winnie was her sister. Now she was her mother.

Winnie finally walked through the door of the diner and then stopped for a moment. Heads turned. She wore a white business suit trimmed in navy blue. Her brunette hair had a poodle-cut look to it, and her dark blue high heels had a white etch to them. She still looked like a million bucks. Winnie stopped for a few moments to chat with two men. She waved to some other people and then joined Lottie.

"It's so good to see you, Mom."

Lottie stood up and gave her a hug. Winnie kissed her on the forehead. They sat and held hands for several moments.

"Seems like you have some admirers over there," said Lottie.

"I really don't know them, but I appreciate their attention. I got a little mobbed at the bank, but that's fine. I'm lucky that people still think of me."

"You were never stuck up, Mom. It's nice that you talk to everyone when you can. You're sure dressed to the hilt today."

"Just some clothes I threw on that I had in my old trunk."

"Of course," said Lottie with a grin.

"I'm sorry that I couldn't make it to the hospital, Lottie. I was in LA on my last audition. Please forgive me."

"I understand, Mom. I'm okay. The doctor ordered me on bed rest for a few days. I guess I needed rest. Gloria and Rosa stayed with me for a few days. Linda helped too."

"It's really nice to come home and have nothing to hide," said Winnie. "I'm having such a great time being your mother instead of your sister. You're being so good to me, Lottie. I missed out on a lot of things for not being honest with you and everyone else. Since my work kept me away, I didn't see you grow up like Ingrid did. Acting like your sister was hard on me, but it was my choice to be that way."

"But I think you're catching up, Mom." Winnie smiled. "I can't complain. You were the best sister one could have. I wondered why you spent so much more time with me than with Gloria or Rosa. But then again, I was the youngest. And you did write me when you were away. I still have some of those letters."

"You know, I always played the part of a woman who was pure as the driven snow, Lottie. If word got out that I was an unwed mother, the scandal magazines would have torn me up real good."

"I'm glad you were never in one of those magazines, Mom. There's enough gossip around town about our families. There was an article in the Boise paper about Great Uncle Will digging holes everywhere."

"That's what I heard, Lottie. One time, Dad looked me in the eyes and made the comment that he would have loved Bill even if they weren't blood related," remarked Winnie. "I almost fainted when he said that to me. Then I wondered how much he knew about everything else."

"Looks like he might have known, Mom. I forgot to ask. How did the audition go in LA?"

"Very well. I just got a telegram from my agent that I got the part and then some. I'm excited. I auditioned for a supporting role with Victoria Whitman, and I'll play her older sister. The story takes place in a town in the Northwest."

"That's good news, Mom!"

"It is, Lottie. I sure can use the work. Dad sure put us on the map when he found the Nez Perce mask and the rest of the treasures."

"We're sitting in the right town for the movie," said Lottie.

"Perhaps I can suggest that to them," replied Winnie. "Any change in John's condition?" asked Winnie.

"No. Now that we have some money coming in, I'm going to get a specialist from Boise. We have to do something."

"I guess a lot happened after I left a few weeks ago," replied Winnie. "Gloria filled me in on a few things."

"A lot has happened since you were here last, Mom. I don't think you were in town when I was a waitress here for a very short time."

"That was the funniest thing I ever heard, Lottie. You really did the Wart sisters in. You're very special. Bill called me when you exposed Lance. I just don't know why Lance and Zach turned out the way they did."

"I guess we will never know," said Lottie.

"Thanks for getting ahold of me and reading the authentic will over the phone, Lottie. I know you tried several times to reach me. I'm happy for you. You deserve it."

"Mom, you do know that everyone will get a little share of the bank revenue once things get going. Everyone is in agreement."

"That's up to you, Lottie. I'm just glad you're not going to lose everything."

"Oh, here comes my favorite person of the day," said Lottie.

Mr. Wendal walked over to their table with some rolls. "It's a pleasure to serve you, ladies. The rolls are on the house. I'll bring more coffee."

"Thank you," said Lottie.

He gave them a fake smile and left.

"See the way he treats me now that I have the bank. A few weeks ago, I wasn't even allowed to come back in here. I'm still going to be the same person I always was."

"You need to change one thing," said Winnie. "You need to slow down. I worry about you, Lottie. Ever since you were young, you had that drive in you that became your downfall at times."

"A lot of questions go through my mind every day, Mom. What if John never wakes up? What if he dies?

I have to keep busy to keep my mind off of things."

"Sheriff Taylor has been on my mind lately," said Winnie. "I hope to be in town long enough to see him. He's so convinced that John will make it. I hope he's right."

"You do have a shining for the sheriff."

"What do you mean, Lottie?"

"You know...like in love."

"We're close. We care for each other a great deal, Lottie."

"The sheriff knows more than we think, Mom. A whole lot more."

"What do you mean?"

"Mom, you can't get serious with him. Not at all. Your heart will be broken for sure."

"Why is that?" asked Winnie.

"You're going to think I'm crazy, but angels can't get married."

"What angels, Lottie? I think you lost me there. What are you talking about?"

"Mark said that the sheriff might not be the angel that has been helping us. They're mistaken. It's Sheriff Taylor, for sure."

Winnie was silent for a few moments. She shook her head and then laughed.

"Lottie, please tell me more. This is really great stuff."

"It's true, Mom! Just listen to me. All these years, the sheriff pretended to be just an awkward, stumbling sheriff, Mom. You know how he is. Tell me where he came from or what he did before coming to town twenty years ago. Tell me."

"Well, I really don't know, Lottie. This has never been an issue with me. I just never thought about it that much."

"But you must have. I bet he's never shown you pictures of his loved ones. Did he ever talk about his family? Where he grew up?"

"No... I don't think so."

"I think he was in the Boise area at the academy, Lottie."

"Some people say that his birth certificate is flawed, date-wise," said Lottie. "Who knows what else is wrong."

"He never seems to talk about the past. I must admit that, Lottie. Have you confronted him? You know he's easy to talk to, and he thinks the world of you."

"Why is he so critical of me at times, Mom?"

"You and Bill were always a handful. You guys kinda earned the reputation. Both of you were always going the distance."

"Oh, the other day he came out of nowhere and pushed my car off the tracks with his police cruiser just as the train was coming down the tracks. There's other stories floating around about the sheriff."

"I know Sheriff Taylor is quite unique and capable when he wants to be," remarked Winnie.

"The sheriff can be pretty shrewd at times," said Lottie. "Years ago, he tried to confuse me concerning his name, you know. Tell me this. Why does he only have one name? He should have a first and last name like everyone else. Right?"

"Lottie, his first name is Taylor. His last name is also Taylor? Yes, Taylor Taylor. You didn't know this?"

Lottie shook her head. "Where in the world have I've been all this time?"

"Honey, you need to let go of this. He's just a plain nice man and a sheriff of a small town and county."

"I think you're wrong," said Lottie. "The kids say that Blackie can tell if one is an angel. He barks only twice if he's in front of an angel. That's just what the kids say. They just might be right."

"Really?" said Winnie. "I know Blackie is a smart dog and all."

"That's right, Mom. So why does the sheriff avoid standing in front of Blackie when he does visit us?"

"I don't know, Lottie. Maybe he's allergic to dogs. Maybe you need more rest. A few days might not have been enough. You know the time you spent in the sanatorium was tough on you. You were always very intense about certain things."

"Mom, are you saying that I'm making all these things up or that I'm telling lies? I was in the sanatorium because I couldn't handle everything that was happening to us, Mom. You didn't have to directly deal with any of this."

"Lottie, it's not that I didn't feel terrible or didn't care about what was going on."

"You were away most of the time and just too busy playing the Hollywood scene and then some. Both families had to suffer all the heartaches over the years."

Lottie looked away for a few moments. Tears welled up in Winnie's eyes.

"Mom, I shouldn't have said that. I'm sorry. Gloria always said that I had a temper at times."

"That's okay, Lottie. I deserve some of that. I didn't mean to imply that just because you were in the sanatorium you were a complete nut job... I could have used a better choice of words. Please forgive me."

"It's okay, Mom." They sat there in silence for a few moments.

"Anyway, I forgot to tell you, Lottie. It was good to see Bill at the bank. He looked so different without his long hair. I'm worried about him. I hope he can keep off the booze and settle down. The booze almost killed me back in the day. Once in a while, I'll have one stiff drink and then I'll leave it alone. I've seen too many lives destroyed in Hollywood because of money and booze."

"So, what is the verdict?

"What do you mean, Lottie?"

"Is the sheriff an angel or just a nice man who trips over his own feet at times? Mom, you will see. And I still think you're deeply in love with the sheriff."

"The sheriff is very special to me, Lottie."

"And I think you're trying to cover for him," said Lottie.

# CHAPTER 30

## *A DAY FOR JOHN*

Lottie is talking with Jerry in front of his auto repair shop. Mark and Sara are in the car.

"Lottie, it's good to see you. I've been so busy that I haven't had much time to visit people or even spend much time at the diner."

"Uncle Bill said you have a part-time job besides the garage."

"Yes I do. I'm working a few hours at the hardware store. I'm trying to make some extra money to repair this old shop. It's been difficult. My business hasn't been that great since they closed off the old bridge here a few years ago. And not many people use the car wash next to me. People still like to wash their car themselves."

"You're kinda stuck on the edge of town off this dead-end street," said Lottie. "Some people may not know where you're at. You need a sign on the corner before the turn, Jerry."

"I've wanted to make a sign, but I'm not good at that sort of thing," replied Jerry. "Looks like I have to make one."

"You've been good to both of our families. I'm going to have Bill make a sign at no cost to you. He's good at that sort of thing and likes to keep busy. Just try to send some business our way."

"Will do. Thanks, Lottie."

"You're welcome, Jerry. The reason I'm here is to let you know that the bank wants to offer you a two percent small business loan. No collateral needed."

"Two percent! That's a real bargain, Lottie."

"It was really Great Uncle Will's idea. Perhaps you can quit that second job after a bit. I'll have Bill make the sign for you."

"You're very kind," said Jerry.

"That old bridge sure brings back a lot of memories," said Lottie.

"Didn't you almost drown one day when you jumped off this bridge years ago, Lottie?"

"That's true, Jerry. A lot of kids jumped off the bridge all the time but not with their clothes on. One summer day, Bill dared me to jump off the bridge when we were walking back from church. He bet me five bucks that I wouldn't. So I jumped in. I didn't think of it at the time that my wet clothes would weigh me down so much. I had a hard time making it back to shore. Bill jumped in and tried to pull me in but I panicked, almost pulling him down. A man on the river bank swam out and helped us. To this day, I don't know who he was. The man just seemed to come out of nowhere. It sure wasn't the brightest thing I've ever done. I was too big to spank, so I was grounded for a month. Bill still owes me the five bucks."

As Lottie continued to talk to Jerry, Mark noticed a man dressed in railroad work clothes standing next to a shed near the car wash.

"I know him, Sara."

"Who?"

"See the man next to the shed, Sara. He's the one that got me out of the river. Let's go over there and talk to him." Mark and Sara left the car and walked up to him.

"Hi. Remember me, Mr. Sam?" asked Mark.

"Yes I do, Mark. I hope you haven't gone over to the river by yourself. You know what happened last time."

"Sir, I've been good. This is my little sister, Sara."

"How do you do, Sara?"

"Excuse me, Jerry. I need to see what the kids are up to." Lottie walked over to them.

"I hope my kids aren't bothering you, sir." "Not at all, ma'am. They're great children." "Have we met somewhere before?" asked Lottie.

"I was at your place a few weeks ago with some friends of mine. You're Mrs. Rainwater. Am I correct?"

"Yes you are," answered Lottie.

"He could be the other angel," said Sara. "His wings are under his coat."

"I'm sorry. My kids are obsessed with angels. They see them at times. Even our dog can spot angels."

"I understand, Mrs. Rainwater. Do you believe in miracles?"

"Well, I do believe in miracles. Why do you ask?"

"I have something for you," said Sam. He handed Lottie a brightly colored folded handkerchief.

"For me?" She carefully unfolded it. "How could this be! Look!"

The kids gathered around her. "It's my chain and cross that I lost."

Lottie looked at the cross and chain for several moments and then looked up.

"Where did he go?" asked Lottie. "I need to thank him." She looked around the corner of the shed. "He left so quickly. It was like he just disappeared."

"So you think he was the angel?" said Lottie.

"Not sure," said Sara. Mark gave Sara an odd look.

"You know, he was wearing the same kind of cowboy boots that the sheriff wears," said Lottie. "That's seems rather odd."

"Was that a special present, Mommy?"

"Not exactly, Sara," answered Lottie. "But it was very special to me. I lost this several years ago when your Uncle Bill dared me to jump into the river with my clothes on. It's still like brand new! How did he know we were going to be here at the garage today? And how did he find it?"

"Why did you get it back?" asked Mark.

"Maybe this is a reminder," said Lottie. "If something is lost or broken, God can fix it. Let's sit down on the bench over there. I need to rest for a minute. It's really hot out. She sat down, leaned back, and closed her eyes.

"Are you okay, Lottie?" asked Jerry.

"I just need to sit for a few minutes."

"I'll get you a glass of water, Lottie."

"Last time when you were real tired, you left us Mommy. You went to that hospital for a long time."

"You know that your Aunt Rosa and Aunt Gloria will always be there to help us out, Sara. Right? And you can count on Uncle Bill and Linda too."

"What about Dad?" asked Mark.

"I'm sure your dad will get better," replied Lottie. "Tell me about your angel friend. I'm ready to listen."

"I think you've seen him before, Mom," said Mark.

"You mean Sheriff Taylor," said Lottie. Sara nodded and looked at Mark. They laughed.

"There's Uncle Bill coming down the road, Mom," said Mark.

Bill stopped in front of the shop and got out of his car and walked up to Lottie.

"The hospital called. There's a change in John's condition!"

"Is he better or worse, Bill?"

"They didn't say, Lottie. We'll go in my car," said Bill.

\*\*\*\*

Uncle Will and his friends stood next to his Mack Truck.

"I'm sorry we're broken down, men. Looks like the fan belt broke. No wonder it was running hot. Luckily we're close to Jerry's garage. It's just around the corner."

The men looked at each and then followed Uncle Will to the garage. A note was tacked on the garage door. Uncle Will read the note.

"Looks like they went to the hospital. Something must be going on. I'd better get there right now. The old truck can wait," thought Uncle Will.

Uncle Will walked over to Lottie's car and looked inside. "The keys are in it." He got in the car and motioned for his friends to get in with him. He made a turn onto Main Street and headed across town.

"I need to go to the hospital first," said Uncle Will to his friends. "And after that, I'm going to pay all of you in advance this week. We're got a lot of digging to do."

"I keep on forgetting that they don't understand English. That's okay. They seem to be happy," thought Uncle Will.

"Uh oh. These brakes aren't good," said Uncle Will.

One of the men spoke to his friends in Chinese. "The car brakes are no good. We should've walked back. Should we tell him that some of us speak and understand English?"

"No," said the other man in Chinese. "It's fun to hear him talk to himself all the time. He seems to say the same things over again. I guess that's what old people do. But he's a good man."

\* \* \* \*

The new deputies from River Falls were standing in front of Bergan's Ferry police station.

"We were supposed to meet the sheriff here, but I guess he just left for the hospital," said one of the deputies. "Let's just stay at the station for now."

As Uncle Will drove past the police station en route to the hospital, one of the deputies became alarmed.

"Did you see that?"

"See what?" asked his brother.

"That Ford that just passed us had several Chinese people in it. A real old man was behind the wheel. Let's go in the office." The deputy took down a small poster off of the bulletin board.

"Looks like him," said the deputy to his brother.

"So that's the man that secretly brings Chinese men in and puts them to work without pay! He just gives them room and board. Let's follow him and then make the arrest. We'll make a lot of points with our uncle if we nail this guy."

\*\*\*\*

Sheriff Taylor parked his police cruiser and walked toward the hospital entrance. He stopped and noticed that Bill and Lottie just arrived.

"Stay in the car for now, kids," said Lottie. "Should I bring the kids in? What if it's bad news, Bill?"

"I'm not sure Lottie," said Bill.

Moments later, Uncle Will drove up in Lottie's car and was unable to stop in time, hitting the back bumper of the sheriff's car.

"No look good," said one of the men in Chinese.

The sheriff rushed down the walkway to the parking lot.

"What's going on here? My car!"

"The brakes aren't good," said Uncle Will. "Nothing I could do."

The sheriff looked at his bent rear bumper. He shook his head and turned to Uncle Will.

"Now I got two bent bumpers," said the sheriff.

As Uncle Will backed Lottie's car away from the sheriff's car, the deputies arrived. The deputies got out of their car. One deputy, with his gun partway drawn, quickly walked up to Uncle Will.

"We got him, Sheriff. This old man is the slave driver of those Chinese people. Get your hands up, old man!"

Uncle Will and the Chinese men held their hands up high. Lottie rushed over to the deputy.

"No one points a gun at my Great Uncle Will, you idiot," said Lottie.

As Lottie kicked the deputy's leg, his gun fired. The bullet glanced off the pavement and hit the back window of Sheriff Taylor's police cruiser.

"Put the gun away before you kill someone!" shouted the sheriff.

"That's Great Uncle Will. He's not the slave driver! He's just an old man who cheats at checkers."

"Can't you control these deputies?" said Lottie.

The deputies looked at each other and then stepped back away from Lottie's car.

"Men, you can put your hands down," said Uncle Will to his friends. "They were really after me." One of the Chinese men sitting in the back seat tapped Uncle Will on the shoulder.

"Who's the tall crazy woman who kicked the deputy?" asked the Chinese man in English.

Surprised, Uncle Will turned around. "What? You guys understand English?"

"The sheriff is going to arrest us all," said Lottie to Uncle Bill.

She quickly went up the walkway and into the hospital. Bill, Uncle Will, Jerry, the Chinese men, and three women from the church followed her. The sheriff walked as fast as he could behind them. He seemed to be talking to himself. The two deputies followed him.

As Lottie walked by the critical care station, a nurse attempted to get her attention. Lottie turned down one hallway and stopped at John's room. She opened the door and slowly walked into the room. The bed was empty.

Lottie's eyes dimmed. She dropped to her knees in tears.

"They've taken you away," thought Lottie.

"Oh John, you're gone!"

The sheriff and the nurse pushed their way through the crowd to where Lottie was.

"Lottie, you're in the wrong room!" said the sheriff.

"Wrong room?" replied Lottie. "Oh. I'm sorry."

* * * *

Lottie is in John's room with the doctor and everyone else. She embraces John.

"You're back with us, John," said Lottie. "Thank you, God."

She kissed John and held his hand. "It's good to see you," said John. "You're a beautiful sight. How's the kids?"

"They're fine. They miss you, and so does everyone else."

"I guess our prayers wouldn't let you go, John."

"Did you see him, Lottie?"

"Who do you mean, John?"

"In my dream, a man touched my head and said that all would be restored and much more. I woke up and there he was in front of me."

"No one saw a man in his room, Mrs. Rainwater," said the nurse.

"It must have been an angel from heaven," remarked Lottie.

"I believe so," said Sheriff Taylor.

"This has been a lot for John," said the doctor. "Please come back later in a few hours after John has rested. We need to do some further examinations right now, Lottie."

"But my kids need to see him. He's been away from us for a long time, Doctor." Uncle Will took Lottie's hand.

"Lottie, the doctor is right. We can come back later. John needs the rest. Let's go. He will be just fine. Come on now."

"Well, okay," said Lottie. "We'll be back later tonight, John."

"And don't bring half the town with you, Lottie," said the doctor. "This is a small room, not an auditorium."

The family gathered in the parking lot while the sheriff looked at his patrol car.

"These people just love to destroy my car." The sheriff turned to them.

"Now I don't even have a back window," said the sheriff. "This time, the law will be enforced. I don't care who I write up or put in jail. Today blood isn't thicker than water."

As the sheriff got in his car and feverishly looked for his ticket book, everyone got in their cars and drove off. The sheriff finally got out of his car with his ticket book and looked around.

"Where did everyone go?"

# CHAPTER 31

## *WINNIE AND SHERIFF TAYLOR*

Winnie and Sheriff Taylor were in the Doughboy sitting in a booth near the jukebox. The lights were dimmed, and the diner staff had gone home for the evening. At ten, the cuckoo clock sounded.

A candle with a jasmine scent lit their table. Winnie had a glass of wine in front of her, and the sheriff had a bottle of Hires root beer. A dish of German chocolates was off to the side.

Winnie wore a deep blue evening dress with a white shawl. Her hair was in a ponytail, and she was the type of lady who didn't need a lot of makeup to be attractive.

The sheriff had a dark brown leather jacket with a jade green western shirt. His long silver-blond hair glistened from the candlelight. Winnie was moved by the sheriff's gentle smile. They sat there in silence for several moments.

It is said that when Sheriff Taylor and Winnie were together in the diner, people purposely sat close to them and tried to overhear their conversations, but for some reason they couldn't hear much of anything. Lottie and Bill said that it was like a wall of silence that surrounded the two. They couldn't hear a thing either.

"It's sure quiet here," remarked Winnie. "How did you arrange for us to be here after hours all by ourselves, Taylor?"

"Oh I just said to the owner that I needed some quiet time with a special person. He happened to be in town the other day."

"You seem to have a lot of pull around here at times," said Winnie. "You never talk about it very much."

"A while back, the owner of this diner and the mayor knew that I saw them one night in River Falls, Winnie. They were in the gambling part of town late at night. They wanted that to be kept quiet from the public. I know what's going on in this town and county."

"So you do know what's going on, Taylor."

"I guess I do, Winnie. This diner seems bigger than it is with just us sitting here."

"It's been the center of town for a long time," said Winnie.

"It seems if you wanted to meet someone you haven't seen for a while, this is the place to come," said the sheriff.

"And this is where I met you," said Winnie.

"Lottie asked a lot of questions about you the other day. I didn't have very many answers to give her, Taylor. She means well."

"Winnie, Lottie has been full of questions ever since I've known her as a young girl."

"Lottie thinks you're the angel who has helped us through all these hard times, Taylor. What do you think about all that?"

"Me? I'm just a simple old sheriff with a badge. I'm just trying to keep this town and county safe from the undesirables. And according to Lottie, I'm a stumbling sheriff at best. Maybe the whole town thinks that, Winnie."

"Lottie thinks the world of you. You know that."

"Well, I suppose so, Winnie. She brings me a piece of blackberry or rhubarb pie at the station at times."

"You and my dad are the only ones she does that for. I know Lottie is a little tough on you at times. You know she's high strung and all that. It's just her nature."

"She got that from her mother, Winnie."

"Well, maybe a little bit, Taylor."

"But I guess I love her as if she was my daughter. But she needs to be disciplined all the time to keep her on an even keel."

"She's not a ship or a little girl, Taylor."

"I know, Winnie. But she can be a little aggressive at times."

"Lottie may be on to something," said Winnie. "I think you may know more than what you let on. Right?"

The sheriff became a little uneasy as Winnie spoke. "And how is that, Winnie?"

"No one seems to know much about you when you first came to this town twenty years ago. You never showed me any pictures of your loved ones. And when you did come to town, you acquired your job as sheriff in more than a timely manner."

"What are you trying to say, Winnie?"

"Lottie said that you don't have much of a past, Taylor."

"And you seem to be in a real serious mood tonight. You only call me Taylor when you're upset or very serious about something."

"I know," said Winnie. "Maybe it's just a habit that I normally call you by your title."

"I always wanted to be a lawman. I guess at times the title just goes to my head. I don't mean to be uppity."

"Let's get back to you being our angel. Please don't get me wrong, but you seem to handle just about anything around here by yourself. There are some real rough people who travel through this town."

"I know I'm a little old for the job, but I was well trained, Winnie."

"I ran into Henry yesterday," said Winnie. "We had a very interesting conversation. He believes that an angel saved him. When he was pinned under his car that day, he didn't directly see the person's face who stood next to his car. As he laid there, Henry said that the person had squared-toed cowboy boots and tan western trousers. Just before the car was lifted up, a glow came over the person's boots and trousers. You always wear those tan trousers and the same kind of custom boots."

"You know that I'm not the only one who buys clothes at the western store in River Falls."

"But someone lifted that car off him, Taylor. Lottie told me about you being there just in time to push her car off the tracks the other day. Just like Lottie said, you don't spit, cuss, or drink. Your attire always looks like new. You've never been married as far as I know. You're almost too perfect."

"I don't know what to say, Winnie."

"You know you can confide in me, Taylor. In the past year, we had to go to a lot of funerals. Gloria said that you seemed to distance yourself from the people at the cemetery and other gatherings at times. We always thought very well of you."

"I'm sorry if I gave anyone that impression, Winnie. I care more about the two families than one may think."

"How long have we been seeing each other when I come to town?"

"Well, it's been about five or six years, Winnie."

"Before that, I was highly attracted to a leading man in one of the films I was in. He wanted to marry me. I was very impressed by him."

"And I guess you turned him down?" said Sheriff Taylor.

"Yes I did. He believed that money and good looks were the only wealth to have. I believed that for a short time until Dad set me straight one day. You know, your friend who cheats at checkers?" said Winnie with a grin.

"So why would a successful actress, a pretty one at that, spend time with a man like me? I'm not tall, and I don't have much money. I'm just one who happens to be a lawman. And for sure, I'm not a Clark Gable type of guy."

"I know it's common for someone like me to only associate with other actors. I just like being with you and no one else. You're not a shallow person, and you care about people. There's women in this town who think you're handsome and would like to trade places with me. Did you know that? It's true."

"That's awfully sweet to say something like that, Winnie."

"Remember when I hinted around one time that marriage would be good, Taylor? You never gave me an answer. I'm still waiting."

"You wanted an answer? That would have been a tall order for even a lawman like me. This is really some serious stuff."

"After all this time, you never kissed me, Taylor. Other people have noticed that too."

"I don't know what to say, Winnie. I don't really have a lot of experience in romance and the like. I'm just not real fancy in some ways. I never intended to offend you."

"I still haven't gotten a good answer on some questions that I've had over the years," said Winnie. "Of course, if I knew you were an angel, there would be certain questions that would be stupid for me to ask. Does that make any sense?"

"I'm not really sure what you're getting at, Winnie. Let me tell you this. Your birthday is coming up next Saturday. Right?

"Yes it is. Why?"

"You say that I'm not willing to mingle with people, Winnie. Let's have a joint celebration that Saturday. I'll set everything up at the senior center. We can celebrate John's recovery and your birthday. On that date, I can also clear up some questions that you may have."

"Why on Saturday?" asked Winnie.

"That date will work out the best for everyone."

"I don't understand, Taylor"

"Please be patient, Winnie. There's a reason for all this hesitation on my part."

"Well, okay. I almost forgot. I told Lottie that you did have two names. She's the only one in town that that believed you only had one name. How did Lottie ever get that impression that you were Taylor and that's it?"

"I might have told her that one time. I was just messing with her. I never knew she still believed that, Winnie. Just getting back at her, I guess," said the sheriff with a big grin.

"So, no wonder my daughter is a little rattled at times," said Winnie.

Winnie got up and walked over to the jukebox. She put two quarters in. "Any special songs?"

"Anything you pick is fine."

"I'll play some slow ones, Taylor." She returned to the booth and then pulled the sheriff out on to the small dance floor. The music started to play.

"Let's dance," said Winnie.

"I'm not prepared for this, Winnie."

"Angels aren't prepared? They don't dance in heaven? She shook her head. "I can't believe I just said that. Now I'm starting to sound like Lottie."

As they danced, Winnie was surprised how smooth the sheriff was on his feet. He had command of the dance floor and a smile on his face that was priceless.

"How did you ever learn how to dance so well, Taylor?"

"I'm not just a lawman. I have many other talents. I can even ride a horse backwards."

"Sometimes you're just too much for me," said Winnie. "You know that with my heels on, I'm over three inches taller than you?"

"If I didn't have my cowboy boots, on I would even be a lot shorter."

Winnie gave the sheriff a look and stopped dancing. "How's your ankle, Taylor?"

"It hasn't bothered me now for a week or two."

"So next week I'm going to know everything about you. Right?

"Well just about everything, Winnie."

"Will you give me a big kiss next week?"

"You're full of questions, just like your daughter."

# CHAPTER 32

## *NOW SHE KNOWS*

Sheriff Taylor and Uncle Will sat together on a bench near the bandstand at Soldiers Park in town.

"You sit here quite often in the mornings before you go to work," remarked Uncle Will.

"It's quiet here in the early morning. I always liked parks," said the sheriff. "It's a good time for me to collect my thoughts."

"I'm ready for the family gathering at the senior center," said Uncle Will. "And I sure do have an appetite today."

"The diner bakery made the two cakes last night," said the sheriff. "And they're cooking up a great meal for today. As you know, I can only eat a small portion of food at a time. I'm not like everyone else. It's going to be great to see John with both families around him."

"Thanks for coordinating all this with the diner and the senior center, Sheriff. You've helped us so much and a whole lot of other people around here over the years."

"Just doing the job that I was assigned to. Time has gone by so fast. Even for me. One day I came to town and didn't even have a place to stay, so I slept in the jail for a week before I found a decent apartment. I didn't know anyone. Now I know the whole town and county."

"You knew of one person before you came to Bergan's Ferry," said Uncle Will.

"I guess I did. But I didn't know you very well at first until you bought me a root beer at the diner."

"You've became very close to people over the years," said Uncle Will.

"I know, Great Uncle Will. I've let myself become too close to the two families. Winnie wants some answers real soon. She said that Lottie considers me to be like a second father figure to her. I don't know where she got that notion."

"You do look out for Lottie and her family as well as ours. I'm really indebted to you for this. I would hate to see you go. And you just might be the greatest when it comes to playing checkers and gin rummy."

"Being a little sarcastic?" asked the sheriff with a smile.

"Somewhat," replied Uncle Will. "I suppose most of the world would think we're pretty square for entertaining ourselves with games like that. Simplicity has its virtues, and today my firstborn is having her birthday. I didn't think I would ever live this long."

Gloria showed up at the senior center about eleven o'clock and made sure that only coffee, tea, or juice would be served, as she wanted Bill to feel comfortable sitting there. She also made sure that the sheriff had his Hires root beer.

John and Lottie were sitting at the head of the table. He was somewhat overwhelmed by everything. He looked a little thin, but the doctors said he would gain his strength and normal weight back as time went on.

Winnie and the sheriff sat across from Gloria. The sheriff really seemed to enjoy himself, and Winnie held on to him as if she never wanted him to leave.

Uncle Will was at the opposite end of the long table with Greta from the diner. She was tickled to death to be with him.

Rosa walked in with Dr. Rose, and they sat by Uncle Will. Rosa was fascinated with Dr. Rose's knowledge of vintage cars, and he was quite fascinated with her.

Bill looked very comfortable being with Sue Wart.

She was hesitant to talk to anyone at first, but as time went on, Sue opened up. Lottie wasn't crazy about her being with Bill, but Uncle Will said it wasn't any of her business. Bill's sandy brown hair covered most of the scar across the side of his head. He was still clean-shaven and sober, and he even quit the smokes.

Mark and Sara sat at a small table off to the side. They complained that their dog Blackie couldn't sit with them.

As everyone was talking, Linda came in with a present for Winnie. A caterer from the diner brought a large cake on a dinner cart. The cake had fifty some candles.

"Make a wish, Winnie," said Gloria.

Winnie looked at the sheriff and then smiled. She blew out the candles, and everyone cheered.

"It's an honor to be here," said Winnie. "My wish was that my special prayer would be answered today. My thanks to everyone here."

Then Mr. Perkins showed up with a four-layer German chocolate cake for John. It had one large candle on top.

"What a great surprise," said John as he stood up. "Everyone has been so good to me. I'm very thankful to have all of you here."

"Make a wish, John," said Lottie. He blew out the candle.

"My wish was that all of you will be always blessed," said John. "We can save the cakes for later. Let's visit."

It had been a long time since Gloria had any kind of a smile on her face since her husband died a year ago. Ray, from the utility department, remarked one day that he wished he had someone to go to church with, so Bill invited Ray and Gloria last Sunday to tag along with him to church. It seemed to work out well.

Bill visited with Gloria for a few moments, and then they both left the banquet room. Moments later, Gloria walked backed in with Ray and introduced him to the family. Everyone was pleased to see Gloria with a smile on her face. Linda was still upset that her mom was sitting there with another man, but in time she would feel different.

Sheriff Taylor stood up and made a toast to Lottie and John with a root beer in hand.

"May you always be together and have a very long life. And a happy birthday to Winnie. She's a very special lady. I would like to thank Great Uncle Will for helping me arrange this get-together. My job is done here. I have a train to catch. All of you will always be in my heart. Thank you all for coming."

"Did you hear that, John?"

"Hear what, Lottie?"

"The sheriff is leaving for the train station," said Lottie. "He said his job is done here. He's leaving and not coming back! What is my mom going to think about that?"

"Winnie told me all about the angel thing with the sheriff, Lottie. I thought you left that alone for now."

"You have to admit someone has helped this family, John."

"I believe someone has, Lottie. In Indian folklore, many of us believe in angel-like beings. I don't think we will ever know."

"Well, I just know what I know," said Lottie.

The sheriff gave Winnie a hug and then left the room. She sat down and didn't say a word to anyone.

"Look at Winnie's face, John. She's not the happiest person in the room. I just might go to the train station and see him off."

Lottie arrived at the station and hurried over to a conductor helping passengers who were boarding the train.

"Sir, I need to get on this train," said Lottie. "I want to say goodbye to someone. Did you see a sheriff board this train?"

"I believe so. He went toward the second car back, ma'am. If you don't get off the train, the next stop is River Falls. Seattle is the end stop. Go ahead. You have sixteen minutes."

Lottie walked through one car and then through the next railcar and then came upon the sheriff and Agent Ben. Lottie gave the sheriff a look.

"So you are leaving us, Sheriff Taylor," said Lottie. "I knew it! I was right."

Agent Ben, I thought you left weeks ago. Did you know that you're sitting right across from our angel?" The sheriff shook his head.

"The sheriff isn't your angel, Lottie," replied Ben.

"Of course he is," said Lottie. "You don't believe me?"

"I'm the angel," said Ben. Lottie stood there in awe.

"What! But you're Agent Ben from Boise," said Lottie.

"I'm still Ben. I've worn the hat of many people."

Lottie, please sit down," said the Sheriff. "You look like you're going to drop." She sat down and gave Ben an intense look for several moments.

"But Sheriff Taylor did so many unexplainable things in this town," said Lottie. "We've been helped beyond our wildest dreams. I don't know about all of this. If you're our angel what did I lose when I jumped off the bridge years ago? I bet you don't know that!"

"When you were at Jerry's garage I gave you your lost chain and cross in a bright colored handkerchief," said Ben.

"What can I say? The kids were right. But why are you leaving town, Sheriff Taylor?"

"I'm just going to River Falls to pick out a wedding ring. I'm asking Winnie to marry me today. I just like riding the trains."

"You're going to marry my mom. So Angel Ben is leaving and the sheriff is staying. Am I right?" Ben nodded.

"Taylor has been my trusted helper for many years, Lottie. I'm very pleased with him. Great Uncle Will was his contact when he first came here. Your Uncle is a noble man. They've sworn years ago to keep this a secret. Will you remain silent about all this and not a word to anyone to include your family?"

"I can't tell my family? Well, okay. My lips are triple sealed," replied Lottie. "Should I call you Angel, Ben, or sir?"

"Ben is fine, Lottie. I believe you will become my helper in the future and may have a special task to perform."

"I'm going to be your helper?"

"Have you ever been to Seattle, Lottie?" asked Ben.

"No I haven't. I have another question. So who lifted the car off of old Henry? And the sheriff just happened to be at the railroad crossing that day?"

"That too was with my assistance," said Ben. "And I was in many other happenings, Lottie?"

"Why did you let Great Uncle Will fall off his truck back then?"

"That was according to God's plan," answered Ben. "Many things would not have unfolded if your Uncle didn't have that accident that day."

Suddenly Lottie and the sheriff were jolted. They woke up moments later. Ben was gone.

"Ben always leaves in a hurry," remarked the sheriff.

"Was all this real?" thought Lottie. "Why did Ben ask me about Seattle?"

"I don't know Lottie. No need to leave the train. You can help me pick out the ring in River Falls." The sheriff leaned back and closed his eyes.

\* \* \* \*

Taylor and his sister were in an orphanage near Denver. Taylor's younger sister, Tessa, was taken to a foster home when she was six and Taylor remained at the orphanage till he was sixteen. They hardly knew their parents. That was the last time he had seen his sister.

He was fascinated with trains as a child but his first desire really was to be a Policeman. He had a few odd jobs after he left the orphanage and then got on with the railroad as a Conductor.

One rainy night he slipped off the passenger car steps and broke his ankle. He wasn't able to resume his job. Taylor felt that there was nothing left for him. After all these years he couldn't locate his sister.

On a rainy Sunday morning Taylor was sitting on a bench in a park outside of Boise. A well-dressed man sat down next to Taylor and shared an umbrella with him. He held his hand out.

"My name is Ben. And your name, sir?"

"I'm Taylor. Why do you ask, sir?"

"I would like to be of help, Taylor. I have a job offer for you but first you must become an officer of the law. Then you will eventually become a Sheriff in charge of a town and a county. Your duties also will include helping the two families the best you can. They are the Rainwaters and the Lindstroms.

"I don't know a thing about being a lawman. How did you know this was my secret childhood dream?"

"I just knew," said Ben.

"So out of the blue you just walked up to me and offered me a job. The next thing you're going to tell me is that you're an angel sent to help me."

"Yes, I'm that angel." Taylor shook his head.

"Are you for real, sir? Why me?"

"I'm very real, Taylor. I picked you because you're a good man. Go to the police academy in Boise and fill out an application and you will be accepted. All the expenses will be paid. Here's a bus ticket to Boise and a train ticket to the town of Bergan's Ferry. Taylor's hands were shaking as he took the tickets.

"I hope I'm not dreaming. Will I see you again, Ben?"

"Yes, you will see me again. From time to time I will assist you and also insure your safety. Your contact person in Bergan's Ferry is Great Uncle Will Lindstrom."

"You cannot share this experience with anyone else without

my permission. I must warn you, Taylor. Great Uncle Will at times cheats at checkers. That's the only inequality he has."

Taylor was jolted as Ben suddenly disappeared. The rain stopped.

\*\*\*\*

"Sheriff, wake up. We're at River Falls," said Lottie.

"Oh... That's odd. First time I ever fell asleep on the train going to River Falls. We're going to have to pick out a ring for Winnie real quick so we can get back to the party."

"One question. Since you're going to be my step-father, should I call you Sheriff Taylor, Taylor, Taylor Taylor, or just Dad?"

"I don't know. Maybe I can't get too close to you. I might have to throw you in jail again. You ask too many questions. Please ask your mother about all that."

As the sheriff and Lottie got off the train, he looked back at the train.

"There was something about that lady," remarked the sheriff. "Maybe I should've said something to her when she passed by me in the train car. I felt like I knew her."

"What lady, Sheriff?"

"Oh nothing, Lottie. He stopped and looked back at the train again as it cleared the station.

Ben walked into the next railcar and looked for a place to sit. Partway up sat a lady with two children in a booth. They were plainly dressed.

"Camille, did you see that sheriff in front of us when we boarded the train back there? I wasn't paying that much attention, Mom. He looked familiar, kids. He looked at me for a moment as if he knew me. I thought that was odd."

"There's a man who needs a seat. Sit on my side, children. I'm going to motion to him that we have a seat for him." Ben walked over to them and stood there for a moment.

"Please have a seat with us, sir. Hate to see someone stand all day on this train." He nodded and sat down.

"Thank you so much, ma'am."

"I'm Tessa Taylor. This is Camille and Freddy."

"Going all the way to Seattle?" asked Ben.

"Yes we are," answered Tessa. "I hope to find work there. My job opportunity in Boise fell through after we arrived there and then our old car broke down just this side of Boise. We didn't have the money for the repairs. We had to abandon the car. So here we are."

"I'm sorry to hear that. Where is Mr. Taylor?" asked Ben.

"Oh, I'm not married. These kids here are my half-sister's kids. Their mother is deceased."

"Do you have relatives in Seattle?" asked Ben.

"No I don't. The only relative I have is a brother but we haven't seen each other for many years. We both were in an orphanage together. I was six when I was adopted out. I heard that he left years later. I don't know where he's at. I remember him so well. He wanted to be a policeman. His first name is also Taylor. I would give anything to find him.

"Taylor Taylor is a great name. I will remember that name. Miracles do happen. Maybe you will catch up with Taylor in the future."

"Hope so. I'm sorry, sir. I didn't mean to unload our troubles on you. Things just haven't gone our way. I'm still so upset."

"No apology necessary," said Ben. "I really do understand your concerns. May I ask what kind of work you do, Tessa?"

"I've been an aircraft worker at Cessna outside of Cheyenne for a number of years, but then I was laid off. You never told us your name.

"My name is Ben. I'm in real estate."

"We need a miracle or something," said Tessa. "We don't know a single person in Seattle."

The children focused their attention on Ben as he spoke.

"Here's my business card, Tessa. Call the number on the back of the card when you get there. His name is Mr. Daniels. He will help you."

"He will help us? Thank you, Mr. Ben. I sure wasn't expecting this. Don't know if we deserve this great favor. Why us? I haven't been to church for a while. I hope to do better."

"Why not you?" replied Ben. "And I believe you will do better, Tessa."

"You're a godsend. Like an angel to our rescue," said Tessa.

"Mom, I think he is our angel," said Freddy.

"Freddy, that's just a saying. We mean that Mr. Ben is helpful like an angel would be. My kids can really have fantasies. I hope that didn't bother you."

"Not in the least. If they say I'm an angel, then I guess I am one," said Ben with a grin. They laughed.

"It's early, but for some reason I'm so sleepy," said Tessa. A moment later, she fell asleep.

"Mr. Ben, is Seattle a big place?" asked Freddy.

"Yes it is," answered Ben.

"Will we see you there?" asked Camille.

"Do you believe in miracles, children?" They nodded.

"You will see me again," replied Ben.

As Ben gazed out the window, he looked out the corner of his eye and winked. Suddenly the kids fell asleep. Ben got up and walked into the other train car and vanished out of sight.

# More Stories to Come!

*2nd book, The Rainwater Sequel*

*The Elusive Mrs. Hanson The 3*

*Heart Mannequins Jerome's*

*End is Near?*

Fred Rubio

Fred Rubio came from a diverse family. He was raised in an old house next to a railyard in the 40's and 50's in the bleak part of town located in the Pacific Northwest.

As a young boy he escaped reality at times by daydreaming and could relate to the downhearted ones.

Fred's life experiences helped him to create unique comical characters that are flawed but very lovable. His characters stumble through life but become victorious at the end.

Fred can be contacted by emailing him at
fredrubiowriter@gmail.com

Made in United States
Troutdale, OR
07/29/2024

21638639R00159